THE WAGER

THE WAGER

Angela Taylor-Hargett

Cover and interior designed by Megan Katsanevakis.

Paperback ISBN: ISBN:979-8-9941387-0-0

eBook ISBN: 979-8-9941387-1-7

For Mom and Dad

CHAPTER 1

THE ROOM WAS SMOKY and overheated. A fire burned in the hearth, and although she was dressed in a filmy sheath dress that left her long legs and arms bare, Sofia could feel sweat pooling in the hollow of her neck and between her breasts.

The low light of the wall sconces created a sheen along her silky, mocha skin and the shadows sharpened her cheekbones. Deep brown eyes blinked against the constant haze of tobacco smoke that drifted to her place in the balcony.

She lifted her long hair away from her neck and fanned her hot skin, closing her eyes in pleasure at the slight breeze her waving hand made. When she let go of her hair it cascaded in a wave of dark browns and deep reds down her back. Her full lips smiled confidently. She knew every move she made was a distraction to the men below her, but that was part of the fun.

Five men were huddled around a horseshoe-shaped table; cards held in their hands. Two were smoking cigarettes and one a cigar and drinks in crystal glasses or bottles were at their elbows. Their eyes swiveled from her, to their cards, and to each other, all hoping to wager their way into her bed.

A young man in a polo shirt and a pair of khaki pants threw down his cards in disgust and glanced up at her. She smiled and he scowled back. He pushed away from the table, almost knocking his chair over. Sofia saw the two big men at the door stiffen, anticipating trouble, but the young man stumbled past them and out the swinging door.

Too drunk, thought Sofia, classic mistake. Having a couple of drinks to loosen up before The Wager was one thing but those who overindulged ruined their concentration and their faces showed their every thought and emotion.

Four men to go. She knew two of them because they had won so often and they came back again and again. While one man blended into the next and most were unmemorable, there were a handful who had become friends.

Don was around forty; handsome, with salt and pepper hair. He was twice divorced and currently single. He had a condo in the city but never discussed what he did for a living. Sofia sometimes joked with him that he was a hit man, and he never confirmed or denied it. In bed, what he lacked in skill he made up for in enthusiasm.

The other man was older, maybe in his sixties, with thick white hair and a broad, handsome face. His name was Jack and he was married with three kids and two grandchildren. After sex, he liked to show her pictures of his family on his phone. He was very proud of his grandson who had recently scored a home run in t-ball. Jack was the favorite for tonight.

He usually did pretty well, but not always well enough.

She liked following the game; watching the players, seeing if she could read them. She'd gotten pretty good at noticing tells; those little quirks and twitches that no matter how much they tried to control, exposed a player's weaknesses. Don's eyes flicked up to the left when he was bluffing, and Jack's ring finger started to move as if he was tapping a key on a piano when he was undecided. It was so imperceptible that it had taken her a long time to notice it.

Another fifteen minutes passed. Don had lost most of his chips and conceded good humoredly. It was down to Jack and a fat balding man whose large size and sagging jowls made it difficult to determine his age. He could have been anywhere from twenty to fifty.

The dealer, Duke, had worked at The Hotel since it had opened. He had been hired right away for his dashing, chiseled good looks and also for his huge muscles, just in case things got rowdy. He stood in the center of the horseshoe and dealt out the final cards. Jack and the other man placed their bets and then revealed their hands.

Jack roared in triumph when his three fours beat two aces, and the other man put his cards down dejectedly. Jack reached into the middle of the table and dragged the immense stack of chips toward his chest. That was Sofia's cue. She stood up, straightening her dress, and went out the small door of the balcony down the stairs to the first floor.

"Congratulations, Jack!" she said, giving him a kiss on the mouth. He kissed her back, joyfully shoving his tongue down her throat, and planting one hand firmly on her backside.

Sofia giggled and looped her arm through his as he escorted her to his room.

Sofia liked Jack. He smelled like butterscotch and although, like every other man, he was out for his own pleasure, he had a silly sense of humor and would usually tell her a joke that kept her giggling through his grunts and groans.

She rarely spent the night. It was part of her arrangement that if the guest fell asleep, left, or told her to leave, she didn't have to stay. In Jack's case he would leave shortly after two and go home to his wife, who would cook him a hot breakfast in the morning after his rough night on the graveyard shift. Jack worked a lot of overtime.

After a final kiss, she left him looking for his clothes and returned to her room to take a hot, scented shower and sleep the rest of the morning.

It was afternoon before Sofia emerged groggily from her piles of blankets and comforters. She stretched and threw back the covers. Yawning, she went to the window and stared out at the grey skies. She had been hoping for a little sun today, but once again it stayed buried beneath the oppressive clouds that hovered over the city like a shroud.

The sprawling landscape spread out for miles; the skyline crowded with towering buildings gleaming with glass and steel. She looked down at the silvery street, wet and slick, and the people jostling on the sidewalk. Cars and trucks splashed through puddles, and she could almost smell the belched-out fumes and hear the drivers screaming and honking. It was like a silent movie, but she could still imagine the sound of street vendors calling out at passersby, and the smell of grease from grilling meat.

The Hotel was located in what had once been one of the worst parts of the city, rank with poverty, violence, prostitution and organized crime. Over the years it had exploded in popularity, catering to the businessman, the male executive and entrepreneur. Those who worked in or visited the city and needed a place to rest their heads could find a multitude of distractions at The Hotel. Men for whom money was no object, and whose morals were as grey as the city itself.

Soon fancy boutiques and restaurants had grown up around the area hoping to take advantage of The Hotel's success. It was a dichotomy of the poorest of the poor and those who could afford anything. While the elite made billions and chased any number of sins, children begged on the street, their only sin, having been born into poverty.

For the massive population of homeless and low income families, the city could be a death sentence. Men and women fought and competed for the same few jobs they were qualified for; cooks, maids, nannies, cleaners, but for every ten people, one job was available. There had been brawls during job hirings, people who had gone beyond civility in a desperate need to feed their families.

Schools had closed due to a lack of funding, and children were educated at home or not at all. There were a few private schools and the university, but the tuition was more than most made in a year. The result was children running in the streets like a page from a Dickens novel, begging and stealing. Some were contributing to their family's meager income, but many had been abandoned by parents who couldn't afford to keep them under their roof.

Sofia had been one of them once. Orphaned and alone, stealing to survive.

She leaned her head against the window, letting the coolness of the glass soothe her forehead. If she let herself think about it, she could still feel the gnawing ache of hunger in her stomach and the cold that cut to the bone until she didn't think she'd ever be warm again.

Now she looked down on it all from her place in the clouds.

She turned from the window, blocking out the grey and welcoming the golden light the flames in the fireplace cast on the white walls of her room. She sat cross-legged on a rose shag carpet in front of the flames, her toffee-colored skin glowing in the muted light.

The heat on her body was like a warm blanket encircling her as she slid a brush through her long dark hair. She stilled her mind, listening to the crackle of the fire, acknowledging each small pop and whistle, letting the repetitive motion of stroking her hair lull her into a trance-like state.

"One." *Her consciousness swirled above her, separating from her body.* "Two." *Her mind was light as air as it floated out of The Hotel and into the cloudy sky.* "Three." *She pushed through the chilly moisture until she could finally feel the sun, warmth draping across her shoulders.* "Four." *She basked in the brilliant rays, while the flesh of her body sat far far away.*

When her hair hung down her back in a smooth curtain, Sofia slowly brought her awareness down from the skies to reconnect with her body. She opened her eyes, blinking in the muted light. The room was glowing cheerfully from the fire and the two dimmed lights on either side of the room. Fake potted ferns and twinkling lights that she'd strung along the wall made the room a cozy haven. She stood up feeling languid and relaxed and walked barefoot to the bedroom which was separated by a latticed door. She flopped back down on the bed and burrowed into the warm sheets.

She heard a quiet "uh-hem" and opened one eye. Sami was standing at the foot of the king-sized bed holding up a white robe. She had short blond hair that stuck up in messy waves and fluffy spikes. She was thin and waifish and could easily pass for much younger than her fourteen years.

She shared a room with Sofia and took care of any needs she might have; anything from bringing her a cup of coffee to hemming a dress. Sami helped out all the girls at The Hotel. She was a wizard with bobby pins and a curling iron, but her first responsibility was to Sofia.

Sofia gave the robe a mutinous look, and stretched like a cat, arching her back. Sami raised an eyebrow. Sofia sighed and rolled over, pulling off her leggings and sweatshirt.

"Fine," she grumbled, letting Sami wrap the robe around her. "What's the latest?"

"There's going to be a ballroom dance competition this weekend," Sami said, her words tumbling out in excitement as she straightened the covers on the bed. "I love the costumes, but I don't know how those women can dance like that in those shoes. I'd break my neck trying to walk in them, let alone dance!"

Sami continued to talk as she went into the bathroom

and turned on the shower. "Next Friday there's a bachelor party in the casino with strippers and a live band. I bet a lot of them will sign up for The Wager."

The Hotel housed a casino, ballroom, restaurants, bars, and, of course, prostitutes. Sami had lived there her whole life and knew every employee by name and had become well known to the regulars as well. Every month she memorized the event calendar and could recite it on request.

She had been abandoned at The Hotel as an infant. Unnoticed by the staff, who were always busy to the point of exhaustion, a stranger had walked in with a basket, set it in the corner of the lobby, and left without it. It wasn't until the night staff came on, and hunger finally overcame the child's docile nature, that they heard her cries and went to investigate.

The female staff brought her to Rufus, the owner of The Hotel, promising they would take care of her and he would never even know she was there. Rufus begrudgingly agreed, but it didn't take long for the little thing to charm him and everyone else she met. It was all Sami had ever known. The Hotel was her home and the girls were her family. Getting to take care of Sofia was the best life she could imagine.

Sami was cheerful and uncomplicated, but she wasn't naive. She knew what went on at The Hotel. She knew what she was contributing to when she did Sofia's hair and picked out sparkly clothes for her. She had learned about sex a long time ago from the girls who worked there, and apparently men wanted it so badly, they paid a lot of money to do it with strangers. They liked doing it with strangers because they didn't like their wives who they were supposed to be doing it with.

Sami couldn't imagine doing it with someone she liked or with a stranger. The idea repulsed her. Rolling around naked and sweaty with a man did not sound fun, it sounded disgusting. Still, she couldn't help but be fascinated when the girls told their stories.

Learning about the sexual dynamics between men and women from prostitutes had left Sami with a wealth of information that she never planned to use. The girls could giggle all they wanted about penis sizes and prowess; to Sami it sounded like nothing she ever wanted to do and had vowed never to let a man touch her like that.

She put her hand under the spray of water, testing the temperature. The countertop was lined with candles, and pastel-colored soaps nestled in a dish on the edge of the tub. The steam released their fragrance, filling the room with the scented mist of vanilla and lavender.

She looked around, hands on her hips, making sure there were fresh towels and everything Sofia would need in reach.

When Sofia joined her in the bathroom, Sami stood on her toes and kissed her on the cheek. "I've got some errands to run," she said, already trotting toward the door of the suite. "Won't be long!"

CHAPTER 2

THE ELEVATOR WAS ACROSS a small hallway and Sami took it to the tenth floor where most of the girls were housed, some four to a room.

It was that time of the evening when many of them were getting ready to parade themselves in front of the male clientele, and Sami loved helping them get ready. The girls running back and forth to the bathroom, sequined gowns and lacey undergarments scattered on the furniture and on the floor; it was like being backstage at a play or fashion show, the chaos exhilarating.

"Oh Sami, be a dear and zip up the back of my dress," called Debora, a busty brunette with large, sumptuous lips. She was working the casino tonight. Her job was to loiter around the enormous circular bar that took center stage, and wander through the tables for craps, roulette, blackjack and poker. She would flirt with the high rollers, blow on dice, and kiss cards for good luck. Hopefully one of those high rollers would slip her a room key. If a guy won big, he would most likely leave a generous tip.

Sami helped another girl, Zoe, with her hair, securing it on top of her head with rhinestone clips that twinkled in the light. Zoe's station tonight was the lobby where she would stand near the front desk, mannequin-like, wearing a very tight skirt and a lacey top that revealed her stomach, shoulders and most of her breasts. A gold chain was wrapped around her midriff with tiny beads that shimmered with the slightest movement of her slim waist. She was a reminder to guests what delights The Hotel had to offer.

When Sami had helped where she could, she took the elevator down to the first floor, skipping through the lobby, dodging bellboys pushing carts full of luggage. She waved at the harried desk clerks and went down the thick carpeted hall to the casino. She scurried around the slot machines, a wraith unnoticed by the hopefuls sitting on their bar stools, pushing buttons as if their life depended on it, praying for a good line.

At the far end of the casino was a service elevator with a sign on the wall saying Employees Only. She took this to the second floor where it opened to the bustling, frenetic energy of the kitchen. Chef was holding court, with his sous chefs hanging on his every word. He announced the specials for the evening and how he expected them to act like they were in a five-star restaurant not some upchuck hut, where they would soon be employed if they embarrassed him.

A plate of chocolate chip cookies was cooling on the baker's rack and Sami palmed one as she passed by. Several women in various states of attire sat at a scarred oak table set up out of the way of the main kitchen traffic. Some wore evening dresses, their hair done up in perfect coifs, others wore pajamas and slippers, their hair wrapped in curlers. They greeted Sami affectionately as she hurried by on her way to the dining room where Rufus was welcoming the first of the evening diners.

Rufus was a tall man with a good build and a bald head, not so much because he was losing his hair but more for the convenience of donning wigs and other stylish hairpieces. He'd been thirty-something for twenty years and had maintained the same trim physique. He might be considered handsome by some, with his firm lips and aristocratic nose, where a pair of horn-rimmed glasses perched, but his flair for the dramatic and flamboyant behavior was an acquired taste.

Sami trotted up next to him and he put a hand on her back. "Sami, perfect timing!" He had a deep, nasally voice that resonated through the dining room.

He led her to a podium where a beautiful woman stood in a yellow silk dress that flowed down her body like liquid gold. The bodice was discreet, curving gently around her throat, but the back was so low it revealed the dimples at the bottom of her spine.

"Hello Athena, my love. Has the mayor made a reservation for tonight?" Rufus asked looking over her shoulder at the computer in front of her.

"Oh look," he said with a smile. "Yes, he has. Party of one. I wonder who his flavor of choice will be tonight? He seems to have been enjoying Lacy's company of late."

He took an envelope from a shelf in the podium and wiggled his fingers into his skin-tight pants' pocket. They came out holding a small card which he placed in the envelope. He licked it closed, his mouth puckering in distaste.

"This one's for JM Sylvester at Fifth and Pearl. It's his room key. I promised him a complimentary room since we were booked the last time he wanted to stay. And this…" he scribbled some words on a piece of paper and gave it to Sami, "is for Edmond Jones of Jones and Jones, Sixteenth and Magnolia."

Sami committed the information to memory, nibbling on her cookie. When Rufus handed her the messages, she wiped her hand down her jeans to avoid smudging them with chocolate.

"Be back in time for The Wager," he said, ruffling her already messy hair. "And be careful out there."

Sami saluted him and maneuvered around the dining tables, back down the elevator, past the front desk and out the huge glass double doors; the papers tucked safely in a small purse that she wore around her neck to deter pickpockets.

She broke into an easy jog, passing food vendors and breathing in the greasy scent of freshly cooked hot dogs. Magnolia ran parallel to the street she was on and the quickest way to get there was through an alley that ran between a hair salon and a Chinese restaurant.

She paused at the gaping entrance, the way before her filled with shadows. She scanned her eyes over the litter scattered in piles around a dumpster, and the windows of the apartments above. She wasn't really afraid; most everyone knew her as a runner, and they respected the profession enough not to mess with her. Of course, there was always that one desperate vagabond who would nab a runner for the few coins they might have in their pocket, so it was always wise to be cautious.

Ten years before, the postal service had been obsolete; outdated and unused. The internet had become increasingly risky to send confidential information through technological conveniences like email and texts. Hackers had infiltrated data in every corner of the city. With bankers and corporations unable to communicate, too afraid of exposing all their information to some punk on the other end of a keyboard, the business and financial worlds were thrown into chaos.

The mayor, who was up for re-election at the time and was desperate for something big to turn the polls around, came up with a grand scheme to save his city. He cut the traditional mail service, already saving the taxpayers money which boosted his ratings automatically, then assured his citizens that he also had a replacement for communication through the internet.

He rounded up children, any kid who wanted a job, and set them to work running messages back and forth to offices and private homes.

"These damn kids are always under my feet anyway," he'd complained to his assistant. "Why not put all that running around to use?"

Each jurisdiction had a group of children assigned to it and they were tasked with making sure documents and messages were delivered fast, efficiently and discreetly. The scheme was a win-win, the mayor had declared. The city saved money, messages were delivered securely, and the kids had the coins they made from tips to take home to their families.

The mayor was re-elected and strutted through the city as if he'd solved world peace. His plan had worked and the runners' network had become like a spider web that wove its way throughout the city. If a message needed to be sent, or someone needed to be found, the runners were the fastest way to do it.

Sami loved running. If she spent too long in The Hotel, she started to go stir crazy, so Rufus had allowed her to have her side project to keep her busy and out of his way.

She reached Sixteenth and Magnolia, breathing heavily and saw a familiar figure slouched in a doorway. The oversized hoodie and baggy jeans covered up a lean, athletic frame but right now he looked like a pile of someone's laundry. Her heart gave a little skip of happiness at the sight of him.

"Hi, Rhys," she said breathlessly, partly from the running but mostly because that was the usual effect Rhys had on her.

Rhys was eighteen, on the old side for a runner, but still the fastest in the city. His exploits over the years had made him a legend and he was admired by all the boys and worshiped by all the girls. Sami was not immune to his charms or his rich brown eyes, the color of dark espresso.

"Little Sami Sunshine," he said in his British accent that made her knees turn to jelly. "What are you doing on this glorious day?" He waved a hand at the misty air and black thunder clouds. He had an amazing smile with dimples that made her heart somersault.

"Got a message from Rufus to Jones," she said, looking around uncertainly for an address.

"You're at the right place," he said, as he kicked the door

he was leaning against with the heel of his boot. He stood back and in a moment the door was opened by a skeletal man with wisps of white hair clinging obstinately to his scalp. He was hunched over as if his head was too heavy for his spine. Behind him was a dark stairwell that smelled strongly of marijuana.

"Mr. Jones?" Sami asked pleasantly.

The man nodded and held out a bony hand. She gave him the piece of paper from Rufus and the man dropped a handful of coins in her palm.

"Thank you, sir," she said and without a word the man slammed the door in her face.

Sami smiled at Rhys and said, "So, what are you doing here?" And then blushed furiously. It was bad form to ask questions like that of other runners.

Rhys laughed. He was always laughing, Sami thought.

"It's alright, I'm not on the clock. I was waiting for a friend, but he appears to have stood me up." He looked up and down the street, smiled and shrugged. "What about you? Got another run to do?"

"Yeah, Fifth and Pearl," she said, holding up the envelope.

He stood close to her, reading over her head which barely came to his shoulder. Having him so close, his breath in her ear, made her stomach roll in strange waves.

"That's a hike," he said and grinned down at her. Her stomach lurched so hard she was afraid she was going to bring up her lunch.

"Lucky for you I know a shortcut." He grabbed her hand and before she could open her mouth, he was pulling her along down the street.

He led her through a series of alleys until she was hopelessly lost. The air grew thicker and cooler and she could tell from the briny smell that they were nearing the docks. This wasn't her patch, but she knew Rhys had every inch memorized, so she followed him without hesitation.

They slid through a narrow opening between two hulking warehouses that stood abandoned, windows boarded up, left to rust and corrode from the salt spray of the sea.

The water that lapped against the quay shimmered with oil slicks, carrying algae and trash at the mercy of the sluggish tide.

Twenty years ago the port had thrived, but over time businesses had failed and shut down, leaving empty warehouses lining the sludgy water.

It was eerily quiet except for the cry of seagulls. Long-deserted fishing boats bobbed lazily, their hulls chipped and flaking, names barely legible beneath layers of peeling paint. Sami jumped when a huge rat scuttled in front of them and then disappeared into the shadows.

Rhys was still holding her hand as they crunched over gravel and loose boards. Sami wanted to keep walking like this with him forever.

He moved with an easy stride, although inside he was coiled like a spring, ready for anything. His lazy, lidded eyes took in his surroundings, every detail, nothing missed.

"How are things at The Hotel?" he asked casually.

"Fine."

"Anything exciting happen lately?"

Sami slanted her head in thought. "One of the girls, Miranda, got in big trouble with Rufus for giving a freebie to one of the guests that she really likes."

Rhys raised an eyebrow. "A freebie?"

Sami felt her face flush all the way to her hairline. "You know what I mean."

Rhys chuckled. "So, what happened to Miranda?"

"She had to pay Rufus out of her wages what the free night cost him."

"Ouch."

"Actually, Miranda said it was worth it."

Rhys laughed, his dimples flashing. Sami felt herself reddening again.

They had neared a more populated part of the docks with bars and strip clubs, interiors dark, doors padlocked shut, waiting for the night. It was a popular area with the locals who had learned to live with the smell of fish and sour mud.

They ducked through a few more alleys, heading back towards the inner part of the city and ended up on a street she recognized.

"Wow, that was faster," she said, grinning up at him. He winked and her heart felt like he had reached out and touched it.

"Sami?"

"Huh?"

He had stopped and pointed to the building she'd just passed.

"Isn't this it?"

"Oh, yeah," she said, telling herself to get her head out

of the clouds. It wasn't professional to be daydreaming while on the job.

They entered the chrome and glass building and stepped into a large foyer. The lady at the front desk told them to go to the third floor so they took the elevator. They both watched the numbers tick slowly by; piped in music swirling around them. Rhys started whistling, trying to copy the melody, but not doing a very good job of it. Sami giggled.

The elevator opened to a carpeted hallway with several doors to choose from. Sami scanned them until she found the one with JM Sylvester painted on the frosted glass in bold, black lines.

She knocked and heard a mumbled, "Come in."

Inside was a typical office with desk, chairs, a fake plant in the corner and a row of file cabinets. The large man seated behind the desk was staring down at some papers in his hands. He didn't look up as they entered.

"Mr. Sylvester?" Sami approached the desk holding out the envelope Rufus had given her. Sylvester reached out his hand, his eyes still rapidly scanning what looked like rows and rows of scribbled numbers. He looked up when he felt the card inside the envelope. "What is it?"

"It's the key to your complimentary suite at The Hotel, sir." She looked at the framed photo of a woman with tight blond curls holding a baby in her arms. Next to her, laughing, were two small boys with identical haircuts and matching t-shirts decorated with dinosaurs.

"Oh, yes. I'd almost forgotten about it." He glanced at the photo and then quickly looked away again. "Tell me," he said, clearing his throat, "does Gigi still work there?"

"Yes sir," Sami said.

"Excellent," he said, avoiding making eye contact with her or Rhys who had been standing quietly by the door.

Sylvester took a wallet from his pocket and pulled out some bills and handed them to Sami.

"Thank you, sir!"

Rhys and Sami left the office and didn't speak again until they were back on the street. They stopped at a stand selling newspapers and assorted snacks and drinks. Sami insisted on buying Rhys a soda with her newly earned tips and they sat on the street curb enjoying a reprieve from the rain.

"Why do men have sex with strangers, Rhys?"

Rhys choked and swallowed before the soda could shoot out of his mouth. "What?"

"Well, Mr. Sylvester obviously has a wife and kids, why would he want to have sex with Gigi?"

"Maybe they aren't going to have sex. Maybe they're going to play pinochle."

Sami laughed. "Yeah, right."

"To answer your question," said Rhys, looking straight at her. "I don't know. If I had someone waiting for me at home, some beautiful girl who loved me, I wouldn't want to be anywhere else."

He was gazing so intently at her that for a moment Sami couldn't move or breathe; she was caught in those brown eyes and sinking fast.

Then Rhys smiled with amusement and the moment's tension disappeared. "Still, it keeps The Hotel in business so you have a place to live, so I'm grateful for that."

He stood up and tossed his soda can in the nearest re-cycler.

"I need to get back," Sami said, regretfully.

"It was nice to see you, Sami Sunshine. You always make my day a little brighter."

He tapped her on the cheek with a finger, turned and sauntered away, his hands in his pockets.

CHAPTER 3

SOFIA PULLED OFF HER robe and stood naked under the spray of the shower. The water streamed onto her head, neck, and shoulders, the heat stinging her skin. She lathered her hands with soap and raised her arms to wash her hair. She went through her routine, keeping her head clear, not thinking about the upcoming night.

Sleeping with strangers never became comfortable. Even with regulars, there was always a part of her that slipped away into the clouds, so she was not fully present.

Sofia was a very sought after woman. She made The Hotel a great deal of money, thanks to The Wager. That popularity had earned her a suite on the top floor with Sami as a companion. She had come so far from her impoverished beginnings and although most would look down on her chosen profession, she was proud that she'd made such a success of it. She had worked hard to learn to read men and what their desires were. Word had spread about her until The Wager was so successful, there was a waiting list to enter. Rufus was very selective as to who got on that list. Only those who had plenty of money to burn through or could advance Rufus and The Hotel in some way were let into The Wager.

Rufus had thought up the name. He said it sounded expensive, and it was; far too rich for most men's blood. Fifty thousand dollars buy in, winner takes all. Only one man got to take her to bed at the end of the night, and that was if they won.

She slid back the shower curtain and stepped carefully onto the carpet, water dripping down her creamy skin. She was taller than average, with almond-shaped eyes, dark and alluring, and skin with just enough bronze to hint at exotic lands. She was lean and firm and had curves in all the right places, and she knew how to use them.

Being a prostitute hadn't been her first choice, or really a choice at all. In a last ditch effort to survive, Sofia had turned to prostitution at the tender age of eighteen, which made it legal in the city. It wasn't the kind of life a little girl dreams of having one day, but Sofia's dreams hadn't been of castles and fairy tales, but whether or not she would eat that day.

Sofia hadn't needed a job when she was young. Over the years she'd become adept at stealing, but as she grew older and taller it was getting harder to grab from the food carts or pick a pocket. Those activities required small hands, nimble little feet and, most important, the ability to disappear into a crowd. Neither her dark auburn hair nor her height contributed to blending in and she was too old to beg; people didn't give away money to a capable girl who could earn it for herself. She had tried to get a job at one of the market stalls or as a housekeeper, but people were distrustful, and the competition overwhelming.

She didn't find the idea of prostitution off-putting; years of starvation had taught her the ability to separate the pain in her body from her mind; but she'd cried the night when she lost her virginity. The old man who'd picked her up had been kind and patient and had helped her through it. It was a shock to her body and spirit, but she also realized her first time could have been so much worse.

It got better from there. She perfected her mind and body separation until anything happening to her body was like a distant thought, just out of reach. Her mind floated away, oblivious and uncaring until it was over and she could become whole again.

For two years she made money having sex on dirty mattresses; in hallways, alley ways, and motels that rented by the hour. The patch she worked was one of the poorest in the city and for a month she cried herself to sleep.

She'd had to toughen up fast and after seeing these men at their most vulnerable; naked and about to burst with need, Sofia had an epiphany. These slobbering fools who wanted her body so badly were not the ones in control. She had all the power because without her they'd have to jack off while they sobbed into their beer, wishing they had a girl in their arms.

Once she stopped viewing herself as a victim, she began looking at what she did as a business. Cash for services, just like the boot cleaner at the market. She was her own boss, and that made the work more tolerable.

Sofia was twenty when her friend Maryanne convinced

her to go to The Hotel. Maryanne was a bubbly redhead, tall and thin, with skin so fair it was almost translucent. She had run away from an abusive father when she was sixteen, and with nowhere else to go, turned to prostitution to survive. She and Sofia had both been teenagers, learning the ropes together, and they had found kindred spirits in one another.

They'd never been to The Hotel. It was too far off their patch to bother with, especially because it had plenty of other girls to choose from, but they'd certainly heard about it. The lavish parties and gorgeous clothes. At the time Sofia said it all sounded too good to be true.

Once a year The Hotel held a banquet celebrating the anniversary of its opening. They bussed in prostitutes from all over the city to work as topless waitresses or to provide extra entertainment for the evening. Maryanne had applied and got one of the spots.

She had come flying through the door of the tiny studio apartment she shared with Sofia. She was high as a kite, and words erupted from her mouth before she was over the threshold.

"We've got to go to The Hotel!" She grabbed Sofia's arm, her eyes unnaturally bright. She was wearing nothing but a pair of panties and an oversized dinner jacket, her breasts barely contained.

"You've just come back from The Hotel," Sofia reassured her gently.

"No." Maryanne shook her head trying to clear it. A beautiful girl at the party with hair the color of cotton candy had given her some pills, and she was feeling fuzzy, like a peach. She giggled. "We've got to go work at The Hotel. It's amazing! It's beautiful inside and I think the outside's made of gold! You can literally see your reflection in it. You can have food whenever you want, and they pay you on top of that!"

Maryanne's porcelain skin had turned pink and her hazel eyes were like saucers in her head. Sofia was worried she might pass out and encouraged her to breathe. Maryanne took two long breaths and then continued on an excited exhale. "Can you imagine never being hungry, always knowing where you're going to sleep? Some girls even get their own room!"

Sofia had been hesitant. To work for someone else? She had sworn to herself that she would never have a pimp after all the horror stories she'd heard.

"But they're not pimps," Maryanne had assured her. "It's an actual job, with steady pay."

It had been the best decision she'd ever made, Sofia thought, as she came out of the bathroom, drying her hair with a towel.

Sami had come back from her errands with rosy cheeks.

"Why are you all flushed?" Sofia asked, tightening a robe around her waist.

"I'm not. I was running," Sami said defensively.

Sofia shook her head. "I know your running face and that," she said, pointing a finger at Sami, "is not it. That's a cat who's licked the cream face."

Sami, to her utter dismay, blushed deeper.

Sofia sat on the edge of the bed. "Did you see him?" she said quietly.

Sami felt the burning all the way to the top of her head.

She nodded and a slight giggle escaped her lips. She sat down on the bed and buried her face in Sofia's chest.

"He's so cute, and nice, and perfect. Why can't I be older…and taller…and have bigger breasts?"

Sofia laughed. "Because you're perfect the way you are. Anyway, I thought you'd sworn off men?"

"Yeah, but Rhys isn't a man. He's not all hairy and stuff."

Sofia gave her a tight squeeze and kissed the top of her head. "Trust me, all men are the same when it comes right down to it, even your Rhys."

Sami was unconvinced. It was true; she never wanted to be touched by a man with lust in his eyes, but Rhys was different and anyway, he would never see her as anything but Little Sami Sunshine.

"C'mon," Sofia said, nudging her, "help me get ready."

Sami, glad to put her mind on something else, went to the closet to pick out Sofia's outfit for the evening. It was one of her favorite things to do. All the different colors and fabrics; the silks that slid through her fingers and the delicate handmade lace. She chose a pink kimono with bright red tropical flowers and hung it up on a hook by the bedroom door.

Sofia sat down at her dressing table and from the dozens of bottles, tubes and powders she chose her colors and carefully applied them to her face. It was like putting on war paint, preparing for what was to come. She never wore makeup when she wasn't working. It symbolized the barrier she put up whenever she was with a man, never letting them see under the mask to the vulnerable skin beneath.

She had become somewhat of a celebrity thanks to The Wager and her inaccessibility to all men except the final winner. The stories of her lovemaking had become legendary due to the boasts of past victors. Like any rumor, the stories became more ridiculously exaggerated with each retelling. Her lips curled up in a smile as she applied mascara to her eyelashes. Whatever keeps them coming back.

She would get the odd fan who was obsessed with her and would hunt for her throughout The Hotel. They were mostly harmless and just wanted a selfie or a kiss on the cheek.

No girl had been accosted at The Hotel since one particular incident when it first opened. A guest, who after spending the night with one girl, snuck into another girl's room and tried to rape her, went into Rufus' office and hadn't been heard from since. The rumor was that Rufus had chopped him into tiny pieces and buried them under the floorboards.

There was the odd guest who tried to get rough with one of the girls, but Rufus' eye- for-an-eye justice was swift and harsh, discouraging any behavior that was not completely consensual. Of course, The Hotel employed girls with very eclectic tastes, so customers rarely walked away unsatisfied.

Sofia remembered vividly seeing The Hotel up close for the first time. It might as well have been the heavenly gates; it was so different from anything she had ever seen. Even in the gloom of overcast skies, it shone with opulence, causing the buildings around it to look even more dingy by comparison. It dwarfed the boutiques and restaurants competing for attention nearby; every window gleaming, every bit of chrome and brass polished to a brilliant shine.

A marquee shielded the sidewalk from the constant fog and mist. A placard attached to the wall advertised The Wager: Coming Soon in large block letters with the words "Try Your Luck!" underneath them. A woman was featured, wearing a thong and holding a hand of cards which were strategically placed to hide her breasts.

Sofia and Maryanne had nervously approached the doorman, looking dapper in his red coat and white gloves. She thought for a moment that he might stop them, ask them what their business was, but he just smiled and wordlessly held the door open. They entered The Hotel and Sofia's breath whooshed out in astonishment and Maryanne gave a little squeal.

The largest chandelier Sofia had ever seen took center stage; hundreds of tiny crystals spreading a rainbow of color on the ceiling. The floor was a mosaic of black and white tiles. Urns spilling over with ferns, lilies and bamboo filled the lobby with exotic fragrances. White pillars created alcoves where men sat in red plush chairs, laptops open, fingers typing furiously.

The lobby was a frenzy of activity. Bell boys dressed in red and black, hats perched jauntily on their heads, scurried past them, their arms laden with luggage. One wall was taken up by the front desk made of white marble. Five desk clerks dressed all in black stood behind it, answering phones that never seemed to stop ringing. Guests, three rows deep, waited impatiently to be helped. A cacophony of music and bells came from the casino down the hall and Sofia could smell stale cigarette smoke wafting its way from that direction.

She also couldn't help but notice the women who sauntered through the lobby, either decked out in evening gowns or decked out in very little. A blond girl, who looked astonishingly young, despite the thick makeup caked on her face, stood next to the front desk, statue-like, wearing a thong and an unbuttoned man's shirt that reached to her thighs. Her breasts were millimeters from popping out and her nipples showed through the thin material. Sofia wondered if that was why they kept it so cold. She herself was only wearing a miniskirt and t-shirt that made her own breasts holler for attention.

She knew pimps liked to sample the merchandise from time to time, that's why she'd never had one, not to mention their reputation for beating their employees senseless. She wondered what kind of boss this Rufus would be. Handsy? Flirty? Nasty and cruel?

She soon learned there were many sides to Rufus, and she would also learn that he was neither handsy nor flirty. He loved the girls like his children, and he did not believe in incest, he told Sofia.

Sofia had often wondered which way the wind blew with Rufus. It seemed to her that he wasn't interested in men or women. He never had visitors in his suite and from what she'd heard he'd never had a partner of any kind.

The Hotel was Rufus' first love; his bride, his beloved, his everything. The rumor was that he had a rich family somewhere who had bought him the derelict hotel as a project to keep his busy, sometimes destructive, mind out of trouble. The site had been abandoned after a fire and the consequent water damage had left the previous hotel gutted and vandalized. Rufus built his vision from the ground up. He used his family's money to demolish the old structure and start work on a new hotel.

In five years, he had created a businessman's after-hours playground. He got to know the high rollers in town and gave special offers to the elite clientele who would bring in their friends and associates. He gave out free drinks, comped rooms, women paraded the halls in their g-strings. He was like The Fox luring stupid little boys to Pleasure Island.

His family promptly disowned him and cut him off when they found out what he was doing, but it was too late. His seed had grown and was spreading tendrils all over the city. He had made his fortune within a year of The Hotel's opening but then came the moment that he confirmed to himself that he was a true genius.

He was wandering through the casino, stopping at tables, shaking hands, laughing hysterically at jokes and generally making himself visible. He stopped to watch a couple of hands of poker and marveled at the concentration in the men's eyes. Rufus loved games and he loved making wagers, so cards had always been one of his favorite past times. He also loved all the money the house would be making.

He wished the gentlemen a good afternoon and went to the bar. He signaled for an espresso martini and sipped it while watching the men at the table. They threw in chip after chip, all hoping to get the big prize.

They'd had poker tournaments at The Hotel many times and sometimes the house would throw in a special prize. One year it had been a car; had that ever blown his budget. The draw was minimal and he decided it wasn't going to make him any money.

Then it occurred to him, why not throw in a girl for the night? A poker tournament, fifty thousand dollar buy in, winner takes all and the girl. He'd call it The Wager. He thought it had a nice ring to it.

He would have to find the right girl, though. It would have to be someone who would make men bet higher and higher in order to have her. If a man wanted a woman who would fawn all over him there were more than enough prostitutes to choose from, but The Wager was a game, a challenge, a gamble for a woman that only came with victory. The gentlemen ate it up.

Rufus knew immediately when he saw Sofia that she would be perfect. She had a fantastic body, long and lean with good-sized breasts. Skin like creamy coffee, hair to die for and those eyes; he thought, a man, not him of course, but a man could get lost in those brown depths. Yes, she was his Wager girl, no doubt about it.

Meeting Rufus for the first time was an unforgettable experience and whatever Sofia had been expecting, there were no words to compare it to the reality of the man himself. He wore a huge pair of square glasses, tiny diamonds sparkling on the frames every time he moved his head. The immaculate pin-striped suit fit his tall figure like a glove, offset by a large red, polka-dotted cravat.

"The rules are simple," he had said, beaming at her. His hands were in a constant state of motion and the rings on each of his fingers, displaying gems of every shape and size, flashed as he gestured.

"Fifty thousand dollar buy in for the house, five card draw, high hand wins, easy peasy. Last man standing gets the pot, and you for the night."

The Wager had taken off, just as Rufus had predicted, and he'd had to start limiting the initial player count to thirty. The group started in the main casino for the preliminary round, spread out, six to a table. The players were given a five hour time limit, and the man with the most chips from each table was able to move through the double doors into the wagering room, where Sofia sat, tantalizingly beautiful, in her balcony.

It had been three years, and Sofia had made a good life for herself. She had made it off the streets; those unforgiving cement slabs that she thought would be her grave.

She blinked at her reflection, clearing the tears from her eyes and telling herself to focus on the job. She straightened her back and took a deep breath. She tilted her head, letting the light catch her bronzed cheekbones and shimmering lips.

Sami came up behind her and curled a strand of hair over her shoulder. Sofia smiled at her and stood up. The sheer kimono did nothing to hide the curves of her body, naked but for a tiny pair of thong panties. The wagering room was always so stuffy and hot, and short of wearing nothing at all, this was the best she could do to keep cool.

She gave her reflection one last look and said, "Showtime."

CHAPTER 4

SOFIA WALKED OUT OF her room to the elevator. Her fluffy, oversized robe protecting her from the chill of the hallway. There were three suites on the top floor. One for her, one for Rufus, and one for a girl named Meechelle. She was on a special call list that catered to the likes of foreign dignitaries, ambassadors and senators and, according to her, a president or two. She was very good at her job.

The other girls all lived on other floors, depending on their hierarchy. Girls who were being disciplined for some infraction, were designated with the new girls, stacked four to a room. If a girl established a clientele, got positive reviews and stayed on Rufus' good side, she was moved to her own room. That privacy was golden and they all knew Rufus' favor could sour with one bad night.

He loved to lavish his girls with praises and rewards but his retribution for bad behavior was swift. He never hit the girls, they were too valuable to put marks on, but his anger was legendary and his moods unpredictable.

Sofia and Sami got out on the first floor, the elevator opening to a private hallway. They could hear the pounding of music coming from the casino and dance club overflowing with men and women who had come directly from work to blow off some steam or entertain clients.

The hallway ended at a door. Sami swiped her master key card over the lock and a light above the handle turned green. Straight ahead of them was a set of stairs, the carpet the color of red wine, leading to the balcony where Sofia would sit, overlooking The Wager. Sami waited at the bottom and took Sofia's robe. Sofia climbed the stairs and drew back the heavy velvet curtain.

There were two chairs, the same royal blue as the curtain, plush and soft as a cloud. Standing, she could see the room below her. The lights were kept dim and the brass fixtures gleamed in the low light. Duke was standing at the table, brushing the green felt that covered it, removing every speck of lint.

The air was already thick with smoke, and she could barely see the other men on the floor. She had to squint through her watering eyes. Only five players were allowed in the wagering room. Part of the allure was to be one of the five who made it in to see her.

The curtain behind her opened and Rufus stepped in and stood beside her.

"Ok, honey cheeks," he said, putting his arm around her waist. He wore a capacious shawl which he arranged so it was over both their shoulders. He had doused himself in flowery perfume and it hung around him like a physical presence, mixing with the smoke in the air. He towered over her in his high-heeled boots. He pointed down to the men milling around waiting for the game to start.

"Little Pinky Peterson over there is up twenty thousand." He pointed through the fog to a very short man who was chewing on a cigar. "He's been killing it all night. His cousin Paolo is right behind him."

Paolo was only inches taller than his cousin Pinky, with thick curly black hair and a pot belly that hung over his jeans and large silver belt buckle.

When the last three men, none of whom she recognized, came through the swinging doors, all the men sat down at the table. Duke shuffled the cards with expertise and flair and then started dealing.

Rufus left the balcony to get a closer look, and Sofia took a deep breath and settled in to wait.

———————

Sofia took the hottest shower she could stand. She could still smell him on her, cigars and old spice. She scrubbed lavender soap over her body. She could never go to sleep after until she smelled like herself again.

Paolo had won The Wager. He had looked up at her, swaying a little and she clapped and smiled as her job required. He didn't wait for her to descend the stairs but gave Rufus his room key to pass along while he went to celebrate with his friends.

When Sofia came down from the balcony the room was

empty except for Rufus, who was sipping on a fruity drink with a little pink umbrella and five maraschino cherries stuck on a toothpick. He pulled one of the cherries off with his teeth and chomped on it. He handed Sofia the room key.

"Our victor wants to party a bit before he goes back to his room. Hopefully he'll blow all that money he just won," he said with a glint in his eye. "You can meet him there, room 1406."

It wasn't unusual for the winner not to want to go straight back to the room, so Sofia took the key and rode the elevator to the fourteenth floor. She let herself into the room and sat down on the bed, bouncing slightly. She had to give Rufus credit, the beds at The Hotel were very comfortable. She reclined on the plump cushions and closed her burning eyes, grateful for a moment of quiet.

He made enough noise coming in to wake the dead. She opened her eyes to slits and saw him standing over her unsteadily. He pulled his shirt over his head but he hadn't undone any of the buttons so his head got stuck in the narrow gap of his collar. He struggled for a few seconds before Sofia took pity on him and climbed off the bed.

"Hold still, sugar," she purred and released him from the shirt's strangle hold.

Paolo shook back his mop of black hair that matched the thick mat covering his chest.

"How are you tonight, handsome?" Sofia said softly, staring over his right shoulder. She never looked in their eyes. It was too personal, and more often than not those eyes looking back at her were cold and blank, like a dead fish.

He didn't say anything; maybe he didn't speak English, Sofia thought. He stripped the rest of his clothes off ungracefully, muttering guttural curses. He obviously wanted to get right to it, which Sofia didn't have a problem with, so she removed her kimono and panties and stood in front of him naked. He prodded her backwards until the back of her knees hit the bed and she laid down. He climbed on top of her clumsily and entered her with a satisfied grunt.

Sofia thought about windchimes and what she imagined the ocean would look like up close. Paolo was sweating from exertion, beads of perspiration pooling up on his forehead and dripping down the sides of his face onto her chest. He was working himself into a frenzy, panting and grinding.

Sofia had been with all sorts of different men. Some had been gentle and kind and tried their best to make it enjoyable for her. Some were business-like and treated it for what it was, an exchange of money for services. Sofia liked those men. They didn't pretend to fall in love with her, she'd had those too. Then there were men like Paolo, which was more typical; drunk and sloppy, searching out an animalistic urge like cows needing to be milked. She giggled to herself; and she was the dairymaid; that would make a cute outfit.

Paolo heaved into her one last time and then stumbled away from her and collapsed onto the floor. She waited but when nothing happened, she looked over the side of the bed. He was out cold.

She stood up, his sweat dribbling down her chest and along the crease on her stomach. Disgusted, she grabbed her scraps of clothing and threw on one of the complimentary hotel robes.

She didn't have to stay overnight with a guest if they passed out or fell asleep. That was one of the rules of The Wager. It suited her perfectly. She didn't remember the last time she'd spent a full night with a john.

After her shower, Sofia climbed into bed with a romance novel. Sami was out gossiping with the girls, so she had some valuable alone time.

She loved to read. She'd read anything and she liked all kinds of books, but tonight she was in the mood for a good bodice ripper. She opened the book, turning the pages in anticipation.

Marco races across the beach, his trusty steed, Bandit, eating up the distance. The horse's hooves thunder over the ground, each step bringing him closer to his heart, his love, his only reason for living. Gwendolyn. She was being held by the cruel prince, a prisoner of his twisted lust, and as a ransom to finally get a noose around Marco's neck.

A pistol in one hand and a sword in the other, Marco storms the palace, taking out each guard that gets in his way. He doesn't stop until he reaches the throne room and bursts through the doors. And there she is, her porcelain, tear-streaked face drawing his eyes like a moth to a flame.

The cruel prince lunges and they cross swords, thrusting and parring. Gwendolyn gasps as Marco is stabbed in the shoulder but he quickly recovers and pierces the prince in his black heart. Gwendolyn swoons and Marco lifts her easily in his strong arms, carrying her to where Bandit waits outside the palace walls.

They ride across the beach, Gwendolyn seated firmly in

front of Marco as they gallop over the sand. Their bodies meld together as one as they slide in the saddle. Unable to control the heat that is burning through their bodies, Marco reins in Bandit and helps Gwendolyn down. They make love on a grassy bank as the sun sets over the horizon.

Their passion burns as bright as the rays of the sun reflecting off the white sand, as Marco kisses Gwendolyn's heavy breasts and works his way down to her womanhood, his throbbing member...

Sofia smiled as she felt the tension crawl from her own womanhood radiating warmth through her core and out to her limbs. Her insides tingled at the thought of a man touching her because he loved her, not just because he wanted her.

She wondered if such a thing was possible or if that kind of passion between a man and a woman was only found in books. To be gazed upon with love and longing rather than lust and greed was a fantasy.

She'd had orgasms with johns before, but it had never been anything more than a sexual release. Never a heart pounding, name screaming, declaration of love. Never that. Sofia would die before admitting it to herself, let alone anyone else, but she was a true romantic disguised as a cynic.

Sofia turned the last page of the book and sighed happily, stroking the cover. It depicted a swarthy man with chiseled features and long hair that was being blown back by some unknown breeze. His chest was bare and his pectorals ridiculously huge. Clutched in his bulging biceps was a swooning woman dressed in Regency fashion, her blond hair tousled, her overwhelming bosom all but spilling out of her bodice. In the background a ship with sails unfurled, waited in the sea.

"The Pirate's Bounty," Sofia whispered. "Well done, Marco."

She put the book aside and turned out the light. She fell asleep smiling.

CHAPTER 5

THE NEXT MORNING SOFIA was up and dressed by ten. Sami had been running since seven and they met on the sidewalk outside The Hotel.

The warm breeze smelled of smog and diesel fumes and the air was thick with humidity. The sun had made a surprising appearance, unusual for May, and intrepid dandelions pushed their way up through the dirt and broken concrete, the only green thing for miles.

The shops were already doing a brisk business and the streets were heavy with taxis and buses belching out their black smoke. Children darted down the cracked sidewalks, in and out of the pedestrians, looking for an easy mark. Sofia and Sami kept their purses clutched close to their chests.

Every Sunday they made a trip to the market. It was located just outside the city limits, where most of the poor lived in run-down apartments or rented houses that were neglected to the point of squalor. Situated in the middle of a five block by five block square with alleys crisscrossing from all sides, the market was accessible from any direction.

It had been designed by vendors who had food or wares to sell but couldn't afford the unreasonably high rent the city charged for business space. Even a permit to sell in the city streets was too exorbitant for those who had very little income, and what they did make was used for food and clothing.

Tired of having no way to support themselves, they came with tents and lumber and built stalls. Anyone who was selling anything to make an honest living could have a stall. There was no tax, just straight across sales.

The city turned a blind eye to this industry because these were peasants selling handmade trinkets and backyard grown food. They weren't any threat to the city's economy. The real money came from the professional class and the commuters, shopping in the upper-end gallerias, eating in exotic restaurants, having clandestine meetings in five-star hotels. They could afford the high prices and would have no reason to visit the market.

The smell of fried fish hit them before they could even see the market. Sofia inspected the money in her bag. Room and board were included in her contract at The Hotel, and whatever tips she made. The Hotel supplied her dresses for formal occasions and all the lingerie she could ever want, but jeans, sneakers, everyday outfits and personal items had to be purchased with her own money.

As they walked, Sami read from a sheet of paper.

"Chef needs extra tomatoes; they didn't send enough in the regular shipment. Um…Roxie wants some more of those soaps we got her last time, and Natalie wants a loaf of rosemary bread."

Sofia and Sami spent the next hour wandering the stalls, spices from every imaginable culture vying for dominance in the warm spring air. The stands were snugged together to fit in as many as possible. Banners and flags waved from the rooftops, adding cheerful color and breaking up the monotony of brown wood and gray concrete. Vendors called to each other over the aisles. Children and dogs dug through garbage cans looking for scraps or dashed among the stalls hoping for a distracted seller that they could relieve of an apple, a loaf of bread or something to pawn.

Many stalls sold homegrown fruits and vegetables and fresh baked goods. Others, homemade crafts and accessories. Anything from earrings to pipes to paintings. If it could be sold, whether handmade or stolen, no one bothered to inquire, it was on display.

Sami looked at the jewelry and chose a beaded bracelet. She pulled some coins out of her little fringed bag and happily handed them over and received her treasure. She put it on her wrist and went to find Sofia who had moved along to the flower seller. Sofia decided on a handful of pink carnations. She had already acquired some new soaps and a small square of chocolate which were tucked under her arm, wrapped in colorful paper.

Sofia remembered the first time she had tasted chocolate. She was twenty, had been at The Hotel for six months and was already dominating The Wager. Men were betting through the roof for a chance to sleep with her.

The winner that night had been a balding, middle-aged

insurance salesman, average in every way. When they got to his room, Sofia had been surprised when he told her it would be "pure heaven" for her to lick chocolate sauce off him.

He had produced a jar from the mini refrigerator and dipped his penis in it, while Sofia looked on, fascinated. When he shoved it in her face she had looked at the brown ooze suspiciously. It didn't look very appetizing. She had given it a tentative lick and her eyes had rolled back in her head. A moan escaped her lips and then…she wasn't in the room anymore.

She was sitting on a green hillside, the breeze blowing through her hair. She was eating a chocolate ice cream cone. Over and around her tongue swirled, licking up the sides and slurping the top. The sweet and bitter taste filled her senses. She sucked up and down, catching the drips on her tongue.

The man was bucking, sliding through her mouth. She came to her senses in time to move her face out of the way.

The man had seemed a little stunned and sat on the bed staring as if he didn't know where he was. Sofia had asked if she could leave and the man had nodded without comment.

Rufus thought it was the funniest thing he'd ever heard and insisted on calling her Hershey girl for weeks.

Sofia and Sami walked through one of the west end alleys on their way back to The Hotel. Despite the bright sunshine of the morning, the alley was dark and damp, littered with garbage and graffiti. The alleys near the market were safe for the most part. People respected the area and the last time someone was robbed the shopkeepers went after the perpetrator like a lynch mob. Not many were brave enough to cause trouble near the market.

It took less than a minute to come out the other side of the alley into an abandoned lot covered in broken slabs of concrete and barbed wire which marked the edge of the city. A set of stairs made of thick mud and stones, with a shaky metal handrail, wound its way up twenty feet to a dusty sidewalk. It was two miles back to The Hotel, but it was a gorgeous morning and Sofia loved the freedom of being outside. Sami skipped alongside her, swinging her purse.

"I heard about Danielle," Sofia said, which made Sami stop skipping and look at her soberly. "Do you know who got her pregnant?"

"It was Michael, the bellboy with the blond ponytail."

Getting pregnant was an automatic dismissal from The Hotel. Rufus always said, "If they don't know how babies are made by now they need to get out of my sight and get a library card."

"Danielle begged him, said she'd get an abortion, but Rufus threw her out," Sami said sadly. "Some of the girls heard Rufus screaming in his office and I was also told Rufus had Michael beat up for ruining one of his girls."

"Really?" Sofia said. She wasn't surprised about Rufus' anger toward Danielle and Michael. It was a stupid thing to have done. Even if she hadn't gotten pregnant, Rufus would have found out about the affair. Nothing happened in The Hotel without Rufus knowing about it, but having Michael hurt? That seemed extreme even for him.

"Have you heard from her?" Sofia asked, concerned about Danielle living on the street and pregnant.

"She and Michael are living with his parents," Sami told her. "They own a stall at the market and do pretty well selling jam that Michael's mom makes. Michael's going to help out. Who knows, maybe everything will work out. Now Danielle doesn't have to be a prostitute any more and they can be together."

Sami could always spin a happy ending out of any situation and Sofia put her arm around her, squeezing her in a hug. "Next week we'll have to stop at their stall and buy some jam."

It was lunchtime when they returned to The Hotel. Their feet ached and they were starving. They dumped their bags in their room and went down to the second floor to the kitchen. There were four other girls already seated at the long wooden table and Sami and Sofia greeted them with enthusiastic hugs. Every girl was on a different schedule, and they all ate and slept when they had the chance.

Chef was English with a pointed nose and a thin mustache that curled up at the edges. He was slender and had long, delicate hands. He grumbled and complained constantly but though he would go to his death bed denying it, he cared very much for the girls.

Day and night he kept soup or something equally warm and hearty simmering for them and they all knew they were welcome to come in and make themselves a sandwich as long as they didn't get in the way of the kitchen staff.

Sofia and Sami helped themselves to soup heating on the stove, and thick slabs of freshly baked bread. Chef made the bread from scratch, of course; anything else would be "peasantry", and it was warm and soft and delicious.

Halo, which wasn't her real name, yawned, her jaw gaping widely. Sofia could see lacy lingerie peeking out of the neckline of the thin robe she wore. She must have just come off a shift.

Rufus came up with nicknames for the girls to make them more alluring for the customers, also to protect what little privacy they had. When they were working they only used their hotel name so the guests never really knew their true identity.

Sofia was thankful for the anonymity. It was one more layer of protection against getting too personal with the customers. Rufus called her Glory because, as he put it, "You came in like a blaze of one, darling and have been ever since."

Sofia had been quite touched.

Halo yawned again. She was twenty but could easily pass for sixteen. She had blond hair the color of gold and with a bow in her hair and a plaid skirt, she looked like a virginal school girl. The guys loved it.

"Sorry," she said sleepily. "Had a wild one last night. He must have been on something 'cause he didn't stop until he saw the sun. I think I'm going to be sore for a week."

"I hope he at least gave you a good tip," Sofia said.

"Yeah, he did," Halo said with a grin.

Sofia stood. "Well, I'm ready for a nap myself."

She and Sami cleared their dishes and took the elevator to the top floor to rest until the evening.

Sofia wore a halter top that tied loosely in the back and sparkly shorts that showed plenty of butt cheek. Black silk stockings rode up her legs, ending mid-thigh.

Rufus was standing against the wall when she came into the wagering room. He was wearing a light blue tracksuit with white stripes down the sides. A baseball hat was perched on his bald head with "Angel" scrawled across the front in bright pink letters. A very large chain with some sort of gold medallion hung around his neck. It looked ridiculously heavy. He was holding court with three men in business suits. When he saw her he excused himself and came prancing over.

"Well, don't you just look like something else, mm.. mmm." He held open her robe, admiring her decalage and giving everyone in the room a sneak preview of tonight's upcoming events. She rolled her eyes and waited patiently for him to finish his soliloquy on the subject of her breasts.

He tucked the robe back around her and pulled her out of earshot of the men who, once her robe was fastened, had gone back to their talking and drinking.

"I'm glad you're looking so smokin' honey cause we are in for such a treat!" He hopped up and down and grabbed her hands.

"Rufus, I am not hopping with you," said Sofia, starting to lose interest.

"Fine," he said sulkily.

"What's the treat?"

His face brightened and he grabbed her by the shoulders whispering, "The infamous Mr. Hardy has placed a wager!"

"Why are you whispering?" Sofia said, laughing

"Because it's so exciting! He's never been to The Hotel, let alone The Wager. He just waltzed right in, asked for a room, and signed up. It was rather rude that he didn't seek me out and introduce himself, but he is a bit of a snob. He lives in the Lake District but also has an office here in the city. I have extended multiple invitations for him to be a guest here but he's always politely declined."

The Lake District, Sofia thought, fancy. It was two hours away by car and only twenty minutes by train, but to most who lived in the city, it might as well have been on the moon. Sofia had certainly never been there, but she'd heard about the lake the size of a city, the scenery awash with color. There was virtually no crime and no poverty since only the very rich could afford to live there.

"If you ask me, he thinks he's too good for us," Rufus continued his rant. "Yet here he is, giving me his money. Who's the big shot now?"

"Rufus, calm down."

"Can't you feel the electricity in the air?" Rufus said, his eyes a little too bright. He started to bounce again and Sofia put a hand on his shoulder.

"And if he doesn't win, he'll come back again and again, they always do. Especially if they make it this far and see you."

Great, thought Sofia. "Who is he?" she asked.

"He's a lawyer, mostly wills and insurance and blah blah blah." He waved his hand in the air. "Anyway, the important point is that he's rich. Very rich. So if he does manage to win, I want you to show him a very good time. Oh, time to scurry on up," he said, patting her butt.

She scanned the room. "Which one is he?"

Each of the men seemed too young to run a business, but it was hard to tell. A teenage boy with enough stubble could put on a suit and impersonate someone important; it didn't mean they were any cleverer than the next guy.

"He's still playing in the annex."

"You mean he hasn't even made it into The Wager yet?" Sofia rolled her eyes.

"Don't underestimate him, my dear. I hear he's very clever. I'm sure he'll come waltzing in through those doors any minute."

This should be an early night, Sofia thought as she climbed to the balcony. The cocky ones were the easiest. They looked at themselves as irresistible to women when really they didn't have a clue. They finished fast and slept like babies.

Sami was standing at the bottom of the stairs, ready to take Sofia's robe.

Rufus sidled up to her. "Be a dear and tell Tom in the bar to lay on the best scotch. I hear our new guest favors it."

Sami nodded. She wondered who the new guest was. She knew all the high rollers who participated in The Wager and usually heard when a new one showed up. She folded Sofia's robe and set it on the bottom step, then took the back, employees only, hallway to avoid the crush of bodies outside the wagering room.

She entered the main casino area. She scooted around banks of slot machines, the sound of pings and bells and chattering voices an ever-present backdrop. A room, separated from the main casino by a sliding glass door, held five tables, but only one was occupied. Sami pushed back the glass door just enough to slip inside.

The room was called the annex, and it was where thirty hopefuls came to play. Most were knocked out in the first hour, some risking financial ruin to keep playing for an opportunity to walk away with a small fortune, and a beautiful woman, but only five went on to the wagering room. Winner take all.

There were only two men at the table; every other player had either lost his money or called it a night. Sami had lost track of how late it was. This was the last table standing. Whoever won this round would move into the wagering room, where Sofia waited.

Sami scanned the faces to see who was new.

Lambert, the dealer, caught her eye and smiled with a little nod. He was really nice and did great impersonations. He'd just moved in with Angie who worked in her father's deli. He was saving up to buy her a ring.

One player was slumped over his cards, his eyes twitchy and dark. He had just pushed his last set of chips into the pile and was muttering to himself. The other man was leaning back in his chair casually; his cards held loosely in his fingers. He turned and saw Sami. He smiled. Sami's mouth opened in astonishment, and she felt the blood drain out of her face.

She watched as he laid down his cards. Three aces; he'd won. Sami didn't wait but hurried to the bar to talk to Tom, then got back to her post at the bottom of the stairs. She couldn't believe he was here, and about to do The Wager.

She felt sick and sat down to wait.

Sofia didn't feel self-conscious sitting up in her box with eyes continually scanning her. She knew she had a nice body and if men wanted to look at it, well, as long as she got paid, Sofia didn't have a problem with it.

The three men who had been alternately milling around and looking at her, took their places at the table. They were carbon copies of each other. Blond hair plastered down with gel, suits and ties; she doubted any of them was Mr. Hardy. They probably all worked for the same advertising firm.

Sofia heard Jack's laugh before he walked through the doors. He looked very dapper in a white sports coat and grey slacks. He winked at her and she gave him a coquettish smile.

The man who came in next was tall with a lean build. He was wearing a button- down work shirt with the sleeves rolled up, revealing strong, tanned forearms. His hair was raven black and when he looked up at her, his eyes were deep blue; every bit as blue as the luxurious chair she was sitting on.

He had a self-assured air about him, almost an arrogance. This must be Mr. Hardy, Sofia mused. He was very handsome, and she was sure he was well aware of that fact. Sofia started hoping he wouldn't win. The cocky ones were easy, but they were also annoying.

He didn't smile, or let his gaze linger, he just did a quick glance and then took his place at the table. He had a glass of amber liquid that he sipped on as the night progressed. One after the other the blond advertising boys forfeited or lost their chips until it was only Jack and Hardy left.

There was no time limit for The Wager, and it was almost

midnight. Sofia shifted in her chair.

Duke dealt the cards and the men examined their hands. She already knew Jack had a good set by the way he stroked his goatee. She studied the other man, but he merely set his cards face down and called Jack's bet. His hands were still, resting on the table, waiting.

Jack asked for two cards, but Hardy seemed content with his hand. Fool, she thought, you could always make a hand better. It was Jack's turn to bet, and he threw a stack of chips into the pile. Hardy set a matching stack on the table and then slid a larger stack next to it.

Jack stared at the pile of chips, his face giving nothing away, but Sofia saw his ring finger start to twitch a steady rhythm. He pushed forward the last of his chips and put his cards face up on the table. He had three kings. Sofia held her breath. She knew Jack, she was comfortable with Jack.

Hardy turned over his cards, revealing a full house.

CHAPTER 6

HARDY SHOOK JACK'S HAND, while Duke gathered his chips together. Rufus came over to congratulate him. Sofia waited for some sort of acknowledgement, but Hardy turned away from Rufus and strode out the door.

Well, he was a cocky bastard, wasn't he? She went down the stairs and found Sami holding out her robe. Sami's complexion was always fair, but she looked particularly pale and her normally upturned lips were pinched in a thin straight line.

"What is it, Sami? Are you sick?"

Sami just shook her head and helped Sofia with the tie to her robe. Rufus trotted up to them.

"Wasn't that exciting? A very tense stand off. Mr. Hardy has requested that you change and meet him in his room."

"Change?" Sofia said, looking down at herself. "Change into what?"

"I don't know. Maybe he wants to take you dancing."

Sofia sputtered out a laugh. "Yeah, right."

"Just wear something pretty," Rufus said impatiently, flapping his arms.

She and Sami returned to their room, Sami uncommonly quiet. When they got to the tenth floor, the elevator stopped, letting on a full-figured woman with long blond extensions that fell to her well-rounded butt. This was Bea the Beautiful, a very unoriginal moniker one of her regulars had come up with.

Bea, whose real name was Evelyn, opened her mouth in a huge yawn.

"Just starting?" Sofia asked sympathetically.

"Yeah. I woke up like thirty minutes ago. Now I gotta go drink champagne and kanoodle. What I could really use is a vat of coffee."

"I hear you, sister," said Sofia.

The elevator stopped at floor fifteen and Bea got out, blowing them a kiss.

"Ok, Sami," said Sofia as the elevator started moving again, "what's bothering you?"

"Nothing, I'm just tired."

Sofia didn't argue. She knew it was more than that, but the poor thing did look exhausted, paler than usual with dark circles under her eyes.

Back in the room, Sofia reapplied makeup that had smudged and brushed her hair.

Sami was staring out of the window. It was dark so she couldn't see anything but flickering lights, and her own reflection. The windows drizzled with rain, hiding her tears. She felt so badly for Sofia having to be with all these men, and this time it was her own actions that were the reason.

"Is wrinkled ball the new look we're going for?" Sofia asked from behind her. Sami started and turned around guiltily, wiping her face. She looked down and saw the bunched-up dress in her hands.

"I am so sorry!" she cried, rushing for the ironing board.

"No, don't." Sofia laughed. "Sami, don't. I'll just wear a different one." She took the iron out of Sami's hand and set it carefully on the board. She looked into Sami's red- rimmed eyes. "Are you crying? You're not upset about the dress are you, because it really doesn't matter."

"I'm not crying," said Sami, wiping another tear off her cheek.

"Oh, come here, sweetie," Sofia said, holding out her arms. Sami went to her and they sat on the bed; arms wrapped around each other tightly as if they could make each other's demons go away.

Sami sniffed. "I just feel so bad that you have to go through this tonight. I feel like it's my fault."

"How on earth could it be your fault?" Sofia hugged her. "Sami, this is my job. Why is it upsetting you so much this time?"

Sami shrugged, picking at the bedspread. She had never lied to Sofia, never withheld anything important from her, but Sami was too ashamed to tell Sofia what she'd done.

"It's nothing," Sami said, taking a deep breath. She smiled at Sofia and wiped her face. "Sometimes the whole thing gets to me, you know?"

Sofia looked at Sami with concern. She was such a happy

girl that it was easy to forget that she was surrounded by a world of greed and sex, and how that might affect her.

"Is there something you want to talk about? Is it about Rhys?"

Sami shook her head adamantly. "No, nothing like that. Never mind. I'm really ok."

"You're sure?" Sofia said doubtfully.

"Absolutely," Sami said, jumping off the bed and pulling Sofia to her feet. "Now let's find you something gorgeous to wear for the oh-so mysterious Mr. Hardy," she giggled.

His room was on the twenty-fifth floor. Sofia straightened her dress and ran her fingers through her long hair, cascading in bouncy waves down her back. She felt a little nervous, and she wasn't sure why. It was always an unknown approaching a new john. Would he want her to be rough, submissive, playful?

She took a deep breath and knocked. She heard him come to the door. It opened and there he was, just as she remembered, raven-black hair and piercing blue eyes. He wore jeans and a button-up shirt. She could see a chain at the V of his neck. His hair was wet like he'd just gotten out of the shower, and it was slicked back messily. He looked young. She doubted he was thirty yet.

She felt a wave of self-assurance. He wasn't that big of a deal, she thought. Sure, he was good looking, but that was just the way his face was arranged; it had no power over her. She was still the one in control.

"Hello," he said, smiling. "Please come in."

Sofia stepped inside and he held out a glass of champagne. She took it, thankful that her hands weren't shaking. She looked around the room. It was one of the nicer suites, spacious with a sofa, large screen tv, desk, computer. The bedroom was separated by a shuttered door and there was a small kitchen with a microwave, stove, refrigerator and dishwasher. Everything a working man needed to mix business with pleasure.

The rooms were designed specifically for men who chose to spend their nights at The Hotel rather than go home during the week. Many didn't go home until Friday night. Was that the case with this guy? Did he have a family somewhere waiting anxiously for the weekend so they could see hubby and daddy? There were no pictures that indicated whether he had a family. The room was bare of anything personal except his suitcase, dug through but still packed, two dress shirts on hangers in the closet, and a laptop.

She poked her head in the bathroom; it looked similar, if a little smaller, to her own. Toothbrush and paste, a razor, deodorant and cologne were filed neatly in a row on the counter.

She turned to look at him. He was still smiling, and she could see faint crinkle lines near his eyes. He had a nice smile, she thought.

"Does everything meet your standards?" he said, taking a sip of his drink. She noticed he wasn't drinking champagne but the same amber liquid that he'd been drinking during The Wager.

She smiled. "Oh, I don't have standards, believe me."

He laughed and held up his glass. "Cheers," he said.

She drank and felt the bubbles bounce happily to her head. She tipped back the rest of the glass and held it out to him. He poured more champagne, watching her as he did.

"Come sit down, please," he said, setting his own glass on a table and leading her to a small leather sofa. "My name is James."

"Why, hello James," she said, putting on a slight southern drawl. She sometimes liked to pretend she was someone else, from somewhere far away. "I'm Glory. It is such a pleasure to meet you."

"Glory, huh?" he said with a teasing grin. "That name doesn't really suit you."

She wanted to sneer at him, but she clenched her teeth and said, "Well, that's my name, sugar, so you'd better get used to saying it."

He put his arm on the back of the couch and turned to her, with that provoking smile that was really starting to irritate her. She batted her eyelashes but lowered her eyes, avoiding meeting his. She trailed a finger along his thigh and when he took it, holding it there, resting on his leg, she looked up at him.

His eyes were bluer than any body of water she'd ever seen, even in pictures. He looked back at her, not with greed or lust, but something else; a familiarity that had her heart thumping heavily in her chest and a flush creeping up her neck.

Before it reached her cheeks in a full blush, she hiked

her dress up to her thighs and straddled him. She leaned into him on her knees, until her breasts were at his eye level and her hand was on his crotch.

"So what do you want, sugar?" she said, her voice lowering and flowing like silk.

He frowned at her and stopped her hands, pushing her back slightly so her butt landed back on the couch. She bit off an expletive.

"I thought we'd just talk for a while," he said mildly.

Sofia blinked. "Talk?"

James laughed at her expression. "You do know how to carry on a conversation?"

"Yes," she said indignantly, undoing her sandal straps so she wasn't tempted to gaze at his beautiful smile. She stretched her feet in front of her until they were resting on his thigh, and smoothed her dress over her knees, trying to think of something to say.

He watched her with an amused expression that she wanted to slap off his face.

"So James, what brings you to the city?" she said, rolling her eyes and huffing out a sigh.

He grinned and rubbed his hand down the side of her foot making her flinch in surprise. He stroked from her toe to her heel, trailing a finger along her arch. As he slowly worked his hand to the bottom of her foot, rubbing gently, she felt her tight muscles start to relax.

"I had to be here for business," he said, dragging his thumb across her smooth skin.

She closed her eyes and when his other hand joined the

first, his fingers kneading into her flesh on the sole of her foot, a soft moan escaped her lips. He watched, fascinated as her face relaxed and the hard mouth softened.

"I'm supposed to be working." He laughed quietly.

"And what brought you to The Hotel?" she said, her eyes still closed. She was practically purring under his touch. "Rufus said it's your first time."

"Curiosity, I guess."

"What do you mean, curiosity?"

He was quiet for so long that Sofia opened one eye. He was still gazing at her with that lazy smile while his hands worked magic on her feet. His eyes were electric and when she forgot to look away and found herself staring into them, her chest began to pound uncomfortably.

"Do you have any family?" he asked.

The change of subject was so sudden that she had to clear her throat before answering.

"Well, the girls are my family, but if you mean a regular mom and dad, no they died when I was really young."

"I'm very sorry to hear that."

Sofia shrugged. "It turned out for the best. We all would have been miserable if they'd lived."

He looked down at her feet and stroked a palm over the top of one.

"My parents died when I was young too."

"You didn't grow up on the streets, though," she said, already knowing the answer. People didn't get to be like him fighting for survival as a child. Rufus said he had come from money. She wondered who had taken care of him when his parents had died.

"No, I was fortunate to have our house in The Lake District to grow up in," he said. For a moment his hands stilled and his face changed. Sofia breathed in quickly at the sadness and frustration that crossed his features. She blinked and it was like those lines and angles that distorted his face into something tragic, had never been there. His eyes were soft and inviting, a smile quirked on his lips. "Anyway, I was lucky. I'm sorry you can't say the same."

His hands continued to move expertly across her feet. He dug both his thumbs into the pads below her toes and she closed her eyes again and leaned her head back.

"Who says I'm not lucky? I get to spend the night with you, sugar." She drawled out the last word and James laughed.

They were quiet for a while and usually Sofia would avoid long silences. With johns it was awkward as hell, but she didn't feel that way right now. It was like she was alone, but better because she was getting a foot rub. She smiled and felt herself drifting, floating away on a champagne bubble.

James wondered if she knew she was smiling. He watched as her chest took on a steady rhythm, rising and falling. Her face relaxed and she was no longer the hard ice- queen sitting on her throne, or some coquettish chameleon who changed identities depending on the audience. She was soft, her jaw loose like she'd finally let go of all the tension she held clamped behind her back molars.

James continued the slow, lazy circles he was making with his thumbs on the bottom of her feet, watching her sleep. He thought he knew what he was doing when he'd come to

The Hotel tonight, but now the only thing he knew was, he was in trouble.

Sofia was dreaming of sunsets, the yellows and reds swirling beneath her closed lids. She wasn't so far down that she couldn't feel the pulsing bliss on her feet and when her eyes fluttered open for a moment she'd forgotten where she was.

She blinked over at James who was still watching her with an amused expression on his face.

"What?" she said defensively, running her fingers through her hair.

"Nothing. Did you have a nice nap?"

She cleared her throat and sneered at him. "I wasn't sleeping. I'm just bored."

James chuckled.

"So what do you do? Rufus said you're a lawyer," Sofia said, yawning.

"Yes, I'm a lawyer. I mostly work out of my home in The Lake District, but I have to come to the city for meetings sometimes." He moved his hands to her ankle.

"Sounds exciting," she said, sighing as he rubbed his hands farther up to her calf. He stopped there, massaging the muscle, squeezing just hard enough to send an aching pleasure up her leg.

When he touched the back of her knee she felt a jolt go through her and suddenly she was wide awake. She purposely closed her eyes again, keeping her face relaxed, not wanting him to see how much his touch was affecting her. He trailed his fingertips in a swirling pattern, feathery light under her dress and up her inner thigh. "It's actually quite boring," he said. "A lot of time on the phone."

"Do you ever go to court?"

"Sometimes."

She smiled and opened her eyes. "Have you ever been in contempt of court?"

He laughed. "Do you even know what that means?"

"Hey, I watch tv."

As James Hardy caressed her leg and they talked about stupid things like television shows, and their favorite food, Sofia was fully aware that she'd dropped the southern belle charade an hour before. What's worse, she had been looking straight at him, gazing into those sapphire eyes and memorizing every facet of them.

She couldn't believe she'd let it go on for as long as it had as she closed her eyes and didn't respond to his last question. She let a heartbeat go by and then opened her eyes and, pulling her legs away from him, crawled on her hands and knees toward him. She climbed in his lap so their faces were level; but she avoided his eyes, staring intently at his right shoulder.

Her skirt bunched up around her thighs and he could easily see the miniscule pair of panties she was wearing.

"What do you want, sugar?" she drawled.

James frowned and put a fingertip to her chin. "Don't do that with me."

She blinked and opened her mouth without knowing what she was going to say.

"Look at me," he said quietly.

She did and immediately regretted it. Her eyes met his and he held her gaze for a long moment before bringing his glance down to her mouth. She parted her lips without thinking and he leaned forward and kissed her.

He tasted like alcohol, and his lips were soft. As he deepened the kiss his lips became more insistent and when he swiped his tongue into her mouth, she plunged her hands into his hair and kissed him back, enjoying the heat that was building inside her. It was so unexpected that she gave into it, not even trying to temper the burn of passion that throbbed in her core.

He pulled away and ran a finger down the side of her face to her neck, and his hand moved softly down her throat. He brought his hands to her shoulders and slid the straps of her dress slowly down her arms until the tops of her breasts were exposed. Her heart thumped violently as he kissed her neck, and she tingled in all the places that she wanted him to touch her.

The ice wall that Sofia had built and fortified over the years started to seep under his mouth as he moved to her collarbone where her breasts were almost spilling over the top of her dress. She couldn't stop the shiver of anticipation that went through her body like electricity when James took hold of the straps of her dress. He surprised her by pulling them back onto her shoulders, lifting her off his lap and standing up.

She laid sprawled where he left her, confused and aching with need. He walked to the table and took a sip of his drink.

"I don't frequent these places as a rule," he said, staring down into his glass. He swirled the liquid around and then drained the contents.

Sofia rolled her eyes and straightened her dress.

"This Wager seems to me a bit desperate. I don't like to put my money down unless I know the outcome." He looked at her with a slight smile. She sneered at him. He looked down at his empty glass and set it on the table. He turned to her, his eyes no longer playful. She couldn't have looked away if she'd wanted to, and at that moment, she didn't want to.

"I'm not here to use you. I won't have sex with you unless you want me to. It has to be completely consensual, and I'm not talking about getting paid. I'm talking about *wanting* it."

She let out her breath in a gasp. If it were anyone else she would have laughed in his face, but the fierceness and passion behind his voice and his eyes had her speechless.

He took two strides, and he was standing in front of her. Her breath caught in surprise, and he gestured for her to stand up and turn around. She faced the wall and felt his warm hands on her back as he unzipped her dress.

"Why did you make me change if you were just going to undress me?" Sofia said, lowering her voice seductively.

"Because I wanted to see you in something other than that ridiculous costume you were wearing." He kissed her shoulder, and his breath was warm on her skin. "You're too beautiful to dress like a prostitute."

He moved his hands up her bare back and she shuddered, tiny bumps dotting her arms.

"But I am a prostitute, James," she said, her voice a little unsteady.

"But you're also a woman," he whispered against her neck. "And should be treated as such."

He lowered the dress to the floor, kneeling as he went. He proceeded to kiss and do other amazing things with his mouth. When he reached her butt cheeks, hanging out from her satin underwear, he cupped them with his hands, at the same time flicking his thumbs into the straps of her panties and slowly pulling them down.

She was quivering when he told her to turn around. He was still kneeling at her feet and his eyes took in every inch of her. For some ridiculous reason she had the urge to cover herself.

He stood and scanned her face, her collar bone, her breasts, as if trying to memorize every last detail. His eyes were sparking like blue flames, making Sofia's breath catch. The desire in them was obvious, but it wasn't just lust. He gazed at her like she was some sort of goddess to be worshiped. He reached out a hand slowly and slid his palm down the side of her breast. Sofia was trembling with adrenaline as his fingers traced over her abdomen and down her arms.

He entwined his hand with hers and led her to the bedroom, pushing her gently down on the huge, plush bed. He leaned over her and ran both his hands up her sides until they reached her breasts. A trail of fire burned across her skin, everywhere his fingers touched her.

She tried to get a grip, to shut this seduction down and force him to get it over with, but every pore was soaking up the pleasure that he was giving her and she never wanted him to stop.

She grew impatient, wanting to be closer. She grabbed his collar and pulled his mouth down to hers. She opened her mouth, welcoming his tongue, letting him taste her. His lips were intoxicating, and her arms came around his neck, pulling him in, as if she needed his kiss more than oxygen.

He broke away and looked in her eyes. He was smiling but Sofia couldn't read his expression. She took a deep breath, needing to get a hold of herself. She started to wriggle away but then he was kissing down her body, licking, touching, nibbling as he went until her nerve endings were raw and aching.

He crawled back up; stomach, breast, collarbone, neck, until his mouth was by her ear.

"What do you want?" he whispered.

She laughed and pushed at him. "You bastard." It was as if he was reading her mind, as if he could sense the confusion in her.

He kissed her mouth and started moving his way back down her body. She was on fire, wanting him closer to her, wanting him inside her.

"Fine. What are you waiting for then?" Her hands were in his hair, and he was smiling roguishly at her.

Her nails dragged down his arms and she looked into his eyes. She saw a hot intensity that burned into her like a brand, but also a longing that made her pulse race.

"I want to hear you say it," he said, his mouth back by her ear. She had lost track of where he was because he was *everywhere*.

He took her lips again, kissing her for a long time and before she could stop them her hands were in his hair, clutching at it, pulling him closer.

He drew his mouth away. "Say it," he said in a low growl.

She was shivering now, wanting him. It was exhilarating and terrifying and she gave herself to it.

"I want you to have sex with me," she said, her breath hitching.

"I thought you'd never ask." He smiled and undid the buttons of his shirt and kicked off his pants and boxers.

Her body was pulsing for him but out of habit she closed her eyes. He leaned over her.

"Look at me," he said in a deep voice.

She opened her eyes. They met his and at that moment he entered her. She let out a moan, closing her eyes again and throwing her head back. He began a rhythmic thrust and retreat, filling her up and pulling back, hitting every nerve ending as he moved.

She wrapped her legs around him, tipping her hips so he'd go deeper. They were both panting, and still James never looked away from her. He was watching when her core came unraveled and her body shuddered, gripping her in waves of pleasure.

When he heard her breathless cries and knew she'd gone over, he let himself go over with her.

CHAPTER 7

SOFIA LAY IN BED, looking at a small crack on the ceiling. She'd have to tell Rufus about that she thought, almost numbly. She watched the room lighten as the sun came up and spread its glow through the windows.

She turned to look at the man sleeping next to her. His breathing was deep, and he had such a look of peace on his face. The sleep of the untroubled, she thought. He wore a chain around his neck with a small round pendant. One arm was cradled under his head, his other resting on his chest.

After they'd had sex, James had stayed awake drinking coffee and talking to her, not wanting her to go. He asked about her childhood, and she'd given him vague answers, not wanting to say too much. He'd finally given in to exhaustion and fallen asleep. She'd stayed and watched him sleep for an hour.

Disgusted with herself, she threw off the sheet and walked naked to the bathroom. Last night had been a mistake. She had let it get too personal and she'd enjoyed herself way too much. She was fond of some of the regulars, but this was different, and dangerous.

She stared at her reflection in the mirror. Her hair was disheveled, and makeup was lining her eyes. She hadn't once tried to stop him, hadn't let her mind float away to the clouds. Between the conversation and the captivating use of his hands, she had completely forgotten to distance herself. She hadn't wanted to, and the thought pressed into her, making her want to throw up.

She had never become emotionally attached to a john and she wasn't about to start now. It was morning and it was time for her to go. Hopefully he'd got his curiosity about The Wager out of his system and she'd never have to see him again.

She splashed cold water on her face and combed her fingers through her hair. She went back to the bedroom and started looking for her dress.

"I want to see you again."

She jumped when he spoke. He was watching her, propped on one elbow.

"I'm sure you do, James, but you only get the one night." She found her dress inside out on the floor.

"No, I mean see you. Go on a date. Maybe meet in the market and have a coffee."

She laughed at the absurdity of the idea. "Sure," she scoffed. "I can just picture us walking hand in hand through the market like two little lovebirds. Listen, I appreciate the gesture, but lots of people want to buy me things or take me places. It doesn't mean they get to do it. This is my job. You want to see me again? Play The Wager like everyone else."

"Don't you ever do anything outside of The Wager? You're not a prisoner here?" he said, propping himself up with pillows so his back was against the headboard. Sofia flipped the dress in her hands back and forth trying to find the opening.

"Not wanting to go out with you does not make me a prisoner."

"So you do go out?" he said.

"I have friends, if that's what you mean."

"Well good, let me be your friend. Meet me at the market as friends."

She'd managed to get the dress over her head and zipped up halfway. That would have to do. Her shoes in hand, she turned toward the door. He got out of bed and slipped on his boxers.

"What are you afraid of?" he asked, coming toward her.

She shot him a filthy look. "I'm not afraid of anything. The night's over. I don't have to stay here any longer."

"Sofia, please," he said quietly.

The shock of hearing her name made her heart lodge in her throat. Turning on him she said, "How do you know my name? Who told you?" She pointed a finger at his bare chest. Had this been some sort of set up? Was this one of Rufus' tests?

"Sami," he said

"What?" she shouted.

"I know Sami. She delivers messages to my office."

That must have been why Sami was so upset; she had recognized James. "And what's that got to do with me?" Sofia asked, holding her chin up.

"I saw her walking with you at the market the other week and I asked her who you were."

"She told you my name, where I worked?"

"She told me your name and that she lived with you at The Hotel. The rest I found out by myself. You're a very hard woman to get a moment alone with. Was The Wager Rufus' demented scheme?"

"Anything it takes to spice up his life. I think he's so high all the time, nothing really excites him anymore."

"That's a sad way to live," James said, looking at her mouth.

"What were you doing at the market?" she said, looking down at the shoes in her hand, afraid to let him see how much she wanted his lips on hers again.

"I like to support small business owners; plus the food there is better."

She cast her mind back, trying to remember if she had seen his face before, but she knew she would have remembered him. He was looking at her with those eyes and that half-smile. He was such an arrogant bastard, she thought. "So, what? You placed a wager to have sex with me?"

"Only to see you, to talk to you. The rest was just a side benefit," he grinned.

She really did want to punch him.

"Why didn't you just come up to me?" she asked.

"Rufus wouldn't tolerate me spending time with you if he wasn't making a profit. Anyway, would you have talked to a complete stranger who came up and said he wanted to get to know you?"

"No. I would have kicked him in the balls."

"My point exactly." He traced his fingertips down her neck. She felt a twinge of pleasure and the hairs stood up on her arms. "Maybe now I'm a paying customer he won't mind us going on a harmless date." He took her hands and drew her closer to him until their mouths were inches apart. "Will you see me again?" he whispered, his lips brushing against hers.

She leaned into him and kissed him back for a long time. His hands were in her hair, and her shoes were clutched painfully against her chest.

She pulled away and looked into his eyes and said, "I can't," and slipped out of the room. She wasn't sure why she felt tears stinging her eyes.

The trip to the thirtieth floor seemed to last a lifetime.

Sami was folding clothes and she was shocked by the look of exhaustion on Sofia's face. She ran her a bath and made sure the bed was ready for her.

Sofia sat in the water until it went from hot to tepid, her arms wrapped around her knees, replaying what had happened last night. She thought about his lips on her body, scorching her skin.

She closed her eyes and laid her head down on her knees. She could smell his expensive cologne on her, but she didn't wash it off. Instead she inhaled deeply letting the scent transport her back to when she was in his arms. She hadn't even cared; she'd wanted him so badly.

She was used to that look of lust in a man's eyes and at first James had been no different. She knew he wanted her body like they all did, but then he had knelt at her feet and gazed on her like a precious work of art. He had brought out desires and longings in her that she had buried long ago.

Afterwards he'd listened to her silly ramblings with real interest, and she had found herself soaking up that attention like parched ground when the rain finally falls.

Shivering in the now cold water, she got out of the tub and padded out of the bathroom naked, leaving her towel lying on the floor. She walked to the full-length mirror, leaving wet footprints on the carpet, and studied her reflection.

Her skin was smooth, and the morning sunlight cast shadows off her curves and angles. Nothing had changed. She thought she'd look different, as if the signs of what he had done to her would be burned into her skin. Her body had joined to his like it was the most natural thing in the world.

Sami tried not to think too much about what Sofia did when she was with a guest, but this morning she couldn't help it. She couldn't remember Sofia ever spending the night in a man's room, and had woken up early in a panic when Sofia wasn't beside her.

Then Sofia had come back looking pale and shaken. Sami felt a knot of guilt in the pit of her stomach for what she had done. It had been a horrible mistake and now Sofia was paying for it.

Sofia felt relief as she laid down on the soft sheets and pulled the huge comforter to her chin. She started to think of him again and then her mind slammed down a steel barrier between those thoughts and reality. He was a john, that's all he was and there was no way he was going to rattle her. She could forget all about Mr. What The Fuck His Name Was and get on with her life.

Sami came and lay next to her. She reached out and brushed Sofia's hair with her fingers. She stroked slowly and rhythmically until Sofía was floating again, this time into the sweet oblivion of sleep.

CHAPTER 8

THE NEXT TWO SUNDAYS Sofia scanned the market looking for James. She knew deep down that she hoped to see him. She couldn't stop thinking about the way he looked at her when he said he wanted to see her again. Every part of her had wanted to say yes, but she knew it was impossible. They'd go on a date and then, what? Become a couple? She laughed out loud at the idea and Sami gave her a strange look. Besides, Rufus would never allow it. She'd lose her standing at The Hotel and possibly her job.

She hadn't mentioned to Sami about talking to James. She realized that's what Sami had been upset about the other night and Sofia knew she was already punishing herself far more than anyone else could. Sami prided herself on her hard work and professionalism. Telling James about Sofia had been out of character for her. Sofia wondered why she'd done it but didn't want to embarrass her by asking.

Sundays were Sofia's days off and now and again she liked to visit her old patch where she'd lived before she went to

The Hotel. She knew many of the families and prostitutes living there and tried to help out where she could. She'd heard Grandmother Linnie, as everyone called her, had been ill and her granddaughter Maria had just had a baby.

Sofia had asked Rufus if she could make sandwiches for them or bring them soup from the kitchen, but he had laughed in her face telling her he wasn't running a charity, so she began hoarding food from her own meals. She wasn't restricted to how much she ate so it wasn't difficult to gather a significant amount of food by the following week.

Sofia went in the morning when most of the undesirables like pimps and muggers were catching up on much needed rest after their nocturnal routines. It was drizzling so she put on her raincoat and bundled the food into a plastic bag.

She took the bus and was let off in a neighborhood where houses with overgrown lawns pressed against a row of three-story apartment buildings that had seen little if no upkeep for years.

Sofia entered the stairwell of one of the buildings and climbed to the second floor. The surrounding walls smelled like urine and there was an unidentifiable substance splashed on the concrete slab of the landing.

A baby was howling behind the door where Sofia stopped and knocked. The door opened and the bag of food slipped out of her hands and onto the ground. Her eyes widened in shock and her pulse thundered in her throat.

"James?"

It was him, there could be no doubt, standing in the doorway of Grandmother Linnie's apartment, the smell of dirty diapers and onions wafting behind him.

"What the hell are you doing here?" she spluttered, hardly able to get the words out.

"I, um…" His face had gone pale when he'd opened the door and now it was a deep shade of pink, darkening his already tanned skin. "I was just leaving."

He bent down and picked up the bag Sofia had dropped and handed it to her. She took it in stunned silence. He put a hand on her shoulder and squeezed gently, then he sidled past her and was down the stairs and gone before she could utter another word.

She stood looking after him with her mouth hanging open.

"Sofia?" said a voice from inside. Sofia went in and closed the door behind her.

The room was small with an adjoining kitchen. Sofia had been there before so she knew there were only two bedrooms and one bathroom. Last time she visited, Linnie was living there with her granddaughter, Maria and her newborn, two nieces and a distant cousin who also had a three year old.

The floor was covered with colorful toys scattered like a minefield. Jumbles of clothes layered every surface, and dishes were piled high on the counter. Grandmother Linnie was sitting at a card table positioned in the small space between the entryway and kitchen, a cup of coffee in front of her. An abandoned cup was across from her.

Maria was standing by the window bouncing a small bundle in her arms. She was a petite girl, only nineteen, with fair skin and flaxen hair cut in a bob along her chin.

"Sofia, how nice to see you," Linnie said. She spoke with a juicy smacking sound, her lack of teeth collapsing her lips. "Is that for us?" she asked, pointing at the bag.

"Oh, yes, sorry," Sofia said, setting the bag on the table absently. She sat down in an empty chair, her wobbly legs no longer able to support her. "Why was James Hardy here?"

Linnie smiled, her face scrunching up so her lips disappeared. "Isn't he just wonderful? He's so attentive, and very good with the baby."

Sofia felt her stomach drop. "Oh my God," she said aloud without realizing it. "James is the father?"

Linnie stared at her a moment, her mouth slack, then she threw back her head and laughed. Even Maria started chuckling as she continued to bounce.

"No! He's helping Maria get her hospital bills paid since her insurance denied her. He's a lawyer, you know, and very smart."

Sofia closed her eyes as a wave of relief washed over her. She didn't want to think about why she was so relieved but then she said, "How on earth can you afford a lawyer, Linnie?"

"It's free," Maria said in her quiet drawl. Sofia turned to look at her.

"Free?"

Maria nodded. "He isn't charging us anything. Isn't that sweet?" she said, still bouncing. The baby had stopped wailing and cooed quietly in its mother's arms.

Sofia turned back to Linnie. "How did you…I mean how do you even know him?"

"Didn't you know, dear," Linnie said, "he helped put

Hector Faxen away."

Sofia didn't think she could take one more shock. "What do you mean? I thought Ebony had some public defender?"

Ebony's story was renowned in the prostitution circle although the case had gotten very little media coverage. It had been a year ago and Sofia had heard through The Hotel grapevine that Hector Faxen, a pimp notorious for beating his girls, finally had one of them turn on him.

Sofia could count on one hand the number of girls who went to the cops for being mistreated by their pimp or a john. Everyone accepted that it was the risk of the job and the backlash was usually worse than the original offense. But Hector had gone too far and raped Ebony, which was not unheard of but frowned upon, and Ebony was pissed.

She turned Hector in, and the case went to trial. Sofia didn't know the details of what happened in the courtroom, except that Ebony had won the suit and Hector had gone away for eighteen months. Apparently, when he gets out, if Hector goes near Ebony again, he faces serious prison time. Ebony moved to a different part of the city, just to be safe.

Linnie shook her head and dug through her purse, pulling out a crumpled pack of cigarettes. "She was going to have a public defender, some pimply-faced kid straight outta law school, but Mr. Hardy stepped in and said he would take the case. He was something else. The other lawyer was trying to make out like it was Ebony's fault, like she deserved it or something for being a hooker, but Mr. Hardy straightened them out."

Sofia sat in dazed silence and watched Linnie light a

cigarette. The old woman held it in two crooked fingers and blew out a long stream of smoke.

"Didn't charge Ebony nothin'. So when Maria was gettin' the run around by these damn insurance fellas, I gave him a call."

"And he came and helped you, just like that?"

Linnie nodded and sucked on her cigarette. "Just like that. He's already gotten them to cover the hospital costs and now he's going after them for hardship and trauma on a new mother." She cackled. "He says we'll be set up with diapers for years. Like I said, he's a smart one. He may look pretty on the outside, but there's one tough son of a bitch underneath."

Sofia felt numb as she said her goodbyes and made the trek back to The Hotel. She was glad her mind hadn't finished processing this new information yet because she didn't think she could handle it. She was already on a double-edged sword when it came to James Hardy. She felt that ice wall around her heart weakening and she mentally pushed against it, holding it in place.

The best thing to do was to put it out of her mind, and for the most part she was able to because it was May and time for Rufus' Spring Ball. Rufus adored parties and threw them whenever possible, but the Spring Ball was an event that people paid thousands to get into. The decorations and the women decked out in their finery was worth the price of admission, but it was also a chance for the upper echelon of the city to rub elbows. This included crime bosses, celebrities, political figures, and anyone else Rufus thought could make him money. It was an opportunity to show off his girls and all the many pleasures to be had at The Hotel.

"The girls will be glowing and the champagne will be flowing," Rufus boasted.

The night of the ball, Sami was in her element. When Sofia didn't need her she was dressing one of the other girls, or helping Chef put out food or watching the last of the ice sculptures being crafted. She was too young to attend the ball so she soaked up as much ambiance as she could beforehand. She especially liked watching the seven piece orchestra tune up. The music was the best part.

As guests began arriving, the atmosphere was electric. Girls in gorgeous dresses held trays of champagne and offered them to the men and women, but predominantly men, coming in the door. This wasn't the sort of ball where men brought their wives to dance the night away; this was an opportunity to network with other like-minded entrepreneurs and end the night in bed with a beautiful young prostitute, all in the name of business, of course.

Sofia was wearing a form-fitting green dress that cascaded to the floor and shimmered like liquid emeralds. The bodice was a corset that laced up in the back, cinching her waist and leaving her breasts barely contained. Sami had ironed her hair straight and it hung down her back like silk.

Maryanne met her at the entrance to the ballroom. Sofia's friend was bouncing with excitement and looked stunning in a long black dress with a slit that went all the way to her thigh and beyond. Her long red hair was tied up in a twisted knot.

"Who do you think will ask us to dance first? I hope

it's no one who comes to The Hotel already. I want to meet someone new. Maybe a foreign ambassador or a movie star."

"You'll have plenty to choose from. Look at how many people are here."

The ballroom was a crush of bodies. Women in a rainbow of sparkling dresses and men in black tuxedos danced, while others stood away from the dance floor alone, glancing hopefully at members of the opposite sex, or in groups discussing business, politics, or the latest scandal.

Every year it seemed Rufus' ball got bigger. He liked to surround himself with influential people and this was a major night of networking for him. Sofia, Maryanne and dozens of other girls were there to mingle, flirt and dance with as many men as possible.

That night they were all for sale, no matter their status. They were there for the sampling so the gentlemen would want to come back. She saw Meechelle on the dance floor, her hips crushed up against an older man with a white beard. Even without her five inch stilettos she would have towered over him.

Sofia's strategy was to be pleasant and show the guests a good time but never spend long enough with one man that he had an opportunity to ask her back to his room. In past years it had worked like a charm.

Rufus came up behind where Sofia and Maryanne were standing, and inserted himself between them, taking their arms. He was wearing a white tuxedo with sparkling blue buttons and blue platform shoes. A white top hat with a glittery blue bow was perched dashingly on his shiny bald head.

"What do you think ladies? I say, spectacular!" He gestured to the room where candles lit up every surface, their glow reflected in the crystal chandeliers hanging from the ceiling.

Tables were laden down with meats, cheeses, seafood, fruit, pies and cakes, all catered by the best restaurants the city had to offer. Huge pots overflowing with blue hydrangeas, brilliant green roses, lilies and hot pink miniature carnations released an intoxicating perfume. Chairs were lined along the walls for those not dancing. Champagne fountains, chocolate fountains and ice sculptures created focal points around the room.

Several girls were positioned around the room, unmoving, like statues, their naked torsos painted gold. Little bowls with tickets sat in front of them; the girls would be raffled off at midnight.

"Très Magnifique!" he cried.

"You've certainly out done yourself, Rufus," Sofia said.

"Haven't I just! Well, don't cower in the doorway. Get in there and mingle, you beautiful creatures." He gave them a little shove and they moved forward into the crowd.

Maryanne tottered away, making a beeline for a group of handsome men huddled in a circle, smoking cigars.

Sofia walked around the room slowly, talking to gentlemen as she went. A few she knew, most she didn't. They all could have done The Wager for all she knew. For the most part she blocked out faces to keep things impersonal, so she often didn't recognize men, even the ones she had slept with.

She complimented them on their tuxedos, giggled at

their jokes, touched their arms and caressed their shoulders, and then quickly moved on to the next one.

She watched the dancers moving across the floor or swaying in their own bubble to a jaunty jazz tune. A waiter came by with a tray of champagne. She took one of the flutes and gave him a sympathetic smile. The waitstaff worked harder than them all. She sipped on her drink, scanning the room.

Straight across the floor, partly obscured by the dancers, she saw James, talking to a man wearing a pin-striped suit and a polka-dot tie. Her reaction was startling. Within seconds her heart started pumping in her chest and she felt slightly off balance. She watched for a moment as he laughed and nodded, the corners of his eyes creasing in amusement. His eyes were piercingly blue contrasted by the black of his suit. The other thing Sofia had learned after years of doing The Wager was the difference between an expensive suit and a cheap one, and this one was as high end as they came. He had a glass of something in his hand and he gestured with it as he spoke to the other man. His lips looked soft and warm. The music slowed and couples moved closer to each other.

Sofia realized she'd been gaping at him with her lips parted. She started self-consciously and turned her head to survey the rest of the room, hoping no one had noticed her staring. She watched the dancers for another few minutes then let her eyes glide back to him. He turned his head at the same moment and their eyes met. A faint smile came to his lips and he winked at her. Sofia looked away.

She tried to focus on the music and let it wash over her. She concentrated on picking out each instrument, the violins, the clarinets. She swayed her hips and closed her eyes.

"Do you like to dance?"

She jumped. James was suddenly standing next to her, twirling the ice in his glass.

"Not really," she replied. She felt her body respond to his closeness. The hair rose up on her bare arms and a ball of excited tension formed in her stomach.

"It looked like you were enjoying the music," he said. He was leaning down and talking in her ear to be heard over the orchestra and other voices. The warmth of his breath against her skin made her shiver.

"You can hardly call that dancing." Her eyes darted to him and then away. He was looking extraordinarily handsome in his suit. Leave it to him to look dapper in a suit amongst a room full of tuxedos. She felt herself blushing.

"Would you like to?" he asked.

"What?"

"Dance, my little idiot."

She hesitated and then took his hand and let him lead her to the floor. She could feel her pulse pounding in her throat, her breath coming in quick, silent gasps. He put a hand on her waist and his palm seemed to burn through her dress and into her skin. He held her other hand firmly and they began to move. Their bodies swayed slowly to the music and Sofia looked into his eyes. Her heart fluttered wildly at what she saw there. They were blue and soft but there was a spark of brightness behind them; a passion that pierced into her.

He put his mouth to her ear and said, "You look very beautiful."

"Thank you."

"About the other day," he said, "I'm sorry I was so rude. You just…caught me off guard."

She smiled. "Grandmother Linnie told me what you did for Ebony, and now you're helping Maria. Why didn't you tell me?"

He frowned. "I don't make a habit of telling people."

"Why not?"

He shrugged. "What I do during my off hours is my business."

"Your secret's safe with me. It's very…kind, what you do."

"That sounded like it was hard for you to say," he said with a smile.

"I don't get a chance to say it very often. I don't see a lot of kindness in my line of work."

His hand squeezed her waist gently. "I'm sorry, Sofia."

She shrugged. "It's ok. Can we just dance?"

His eyes sparkled and he pulled her close. The music swirled and she imagined they were the only two in the room. The rest of the people faded away and all that existed was their bodies moving together. For this moment, she thought, just for this moment, she would let herself enjoy being held in his arms. She put her head on his shoulder and let him lead her.

His hand moved from her waist to her back and he stroked down the silkiness of her dress. She shivered a little and nestled closer to his neck. He smelled like the scotch he had been drinking and his own natural scent that was becoming far too familiar to her. He brushed his lips on her hair and it felt like the most natural thing in the world.

The song ended and melded into more soft jazz, and they continued to dance.

"Why won't you go out with me?" he whispered.

She laughed at his persistence and looked up into his eyes. "I'm a working girl, James. I don't go on dates. I told you it's a ridiculous idea."

"No more ridiculous than me coming to a ball just so I can dance with you." His arm tightened around her waist. She swallowed hard.

"Then you're a fool," she said matter of factly, but she was having trouble keeping her voice steady.

"It's never foolish to go after what you want."

"And what do you want?" she asked, her breath coming fast.

"I would think I've made that pretty obvious," he said.

"Sex." She scowled at him.

"Get your mind out of the gutter. I'm talking about an evening at the market."

The music stopped and they stood on the dance floor staring at each other. She didn't know what to say. If she said no, that would be it and she would never see him again. But saying yes would open a pandora's box of emotions that she just wasn't ready to face.

"James," she said, swallowing hard, "I think you need to leave me alone. You're getting the wrong idea about me. I don't go on dates. I don't see men outside of The Wager. I think it would be best if you stop coming to The Hotel."

She realized another song had started and James was still holding her hands. She pulled away, almost colliding with a couple behind her. She mumbled an apology, and, not looking at him in case her resolve crumbled, she dodged into the crowd. She felt flushed and overheated. She needed some air.

She tracked down Maryanne who was flirting with a man at the bar. He was short and stout with a white handlebar mustache. He was sitting on a stool and with Maryanne standing, was at the perfect height to talk directly to her breasts. Maryanne didn't seem to notice; it was obvious she had been enjoying the complimentary champagne.

"Having fun?" Sofia asked, standing next to them.

"I'm having an amazing time!" Maryanne chirped. "This is Schmidt, he's from Europe."

"Brussels, my dear." The man sitting next to her said in a thick accent. He stroked his moustache lovingly.

"Brussels!" Maryanne giggled. "Like the vegetable."

Schmidt smiled indulgently and patted her arms with a chubby hand.

Sofia laughed and snuck a look at the dance floor. James had taken the hint and walked away, and she couldn't see where he was. She felt an idiotic desire to cry and then a voice said behind her, "A beautiful woman should never look so sad."

She turned and looked into a pair of hazel eyes, with thick brows and ridiculously long eyelashes. He had salt and pepper hair, the grey thicker on the temples, a tan, an exotic-looking face and a smile that showed off very white teeth.

Sofia cleared her throat and regained her composure. "I'm not sad," she said, smiling back at him, grabbing two champagne flutes off a passing waiter's tray. "I was just lonely, but now you're here, I don't have to be any more." She handed one of the glasses to the man and held hers up. "Cheers."

She forced herself to swallow the champagne even though her flirty words burned like embers in her throat. Get a grip! She shouted in her head. She was a professional and she needed to start acting like one. She had everything she wanted and she was the best at what she did. She needed to remember that she'd made a success from being a seductress and her words were like a siren's song to the opposite sex. It was time to shake off whatever grip James Hardy had over her and get back to business.

"Glory," she said, holding out her hand. He leaned down and kissed it.

"Beautiful name, it suits you. I'm Jeremy Paulsen"

She inclined her head and smiled at him. "What do you do, Jeremy?"

"I'm fairly new in town. Just opened my own financial consulting business."

"How fascinating!" she said, and blinked several times, fluttering her eyelashes.

He continued on for the next few minutes, throwing out words like mergers, acquisitions and equity. Sofia drank her champagne and sat with her chin in her hands, watching him with wide-open eyes. One of the things that set her apart in her profession was her ability to listen with rapt attention, no matter how boring the subject.

"I'm sorry," said Jeremy with a charming smile. "It's just all so new and exciting I get a little carried away."

"Oh no, it is very exciting, and so interesting," Sofia

said. "So what brings you to The Hotel?"

"My friend brought me here six months ago when I got to town. It's very unique, isn't it?"

Sofia laughed. "You could say that."

Jeremy gazed at her and shook his head. "You are an incredibly beautiful woman, Glory." He rubbed a finger along her arm and his eyes flickered to where the top of her breasts strained against the bodice of her dress. She wanted to grab his chin and drag his eyes back up to her face.

He moved his head closer and his eyes locked on hers. They were interesting eyes, different shades of browns and greens; they focused in on her mouth.

"Would you like to dance?" Sofia said, before he could kiss her.

The slightest look of irritation crossed his features before he smiled and nodded. He led her to the dance floor and held her close; his arms wrapped around her waist.

James drank his scotch and watched Sofia be led to the dance floor.

"What do you think, Hardy?" said the man standing next to him in the ill-fitting tuxedo, but James had no idea what he'd just said nor did he care. He had already forgotten the man's name.

He excused himself, saying he had a phone call to make, and made his way through the crowd to the ballroom door. Just inside was the coat check and he pulled his ticket from his pocket.

"James!" A voice cried from within the forest of leather and fur. Sami popped out wearing a beautiful pink dress that brought out the green in her eyes. She was hopping from one foot to the other. "Guess what?" He looked at her, raising his eyebrow in curiosity. "I wasn't supposed to be at the ball tonight but one of the coat checkers got the flu so they let me fill in."

"That's great. It looks like you're having a good time."

"I love the music!" she practically squealed. "It's so beautiful. I wish I could dance, but I'm not old enough."

"Don't wish yourself into adulthood, Sami. It's a real bitch."

Sami giggled.

"It's been awhile since I've seen you," he said.

Sami thought of the last time she had seen him, leaving the wagering room to spend the night with Sofia, and blushed furiously.

He laughed and held out his ticket.

"You're not leaving yet!" she cried. "You've only danced once."

He narrowed his eyes at her. "Sami, are you spying on me?"

She laughed and took his hand. "You have to stay."

He turned and could see Sofia dancing. Her partner had a firm hold on her butt and her arms were around his neck.

"Maybe another time, Sami," James said. He took his coat from her and stuffed bills in her little tip jar, overflowing it.

CHAPTER 9

JEREMY PAULSEN STROKED HIS hands down Sofia's hips and cupped her bottom. She didn't say anything, just put her arms around his neck and continued swaying to the music. Encouraged, by the close contact, he ground his hips into hers and pressed against her, so her breasts were squashed to his chest. She sighed and allowed it for the moment; it was her job after all.

She looked around and spotted James talking to Sami. He was laughing and she was bright-eyed. When Sofia saw Sami hand him his coat, her heart fell into her stomach, leaving an ache in her chest. She sighed in resignation, knowing it would have eventually come to him leaving, and most likely never seeing him again. It was better that it happened now than let whatever it was between them go on any longer.

The song changed but Jeremy showed no intention of letting her go. He smiled down into her eyes. He was quite good-looking. Maybe the best way to forget about James Hardy was to enjoy a flirtation with someone else. That was what she was here to do tonight. She was a professional and took her job seriously. James had thrown her off her stride but now she could move on and get back to business.

Jeremy kept one hand tightly grasping her butt while the other came up and caressed her cheek. She let him take her mouth softly with his as she let her mind go somewhere else. His tongue caressed and teased but she was miles away in the clouds.

She was brought back to earth as his tongue dove deep. His lips became more insistent and his hand clutched the back of her neck, his fingers digging into her flesh. She struggled but he had her locked against him. She tried to move her mouth away from his, but he bit down on her lip until she tasted blood.

"Hey!" She yelled and fought harder to get away from him. He grabbed the bodice of her dress and tugged it down, exposing a breast. She slapped him as hard as she could, knocking him away and off balance. He fell to the ground, scattering the dancers who quickly moved to the sides of the room to observe the drama from a safe distance. The orchestra stopped playing and Rufus scurried over in a panic.

"What's going on?"

"This bitch slapped me," cried Jeremy, jumping up and pointing at Sofia furiously, holding a hand over the red mark on his cheek. She stared angrily back at him, pulling her dress up so she was covered.

Rufus looked from Sofia to Jeremy with an astonished expression on his face. "My good sir, my sincerest apologies. I don't know what could have gotten into her." He looked at

Sofia, his eyes bristling with rage, but then they turned cool and icy and she shivered.

Rufus gestured them to the side of the dance floor. "Please," he called to the rest of the room, "continue dancing." The musicians nodded to each other and picked up their instruments. Couples moved back to the floor, casting curious glances at the scene that was taking place on the sidelines.

"Sir," Rufus said, bowing profusely, "again, please forgive Glory's awful behavior. I can assure you she will be disciplined."

"I should hope so," said Jeremy, straightening the cuffs on his jacket. His cheek still had the faint imprint of Sofia's hand.

"In the meantime, we appreciate your business more than you know; half off for the night," Rufus said, stepping back and bowing, gesturing to Sofia.

Jeremy looked her up and down as if appraising a horse he was about to buy. He shrugged. "Done!" And shook Rufus' hand.

Sofia felt the blood drain from her face, and black spots in front of her eyes threatened to overwhelm her. She honestly thought she was going to faint. She looked at Rufus in shock but he raised his eyebrows, giving her a "you made your bed…" look.

Jeremy moved to grasp Sofia's arm.

"I believe I've already booked this lady for tonight," James said, suddenly appearing at Sofia's side. She looked at him in surprise, but his attention was on Rufus. James held up a wad of money and Rufus gazed at the roll of bills, licking his glistening lips.

"Mr. Hardy, did you indeed?" he said, grabbing for the money. James pulled it out of reach.

"Did you forget?"

"Of course not. This gentleman was just dancing with Glory until you got here. No harm done."

James lowered the cash and Rufus snatched it, tucking it into his waistcoat pocket.

"What is this bullshit?" Jeremy growled. He grabbed onto Sofia and jerked her arm as if to pull her out of the room. James took a step forward, looking thunderously from the man's hand to Sofia's eyes. She shook her head slightly.

"He's right. He did reserve her," Rufus told Jeremy hurriedly, worried that the two men staring each other down like dogs marking their territory, were going to ruin his beautiful ball.

Then his eyes lit up and he clapped his hands. "Have I got just the girl for you." Rufus put his arm around Jeremy's shoulder and led him away. "Her name is Monica and she is a former acrobat, very flexible."

James held out his arm and Sofia took it, too shocked to speak. She looked up at him. His eyes were focused straight ahead but he had that half-smile on his face that she had come to recognize as his pleased with himself expression.

She shook her head and smiled, feeling some of the tension release. On their way to his room, James stopped a bellboy and whispered in his ear, handing him a bill. The boy scurried off. They took the elevator in silence, James sensing Sofia's need to process the events of the night.

When they got to his room he waved his keycard in

front of the handle, unlocking it. The room was so familiar to her that she immediately felt comfortable. She stumbled to the adjoining room, sat on the bed, took her shoes off and rubbed her tired feet.

"My feet are killing me," she said looking at James. "Were you really going to fight that guy right there in the ballroom?" she asked. James had followed her in and had gone to the bathroom and was running water.

"If he didn't take his hands off you," he said, kneeling in front of the bed where she sat. He had a wet washcloth and he touched it to her lip. She winced and flinched back in surprise.

"Your lip is bleeding," he said quietly, his mouth no longer smiling but set in a grim line. She leaned forward and let him dab at her lip. She watched his eyes as they narrowed in fierce concentration. They were so blue and cold, anger sparking in them like lightning.

Sofia stilled his hand with her own and took the washcloth from him. "It's ok, James," she said. "It doesn't hurt."

He gave her a curt nod and stood up, pulling off his tie and suit jacket. He reached out his hands to her and without a word pulled her to her feet. He gestured for her to turn around. She looked at him questioningly but obeyed.

She felt his hands on her back as he unlaced her bodice. He moved slowly, letting the silky strands slide through his fingers. She felt the coolness of the room on her back as more of her skin was exposed.

When the last lace was freed, there was nothing holding her dress up except his hands on her waist. He kissed the side of her neck and Sofia almost came out of her skin. His lips were hot, electrifying her where his mouth touched her. He gently pushed the dress down and it slid over her hips and fell to the ground in a pool of green satin. She wasn't wearing anything underneath.

She turned and he looked at her naked body with a serious, thoughtful expression. He ran his hands from her shoulders down to her waist, sending shivery bumps all over her skin. He stepped away, leaving her trembling in the cool of the room.

He came back with a fluffy blue robe, compliments of The Hotel.

"Here, put this on."

"Why?" she asked, but she stuffed her arms in the sleeves and tucked the belt around her gratefully.

There was a knock on the door and the same bellboy came in with a bottle of wine and a covered tray. James gave him another bill and patted him on the back.

"Because I don't typically eat in the nude," James said, after he closed the door.

Sofia smiled and curled up on the bed, her feet tucked underneath her. James set the tray on the bed next to her and removed the lid. There were various types of cheeses, probably something she'd never heard of, she thought, crackers, strawberries and melons. The food made her realize how hungry she was and she dug in happily.

While she ate James retreated to the bathroom and came out wearing a matching blue robe. He poured them each a glass of wine and sat down next to her on the bed. He leaned back, watching her. There were dark circles under her eyes. He could see she had tried to cover them with makeup, but the bruised skin was starting to show through. He wondered if she'd been getting enough sleep. If she hadn't it was because of The Wager and he felt an unexpected wave of possessive anger, knowing what she was doing that kept her up nights.

He picked up a strawberry and held it by the stem, twirling it absently in his long fingers. Sofia could feel his eyes on her, and when she looked at him he raised the strawberry to her mouth. She watched it, almost hypnotically, and then parted her lips. She took a bite. Crimson juice dribbled down her chin, and she drew in a sharp breath when James leaned into her and licked it, trailing his tongue along her jaw. Little bumps raised up along her arms, a tingling excitement that smoldered in places buried deep inside of her.

He kissed the corner of her mouth, gently, sweetly, and then he was kissing her lips and there was nothing gentle about it. His hand went to her hair, drawing her even closer. Sofia opened her mouth to him, relishing his taste.

James pulled away so abruptly that she almost fell face first onto the bed. He stood up and took a long drink from his wine glass.

"Are you done?" he asked, pointing to the tray. She nodded, too surprised to speak. He set it on the desk and, not sure what else to do, Sofia stood up and reached for the ties of her robe.

"You don't need to do that," James said. "Unless that's how you want to sleep, because that's all we're going to do." He turned down the bed and took off his robe. He was wearing plaid boxer shorts.

"Sleep?" she asked, raising her eyebrows.

"Yes. You may be miss party all night long, but I'm exhausted." He positioned himself under the covers.

She grinned at him, untied the belt at her waist and let the robe puddle around her feet. James took in her naked body, glowing in the low light of the single lamp.

"Vixen," he said and patted his chest.

She only hesitated a moment before sliding under the crisp sheets and positioning herself in the crook of his arm. His heart thumped steadily under her ear. The light dusting of dark hair on his chest tickled her nose and he smelled good enough to eat. She was surprised how natural this felt. Like she'd done it all her life. She let the stress and excitement of the evening float away and she was asleep in minutes.

CHAPTER 10

JAMES LAY AWAKE FOR a long time listening to Sofia breathe. She had a light raspy snore that made him smile. What was it about this woman that lit him up inside? His sister had asked why he had such a goofy look on his face all the time. It had to be seriously noticeable for her to voice such concern. He didn't have an answer for her.

He'd stopped in his tracks when he saw Sofia that day at the market. He had been helping two brothers who owned a bakery stall. They'd been saving for a space in the city but when the time came for them to be licensed, they were denied on some technicality.

James had taken the case before a judge and the brothers not only got their license to sell in the city, but a thousand dollars for potential loss of business while they were in court. James was promised free bread for life.

It was her smile that caught his attention. She was laughing at something Sami must have said and the look of pure, innocent amusement took his breath away. Now that he knew her better, he recognized that she didn't smile like that very often. She smiled, but it was coy and seductive, not the joyful abandonment he'd seen at the market. If he could, he would make it his life's mission to make her smile like that every day.

Her lustrous hair and perfect body didn't escape his notice either, and he had come to The Hotel because he was intrigued and wanted to know more. He hadn't been shocked to find out she was a prostitute. He knew few people were born with the luxuries he had. It had just made his desire to protect spark into flame, and he knew he had to somehow get to her.

He hadn't been worried about The Wager. James had played cards with his dad since he was five. He tensed slightly at the memory and loss that always rippled through him when he thought of his parents.

As he and Sofia talked, his feelings for her had only intensified. She tried to keep up her come-hither but not too close attitude, giving her body while building walls around her heart, but he saw her whether she wanted him to or not.

He saw her strength and resilience; but unguarded, like the day at the market, he also saw her softness and compassion. The way she looked after Sami and cared for the people who had nothing. He felt an unfamiliar ache in his gut.

After the night they had spent together, and her refusal to see him again, James had gone back to The Lake District and tried to put her out of his mind. It was a miserable failure. Her smile, her voice, her smell, her body, everything about her permeated his thoughts.

When he had received Rufus' invitation to the ball he

hadn't hesitated to send a reply. He hadn't even known if he would see her, and having her here in his arms again, was unexpected.

Her head was on his chest, one arm draped over him. Her hair was spread over the pillow next to him and she smelled like flowers. He ran his fingers lightly over her arm and watched the moonlight play on her skin. He would have to leave her in the morning. His jaw clenched when he thought about her going back to The Wager. The thought of other men touching her, even being near her, made him want to put his fist through the wall.

He slipped out of bed slowly and she rolled over onto her stomach with a little grunt. He went to the sliding door and stepped out onto the balcony. The fresh late night air had cleared most of the smog but the city was never silent. He took a deep breath and closed his eyes. He could hear a far-off siren and cars honking, oblivious of the hour.

He hated the city, he always had. He remembered the first time his parents had brought him here. The pollution had clawed at his throat and the noise, after his peaceful home, had been overwhelming. He had told them he never wanted to go back.

But he had come back and had forced himself to see the suffering on the outskirts of the opulence. He had been given so much while so many had nothing. And once he'd seen it, he couldn't look away and was determined to help in any small way he could.

He laughed ruefully. He'd been spending far more time in the city these days than his work required of him. He looked back into the room where the moon shone on Sofia's light mocha skin. What was he going to do with her? If he left her here to do The Wager, it would drive him to insanity.

He was shivering when he went back inside. He slid into the sheets, putting his arms around her and pulling her close.

"Cold," she grumbled sleepily.

"Sorry," he whispered and nuzzled her ear. He closed his eyes and slept.

Sofia woke up with a start, not sure where she was. It was The Hotel but it wasn't her room. She looked at the figure lying next to her and her heart leaped painfully. It hadn't been a dream, she thought with an unexpected relief that left her feeling dizzy.

He was lying on his back, one arm over his face, the other laying on his chest. She smiled and admired his body. He wasn't overly muscular but even relaxed she could see the definition of his biceps and shoulders. His stomach was flat and she put her hand on it gently, feeling the rise and fall with each breath. She trailed her fingers up his tan chest. He obviously spent a lot of time in the sun which he would, living in The Lake District.

He didn't stir as she followed the thin trail of black hair with her hand from his chest, down his torso, pushing the sheet back to uncover where it disappeared into his boxers.

She put her head under the covers and looked at his long legs. She ran a finger lightly across the line of his thigh muscle, smiling when he twitched in his sleep. Slowly and gently, she slid down his boxers. Positioning herself over him, she took him in her mouth and sucked slowly, caressing every inch. She felt him harden causing her own heat to start coiling around inside of her. She had never done this before; given a man pleasure just because she wanted to. It was like taking off a suffocating mask and breathing in the fresh air.

His hands came into her hair as she reached the tip and started down again. He moaned and it made her burn. He put pressure on her head, encouraging her to go deeper. She went deeper, and faster. His hands tightened in her hair and his hips came up to meet her.

"Sofia," he gasped.

She went on, stroking him expertly with her mouth. "Sofia…stop."

She looked up at him. He pulled her up and pushed her onto her back, kissing her with a hunger that took her breath away. His kisses were always passionate, but this was more like a possession, a marking of territory. He traced his lips over her neck and collarbone, and when he took her breast in his mouth, she arched her back and grabbed his hips.

He slipped into her softly, smoothly, enjoying every moment. He kissed her but this time it was gentle as if he were savoring the taste of her. She took him with a want that surprised her. The tension built and they moved faster, breathing heavily. It was coiling in the center of her, tighter and tighter.

Her eyes met his and they burned her with their brilliance. She tried to look away; it was too vulnerable, too revealing and it flayed her open. He watched as pleasure throbbed through her, his eyes never leaving her face; pinning her gaze to him as though her choices were no longer her own. He breathed out heavily and she clung to him as he plunged over the edge.

James was sprawled on top of her, the sheets and comforter were on the floor. She nudged him and he groaned. She laughed and gave him a little shove and he rolled off her onto his back. She looked at his face. His eyes were closed and he was smiling. She brushed the hair off his forehead. She suddenly felt shy and nervous. Almost insecure…almost a fear that he didn't respect her. That made her laugh out loud and he looked at her with one eyebrow raised.

"Nothing, "she said, still smiling. "I'm going to take a shower."

While she showered, James paid another bellboy to talk to Chef. When she came out of the bathroom there was a full eggs and bacon breakfast with toast and hashbrowns, and different types of fruit. Her stomach growled appreciatively. She ate and watched the news while James showered.

How domestic it all seemed, she thought as she nibbled on a piece of toast. Amazing how looks could be so incredibly deceiving. This was going to have to come to an end at some point. She was an idiot to keep fanning the flame that was slowly growing inside her. She didn't recognize the feeling, and it terrified her. She just knew that it would soon grow out of control, like a wildfire, and it would be too late to stop it. Too much more of this and it would consume her.

She finished her coffee and brushed crumbs off her lap. Pushing aside the tray of food, she went in search of her dress.

She found it bunched up, half under the bed. James came out of the shower dressed in a t-shirt and jeans, his hair damp and messy. She thought he looked good enough to devour.

He watched her gather the silky green material, but when she began looking for her shoes, he stopped her and took her hands. He pulled her down until they were sitting on the bed, his gaze so intense that she self-consciously tightened the robe around her.

"I really enjoyed last night." He paused and then grinned disarmingly. "And this morning."

His easy smile was soft and welcoming and Sofia, against all her instincts, found herself hanging on every word he said.

"I want to see you away from this place." He nodded to the room. "Not because I'm paying you, but because you want to. I suggested the market because it's open, there's lots of people around, but I hope you trust me by now."

James spoke quickly, not giving her a chance to interrupt. He needed to convince her that he wasn't a threat. He looked down at their entwined hands. "I'd like to talk to you about some things. Can you get away tonight?"

Sofia hesitated, avoiding his eyes. She realized why it was so disconcerting to really look at him. He had such a tenderness about him; it frightened her. To let kindness or gentleness in was dangerous and she'd already stepped over the line with him. She was letting her feelings for him get in the way of reality.

She thought about kissing him and the feel of his hands on her body. Would it be so bad to go out with him? Just a harmless trip to the market? It wouldn't have to mean anything. He would probably be happier if it didn't.

She looked at the floor frowning and then said quietly, "Alright."

He smiled and kissed her.

———————

Sofia went back to her room. Sami was still sleeping so she quietly changed into a t-shirt and a pair of leggings. She sat down in one of the soft chairs by the window, tucking her bare feet under her.

The spring skies were heavy with rain. Nice days were few and far between this time of year. Summer couldn't come soon enough; she desperately needed some warmth. She thought of James and a quiet peace came over her. After they had talked, they had made love again, passionately, greedily.

She closed her eyes. She was treading on dangerous ground. Being with him made her happy but she was in no position to let a man control her emotions. His hands on her body clouded her mind, his kiss intoxicated her. His mouth, close to her ear, whispering, enticing.

Did she honestly think anything would come of this? He just wanted to possess her like they all did. To claim her, own her, make her his. He wasn't any different from any other man, because if he was, she thought, tears coming to her eyes, if he was, she was in serious jeopardy.

He had opened a crack in a wall that she'd built years ago, and if he was different, then that crack would shatter and expose the one thing that she could not afford to lay bare, and that was hope. Hope meant there was a life beyond this one, and that kind of thinking was the most dangerous of all. She had already gone farther than she ever should have down that road. She had to put a stop to it before she got hurt beyond the point of recovery.

She looked up at the black clouds that stared down at her, taunting. They had no answers for her. They never had. She put her head on her knees and cried as softly as she could so she wouldn't wake Sami.

CHAPTER 11

SOFIA CAME OUT OF the shower wearing a light robe and her hair done up in a bun, damp tendrils hanging down her cheeks. Outside, the sun was setting behind the clouds and the already dark sky had turned charcoal. She sorted through her lingerie, trying to decide what to wear. Sami was arranging dress choices on the bed. Sofia held up a red teddy for inspection. "I hope the wagering room is a little cooler tonight. Lately it's been hot as balls."

Sami stopped, holding a pile of dresses in her hands. She looked at Sofia in surprise. "Aren't you going out?"

"No, it's Saturday. Why would I be going out?" Sofia went to the dressing table and pulled out her lipstick.

Sami stammered, "But I thought you took tonight off. I thought you were going..." she stopped.

Sofia turned and stared at her. "Going where, Sami?" she asked.

Sami looked at Sofia like a deer caught in headlights. Lying was not one of her strong suits, every emotion she had played over her face. "Nothing," she said, picking up the rest of the discarded clothes. "I just thought it was a nice night for a walk."

Sofia snorted. "Yeah, right." She put down her lipstick and sat on the bed. "Sami, I know you talked about me to James. I'm not upset, I'm just surprised. I've never known you to do anything like that before. What happened?"

Sami dropped the dresses to the ground and knelt in front of Sofia, putting her head down and sobbing into her lap. "I am so sorry! It was an accident. I've been delivering messages to his office for two years and we've talked about lots of things. He told me he'd seen me at the market and asked who I'd been with. I was so surprised to hear he'd been at the market that I didn't even think. I just told him who you were.

"I never in a million years thought he'd come to The Wager. It's all my fault that you're so unhappy. I'm the reason you've had to be with him so much. If I hadn't told him, he never would have come here."

For one painful moment Sofia thought about never having met James and it brought sudden, unwanted tears to her eyes. She helped Sami up and they sat on the bed together holding hands. Sami had tears running down her cheeks and Sofia was trying to hold hers in. She felt if she started crying again, she wouldn't be able to stop.

"It's alright Sami, I understand. He can be a charming son of a bitch."

"I've known him for such a long time," Sami said, fresh tears falling. "I couldn't believe it when he showed up at The

Hotel. But at the ball, you danced together, and then I was delivering a message to his office and he was there. He said he was meeting you at the market. He seemed really happy. So then I wondered if maybe it hadn't been such a bad thing that he came here, that maybe you liked him. I mean more than just one of the guests."

Sofia thought about that for a minute. "I think I did," she said, gazing at nothing.

"Then why..?"

"There's no point, Sami," Sofia said, desperately trying to convince herself. "It wouldn't mean anything. It's all make-believe. These men have lives and families away from this place. Here they can be whoever they want to be. They play a part and so do I. They go away thinking they're in love with me and want to rescue me. But it's this fantasy they love, not me. I'm just very talented at making them think they can't live without me."

Sami frowned, staring at their clasped hands. "I thought James was different."

Sofia sighed and patted Sami's hand. "He is different. He's kind and a gentleman, but he's also a man with a man's needs. When he doesn't get what he wants he'll forget all about me, they all do. I'm sure after tonight he will move on to someone who's not so much work," she laughed.

Sami smiled and Sofia kissed her cheek. "You go on being James' friend, but nothing good can come of him and me being friends. Do you understand?"

Sami nodded.

"Good, "said Sofia. "Now help me get ready, I'm late."

———————

"Peter Dillard," Rufus said. His eyes were lined black with kohl, and he waved his hands expressively, his rings sparkling. "An upcoming superstar in the tech field. He developed some gadget that does something important, so now he's out spending money like it's going out of style. He and his buddies are having a stag weekend. The whole nine yards, limo, dancing girls." He rubbed his hands together. "He joined The Wager and has done surprisingly well. I didn't think he had it in him."

He and Sofia turned their glances to a skinny kid who didn't look a day over twenty-one. He wore a green sweater that made his red hair stand out like a beacon. His thick lensed glasses obscured his eye color, and his cheeks and nose were covered in a profusion of freckles.

"He doesn't look like much but apparently his mind is worth millions," Rufus said. He was wearing a floor-length brown coat with fur on the cuffs and a collar like a lion's mane. Several gold chains hung at his neck. So much for not looking like a pimp, Sofia thought. He turned her toward the stairs and gave her a pat on the butt.

She entered the balcony through the curtain and sat down. Peter and two other men she didn't know were at the table. Sofia took a deep breath to steady her beating heart. Would James come through the door? It was better if he didn't, she thought, trying to convince herself. She needed to put some distance between herself and Mr. Hardy.

The door opened and Sofia held her breath. Don and

Jack came in, laughing together. Jack winked up at her and they took their seats, shaking hands with the other men. Sofia felt a moment of disappointment that shook her.

She blinked hard a few times and then held her head up and plastered a smile on her face. She was a professional, for heaven's sake. She looked down at the table, concentrating on the game.

Peter held his own, methodically cleaning out the other players until it came down to him and an elderly man who used a cane and peered at his cards myopically. He had managed to outlast the other men with, as far as Sofia could tell, blind luck.

Peter received the three cards he'd requested and Sofia saw the back of his neck redden. Peter had the unfortunate tell of his skin flushing a distracting shade of crimson when he had a good hand. His opponent could hardly miss the signs and tossed his cards down, folding.

Peter's hand was three nines and he pumped his fists in the air. He glanced up at Sofia and, if possible, turned a darker shade of red. He gave a tentative wave and Sofia blew him a kiss. He grinned at her shyly. Rufus appeared and Peter handed him his room key. Peter opened the door to a chorus of cheers from his friends and Sofia made her way down the stairs.

Rufus chuckled. "Do you think he's a virgin?"

Sofia just smiled and took the key from him.

She found Peter's room and after waving the key card in front of the door, went in. She lit the fireplace and stood in front of it, showing her body off to its best advantage.

Her red teddy had a plunging neckline that left little to the imagination. The firelight flickered over her tan skin. She brushed her hair away from her face and put her shoulders back and her boobs out.

For a fleeting moment, James crossed her mind and she felt guilty. *Guilty*, she thought. How utterly absurd.

The door opened. Peter came in wearing only a pair of white briefs. His long, skinny arms were wrapped around his equally thin body and he was visibly shaking. He would have looked miserable if it hadn't been for the huge grin on his face.

His gaze fell on Sofia and his eyes widened. His mouth fell open like a cartoon character and she stifled a laugh. She put a finger in her mouth and watched him, her eyes half-closed. He made a move forward and tripped over the foot of the bed, falling to his knees.

"Are you alright?" she cried breathlessly, hurrying over to him.

"Yeah," he laughed, standing up and rubbing his knees. He looked up, his eyes level with her breasts. "I'm freezing!" he laughed.

"Well, come over to the fire and sit down, sugar." She directed him to one of the easy chairs near the hearth. "Where are your clothes?"

He giggled and said through chattering teeth, "I lost them in a bet with my friends. They said I couldn't drink ten beers without having to pee." His eyes were glazed, the firelight reflecting off his glasses. "They were going to give me a thousand dollars if I could do it, but I couldn't," he snorted. "I almost wet myself. Anyway I had to give them my clothes because I lost."

She laughed in a low, husky voice and knelt in front of him. "It certainly makes things a lot easier. Do you know how to please a woman, Pete?"

Peter snorted.

"You must because you're so strong!" She massaged her hands up and down his arms. "And muscular." She put her hands on his knees and rubbed up to his crotch. He opened and closed his mouth and then seemed to pull himself together. "I do box twice a week".

She gasped. "I can tell!! And you're smart too. I heard you invented something."

"I did, but I don't want to bore you with the details," he said hopefully.

"Oh, good," she said and reached into his underwear and pulled out his very stiff erection. "I've never sucked off a genius before." She put her mouth on him.

It was over in seconds. Peter lolled his head back and was soon snoring. Wearing one of the hotel's fluffy robes, Sofia slipped out into the hall.

She met Rufus in the elevator.

"Early night, m'dear?" he snickered.

Sofia just smiled.

As she showered that night, she thought of James and for the first time in her life, wondered what it would be like to be with just one man. For a moment tonight she had felt ashamed as she played the bimbo seductress. Which was absolutely ridiculous. She had to get it into her head that

James was just another man who'd gotten lucky at The Wager.

She didn't expect to see him again. She had given him every excuse to give up on her. He had realized, just like she knew he would, that the fantasy did not match the reality. She allowed herself one moment to acknowledge that in some far-off place she was hurting, and then she cleared her throat, buried it deep and got ready for bed.

CHAPTER 12

IT HAD BEEN A week and a half, not that Sofia had been counting, since she'd last seen James. Every day she had to forcibly remove his image from her mind so she could do her job.

Sami was brushing Sofia's hair for the next wager when she mentioned casually that she had seen James downtown the day before.

"Oh really?" Sofia said picking at one of her fingernails like she couldn't care less.

"He was with a lady," Sami said.

Sofia's eyes flicked up. "A lady? Like a woman? A lady woman? In the city?"

Sami paused in her brushing and looked at Sofia curiously in the mirror. "Does that bother you?"

"No," Sofia laughed. "Of course not. I told you he'd move on. It's probably his wife. Most men who come here are married." She tried to calm her speeding pulse. "Did you talk to him?"

"Yeah. He asked about you."

"He did?" Sofia fiddled with the tassel on her robe, trying to appear uninterested. "What did you say?"

"I told him you were fine."

"Did he say anything else?"

"He said to tell you hi and then offered to buy me ice cream. I was running so I said no thank you, and he said see ya and I said see ya…"

"What did she look like?" Sofia interrupted her.

"Who?'

"The woman he was with."

"She was really pretty," Sami said, thinking about it. "I didn't get a chance to talk to her because she went into one of the shops."

James had a wife, Sofia thought. Of course he did. She had come so close to letting him in, she had to hold in a sob thinking about how close.

She got up from her chair leaving Sami holding the hairbrush and sat in front of the fire. She took deep, steadying breaths and let her mind go to another place where there was sunshine, and it was warm. She let go of the disappointment that she cursed herself as a fool for having. She'd known better than to let it get too personal, yet she'd done it anyway. She'd ignored every instinct that had been screaming at her.

She stayed seated on the rug in front of the hearth until her pulse had slowed and all tension had left her body. When she was sure her head was in control, and not any other part of her, she let her thoughts and her body merge, and she sat up and got dressed.

She hardly paid attention to the events going on around her. She went to the wagering room with Sami and climbed to her balcony. The heat and smoke from the fireplace mixed with the cloying smell of cigarettes floated up to meet her, making her eyes water. She had chosen a deep pink, lacey bra and panty set with a filmy white negligee but sweat still trickled down her back.

Four men were already at the table. Jack and three strangers chatting with Duke, waiting for the fifth man to arrive. When the door opened and James walked in, Sofia felt her heart jump to her throat, and she hitched in a gasp.

He was wearing a dark blue dress shirt that made his eyes dazzle in the low light of the room. One hand was in the pocket of his black slacks and the other reached out to shake the hands of the other men. He didn't once glance up at Sofia.

Sofia watched the game in intense anticipation. If James won, what was she going to say to him? Maybe he wouldn't win, she thought; not sure how that outcome would make her feel and not wanting to examine it too closely. Jack had already wiped out two of the other men and James' stack of chips was looking unpromisingly low.

James bet big on the next hand, almost depleting his pile but ended up winning with three tens, cleaning out another guy, leaving only himself and Jack with close to an equal number of chips.

Sofia watched as the hand was dealt and both men examined their cards, seemingly indifferent. Without hesitation Jack shoved half of his pile into the middle of the table. He obviously had a promising beginning hand, Sofia thought.

James gave him a sideways glance and, sorting through his chips, slid the same amount across. Duke turned to Jack, but James raised a finger and slid a third of his remaining chips into the pile. They hadn't even drawn yet and James was betting like he knew the outcome. Sofia turned her head to look at Jack, but he just grinned and called James' raise.

They tossed the cards they were trading toward Duke. Jack asked for three more and Sofia assumed he had a pair and was going for three of a kind. James only asked for two cards and Sofia wondered if Jack was thinking what she was, that there was a very good chance Mr. Hardy had the beginnings of a flush or full house.

When James picked up his new cards the slightest twitch of his lips, hardly perceptible, gave away that he had something good. Sofia's eyes flicked to Jack, but he had seen it. Then James made it obvious by shoving the remainder of his chips into the middle. Sofia felt her stomach drop. It was an amateur mistake. If James had been more subtle with his betting he might have been able to string Jack along until he had nothing left. Instead, Jack immediately folded and laid down his cards; he had two pairs.

James lay down his own cards…Nothing, he had nothing, not even a pair. If Jack hadn't folded, James would have lost all his money…and her. Sofia could tell Jack was angry that he'd been tricked and he pressed his lips together in a hard line as they continued to play.

James dominated the next two rounds and when the last of Jack's chips were huddled in the middle of the table James ended it with a straight.

Jack stubbed out his cigar forcefully into the ashtray but still shook James' hand. He looked up into the balcony and raised his beer to Sofia. She blew him a kiss, and he finished his drink in one long gulp. He set the bottle on the felt table and strode out the double doors.

James still didn't look at her. He handed Rufus his key and left the room. Sofia felt shaky as she descended the stairs. Rufus bounded up to her, his dangly earrings shaped like fish bones swaying with each excited move of his head.

"That James Hardy," Rufus tsked. "He certainly is a sly so and so. I sure wouldn't kick him out of my bed for eating crackers." He snorted and walked her to the elevator, pushing the button for James' floor.

"Have fun, m'dear," Rufus winked. "But not too much fun." His voice deepened and the tone was almost a warning. His eyes flashed as the elevator doors closed and Sofia took an involuntary step back. Sometimes Rufus could look like the devil himself.

She let herself into James' room with the key. The gas fireplace was lit and the room was very warm. She looked around and recognized his suitcase and laptop. A black sweater was draped over a chair and she picked it up and put it to her nose. She recognized the musky scent of his cologne.

The bed was neatly made and she pulled back the bed-spread and the sheets and climbed into the feathery softness.

Sofia awoke to the click of the door as the lock disengaged. James came in quietly, closing the door behind him. He walked towards the desk and hung his suit jacket over the chair. He unbuttoned the cuffs of his dress shirt and rolled the sleeves up to his elbows. His movements were loose like he was completely at ease, as if she wasn't even there. He kicked off his shoes and only then did he stand at the end of the bed and look at her.

She was on her back, watching him through half closed lids. The light from the fireplace cast shadows over his face making it impossible to read his expression. She sucked in a surprised breath when he crawled onto the bed, hovered over her, and kissed her. His mouth was hot and tasted like spicy alcohol. His hips were locked with hers and his chest pressed against her. She responded without a second thought, wrapping her arms around his neck.

He pulled the sheet away from her revealing the swells of her breasts pushing up from her bra. Against the pink material, her skin looked like creamy toffee. He brought the covers down further exposing her body to him. His eyes sparked and she shivered even though the room was oppressively warm.

He dipped his head, kissing along her stomach, and then lower. She caught her breath and shifted restlessly, her fingers entwined in his hair. Perspiration trickled down her sides and collected underneath her as he moved his mouth and tongue over her sensitive flesh.

She almost whimpered when he stopped what he was doing and straddled her. He was still fully dressed but he could feel the sweat between her thighs, slick under him. He leaned down and kissed her until she was gasping, her back arching.

He gripped her wrists painfully and yanked her arms above her head, holding them there. She gasped in shock when she found herself immobile. She tried to wriggle away as panic engulfed her, but his knees dug into her sides, holding her in place. He stared down at her, and she glared back at him.

"Why didn't you meet me?" he said in a rough tone she'd never heard from him before. His breathing was heavy, and moisture glistened at his temples.

She fought against his hands, her arms jerking uselessly against his grip. She growled out of frustration, "I had better things to do."

"This is better? Is this what you want? To be fucked by men who don't give a damn about you?"

She struggled to get a hand free to slap him.

"How dare you judge me, you son of a bitch! You don't know me!"

"I think I do. You hide behind The Wager so you don't have to feel anything. You're scared of leaving this hotel and facing the real world."

"What do you know about me? What do you know about anything?" she spat, trying desperately not to cry.

She tried to buck him off, but his weight crushed her to the bed. He tightened his thighs and kept her arms stretched above her head.

"I don't think so, I won The Wager. You're mine tonight."

She felt a sudden wave of unwanted desire flood her body. She wanted to be his, she thought with a sickening dread as if falling down a bottomless well. She wanted his hands on her skin, his mouth crushed to hers.

She closed her eyes, squeezing away the stinging tears, picturing him with a wife. Her body sagged and her breath released on a sigh. James must have felt the fight go out of her because he looked at her, frowning, his eyes darting over her face. He released her hands and rolled off her.

Sofia swung her legs off the bed and ran for the bathroom, slamming the door shut. For a minute all she could do was lean over the sink and breathe. She splashed water on her overheated face and looked at herself in the mirror. Her lips were swollen from kissing him and she had his scent all over her.

Her chest ached with the effort not to cry as she stared into her reflection. She didn't even recognize herself anymore. Where was the self-assured woman who never let anything move her? Despite the awful things he'd said, her body knew just what to do when he put his hands on her. He had all her defenses crumbling and she couldn't allow that to happen. She stared straight into the mirror, her eyes hardening to steel.

So what if he had a wife? He was nothing to her, just another john who won The Wager. He had no hold over her. She was still in control. She took a deep breath and opened the door.

James wasn't there. The sheets were scattered across the bed in an untidy heap. She found her filmy robe on the floor and noticed his shoes were gone. He must have gone back to the casino. She felt a stab of disappointment, reminded herself that she didn't care, and left the room.

Sofia took a hot shower, rubbing her skin raw until the water burned her abused flesh. She didn't know what time it was when she crawled into bed, but it was starting to get light. Her thoughts were fuzzy as she stared out the window.

She couldn't see any stars through the thick clouds but every now and then the tiny lights of a plane would flicker overhead. She watched it cross the sky, soaring so far above her, until it was out of sight. She wished she could soar through the clouds like that, away from this life, this turmoil inside of her.

She got out of bed and walked to the window, looking down at the lights of the city shimmering in the pre-dawn glow. It was so pretty; she could almost forget how ugly it was close up. The streets were dirty and cracked, the only green thing the dusty weeds that pushed their way through the gray concrete. She wrapped her arms around herself.

She was seven when she had been left alone on those streets. Her parents had died of pneumonia, at least her father had. After he was gone her mother took one look around her; a tiny dirt floor house, a hungry child to feed, bills to pay and decided dying was the better option.

Sofia had lived only to survive, begging and stealing. Sometimes she just wanted to give up from the gnawing pain in her empty stomach and the exhaustion of trying to make it through another day. Just fall asleep and never wake up, she thought, it would be easy. But she was terrified of her dead body being torn apart by the thousands of rats that scurried through the city.

James was wrong about her fearing the world; she'd love to see the world. She'd love to leave The Hotel, but the only way out was back onto those streets, and that was what Sofia was truly afraid of. The starving, rat-infested streets. She wouldn't be alive right now if she'd stayed there. She never thought she'd live much past twenty. It was a miracle she'd gotten out and she wasn't going back. She had security at The Hotel and she couldn't afford to mess it up. She shivered and turned from the window.

CHAPTER 13

SOFIA WAS SITTING UP in bed, bleary eyed, drinking a cup of coffee, when Sami came rushing into the room with a vase full of carnations.

"Look, they just came for you!" She bounced eagerly on the balls of her feet as Sofia took the stunning flowers, an explosion of pink, white and red. "There's a note too," Sami said pointing at the card nestled in the green stems.

Sofia opened it and scanned its contents. Sami was too polite to ask but Sofia could feel the curiosity and impatience radiating off her as she shifted from one foot to the other.

"It's from James. He wants me to meet him at the front of The Hotel at eight."

Sami pumped her fists, unable to control her excitement. "I knew they were from James! I told him carnations were your fave."

"Geez, Sami, what didn't you tell him about me?"

Sami grinned. "So if he sent flowers, does this mean it's like a date?"

"It's definitely not a date," Sofia said, picking up the phone. "I don't know what it is but if he thinks he can summon me whenever he feels like it…"

Sami rolled her eyes and set the vase on the side table. Obviously James liked Sofia and she sometimes got the impression Sofia liked James. So what was the problem? She sighed, thanking whatever gods were listening that she never planned on falling in love.

"Hi Debra," Sofia said over the phone, "can I talk to Rufus? Sure, I'll wait." She fiddled with the phone cord. Finally Rufus' tinny voice came over the line.

"What can I do for you, my dear?" he said, his voice tinged with impatience.

"What's going on with James Hardy? He wants me to meet him but I'm on The Wager tonight. And since when do guests get to meet me outside The Hotel?"

"Since he made an incredibly generous contribution last night. He was drinking like he'd find his dreams at the bottom of a scotch bottle." Rufus snickered. "I love it when rich men drink. They lose all their inhibitions about money. He said he wanted to take you out and slipped me a big enough check that I didn't need to worry about letting you out of The Wager tonight."

"But…" she started to object but Rufus cut her off.

"Gotta go."

The line went dead and she gaped at the phone. Was he serious? She was for sale now? She looked at the flowers and frowned. Did James think he could buy her? If he thought she was going to be some piece on the side, he was sorely mistaken. She might be a prostitute, but she still had some self-respect.

That night she pulled out her favorite dress. It had a floral pattern and was made of soft cotton. Boring. That's why she loved it. No sequins, not a stitch of silk or lace. The bodice complimented her shape while not revealing too much and the skirt hung modestly to her knees. It didn't make her feel sexy or desirable; it made her feel pretty.

She told herself she wasn't making a special effort to look nice for James. Her plan was to play it cool and aloof. She didn't know where he was taking her, it didn't really matter. This was not a date, it was work. If this was how he got his kicks away from his family, that was none of her business.

She greeted the door man and stood to wait on the curb. The rain had stopped, and the wet pavement glistened in the lights of brass sconces lined along the outside walls of the building. A small, dark green sports car zipped up to where she stood and glided to a stop. James got out and came around to her. She was furious to find herself smiling. He kissed her cheek and said, "You look lovely."

She thanked him and let him open the door for her. The car smelled like leather and she sank into the plush seat. He came around and got in next to her.

Before he could go anywhere she turned to him and blurted, "Are you married?"

He lifted one eyebrow and she winced. So much for cool and aloof, she thought. He stared at her, and she resisted the urge to shift in her seat.

The question didn't surprise James, but the intensity

behind it caught his attention. He searched her dark eyes, trying to see past the prostitute and into the woman, but she was far too good at what she did. The look she gave back might as well have been a brick wall. He shoved the car into gear and peeled away from the curb.

Sofia had been in taxis before but never anything this comfortable and smooth. For a moment she was distracted by the way the car seemed to drift through the traffic, then remembered he hadn't answered her question.

"Well?" she finally said.

He smiled and said, "No, I've never been married."

She slowly let out a breath, then her head whipped back in his direction. "Kids?"

"No kids, but I do have a little sister." They stopped at a light, and he took her hand and brought it to his lips. "Why do you ask? Would it break your heart to find out I had a family stashed away somewhere?"

She pulled her hand away. "Of course not. You could be gay for all I care. I just want you to know that I'm not going to stand by and be someone's concubine. I don't care how much money you throw around, I'm not yours. Just because you bribe Rufus doesn't mean I belong to you."

"Understood."

He said it with a straight face, but his eyes seemed to be laughing at her. She clenched her fists in her lap to keep from punching him.

After a few miles, Sofia recognized that they were coming up on her old patch. She got a look at the cluster of girls hanging on the meters and yelling at cars that drove by. They looked so young.

James maneuvered away from the busier streets, picking up speed. They were heading for the ritzy part of the city, she realized. Hookers didn't walk the streets there; they were hired from private escort agencies. The sidewalks and parking lots started to look cleaner and the buildings shinier.

As they sped past stores and restaurants, Sofia could see the bay nestled inside the horseshoe of land. Lights from the city reflected off the water, like a thousand fireflies flittering over the surface. It took her breath away. They pulled up in front of a building with a red and white striped awning. James got out, handing the keys to a young man in a blue uniform. He opened Sofia's door and led her inside.

A pretty woman in a white shirt and black skirt stood at a podium. Before she could greet them, a man quite a bit shorter than James, with tufts of hair on either side of his balding head, approached them with a huge grin.

"James!" he said, extending his hand. "You son of a bitch. It's about time you came back. How long has it been? More than a year? And who is this beautiful creature on your arm?"

He smiled charmingly at Sofia and took her hand in a firm grasp.

"This is Sofia," said James. "Sofia, this is Max, the owner.

"Enchanted, my dear," said Max. "Ruby," he called over his shoulder, "champagne to table sixteen. Come this way." They followed him to the back of the restaurant where a bank of windows overlooked the bay. They were seated in the corner away from the other guests; a candle flickering in a glass holder and the low-lit wall sconces the only illumination.

Outside the lights from small boats could be seen bobbing in the water. The champagne arrived and Max poured them each a glass and laid menus on the table.

"Someone will be with you soon. Enjoy!"

Max shuffled away, and James held up his glass. "To a beautiful night with a beautiful woman."

Sofia rolled her eyes but touched her glass to his and took a long drink. She had never been this close to the bay before and she was amazed at how it seemed to go on forever into the darkness.

James put down his glass and ran his finger along the rim. He frowned and said, "I was out of line last night. I hope you can forgive me."

"There's nothing to forgive, James. You were absolutely right. I do fuck men for a living, but you knew that about me when you met me."

He continued to stare down at his glass with that thoughtful frown on his face. "I shouldn't have said those things and I shouldn't have gotten rough with you. The thing is, Sofia..." He stopped, still not looking at her. Was that a faint blush on his cheeks, Sofia wondered, or a trick of the light? "...I'm jealous."

She laughed and almost spit out her champagne. "Jealous? Of who?"

"Everyone!" he said, slamming his fist down on the table, making the silverware jump. He leaned in and whispered, "Every man you sleep with, every man who touches you, every man who even looks at you. I want to kill them all."

She was stunned speechless. The waitress, who had seen

the two with their heads together, obviously having some serious discussion, took advantage of the pause and said cheerfully, "Are you ready to order?"

James looked at her as if the chair next to him had called him a rude name. Sofia smiled and said, "I think we need another minute." The waitress looked uncertainly at James and then scurried away.

"Get a grip, James, you're being ridiculous. Now figure out what you're going to eat." They picked up their menus.

"I'm sorry," he said, "I don't want to spoil the evening."

"Then let's talk about something else."

The waitress, seeing them put their menus down, trotted back over to their table. James gave her his most charming smile to make up for earlier and Sofia watched as the poor girl practically swooned. They finally managed to order and James poured them more champagne.

"Tell me about your sister," said Sofia, hoping to lighten the mood.

He smiled and his face transformed from serious and intense to a fondness that softened his features and made him look very young. "Her name is India. She's seventeen and a complete pain in my ass. She's always coming home with a new piece of metal sticking out of her face or a new boy who I'm not allowed to talk to because I would mortify her. We lost our parents when she was three, so I've been the only thing keeping her from total catastrophe ever since. I'm away on business a lot and she has a tendency to run wild."

"How old were you when your parents died?" Sofia asked.

"Thirteen."

"What happened?"

He was silent for a moment, taking a long drink from his glass. He set it carefully on the table, turning it so it caught the light from the candle flame.

"My father was a cardiologist. He worked primarily in The Lake District but sometimes he would come to the city for conferences or meetings. It was two weeks before Christmas so my mom took me and India shopping in the city while my dad went to some doctor convention. Afterward we all had dinner and drove back home. It had started snowing and it was dark. We were crossing a bridge at the same time as a truck. It hit a patch of ice and slammed into us."

He could still remember the deafening sound of metal hitting metal and the sickening feeling of spinning as he and his family were propelled off the bridge and into the icy water.

"My parents were screaming at me to get India out. I could barely feel my limbs, it was so cold but I managed to get her car seat unfastened just as her head went under. I was able to get the window down and pull her out. I thought my parents were right behind me but when I got to the surface I couldn't see them."

He'd shoved a hysterical India into the arms of the truck driver who'd called 911 and James had jumped back into the water.

"At this point I had hypothermia and the only thing that kept me moving was spiked adrenaline. I went back through the open window and grabbed my dad under his arms but he didn't move. He was dead weight."

James blinked back the memory of swimming around

the front of the car and seeing his mother's dark hair, flowing around her face like tendrils of smoke, her blue eyes, identical to his own, glassy and unseeing.

"I stayed down there for as long as I could. By the time I came back up the cops were there. They were waiting for divers to arrive but I kept going under, trying to pull my parents from the car. When the divers got there they had to pull me bodily from the river because I refused to stop. I was in the hospital for two days. Turns out even the divers couldn't get my parents free, their legs had been trapped under the dashboard when the truck hit them. I never would have succeeded."

Sofia sat in shocked silence. Anything she could think of to say seemed to fall short so she put her hand gently on his. He glanced up, the faintest look of surprise on his face.

"I'm so sorry, James. What happened after you got out of the hospital?"

"India and I went home. We miraculously fell off the radar and no one from social services came looking for us."

"So you had no adult taking care of you?"

He smiled at the concern in her voice. "We managed. I'd like to say I had a hand in raising India, but she never listens to a word I say."

Sofia could tell by his tone that he loved his sister very much. She saw that fierce protectiveness that she'd seen at the ball when it was all he could do not to put a fist in Jeremy's face. There was also a softness in his voice when he spoke about her, a gentleness that made Sofia's heart flutter in an unusual way.

Their food came and James told her stories about him and India growing up. Sofia couldn't remember a time when she had laughed so much. Eventually he steered the conversation to her and before she realized what she was doing she had told him about her life before going to The Hotel and what had led up to her becoming a prostitute.

A few times she had to blink back tears and couldn't talk because of the large lump in her throat. She fidgeted with the knife beside her plate and James put his hand over hers.

"You are a strong, amazing woman, Sofia," he said softly, and the intensity in his eyes had the blood running hot in her veins.

She was so confused when she was around him. He made her feel strong and confident and at the same time vulnerable and protected. For so long she had buried any memory of her childhood, refusing to let it define her, but James had brought it all bubbling to the surface. She found herself wanting to tell him, to explain to him how life had led her to this point. He listened, and she felt safe.

It also didn't escape her notice how her body reacted whenever he touched her. Even now, with his fingers barely skimming the back of her hand, it was like electricity was flowing up her arm, spreading to her core.

Telling her he was jealous had rattled her more than she wanted to admit. She was starting to lose her heart to him and the words in her head, the words that had raised her, the words that had kept her alive were screaming: Don't trust him! He only wants to use you!

When she was through telling him about her transition

to The Hotel and The Wager, he was silent for a long time. She was starting to think she had been wrong in confiding so much. He wouldn't even meet her eyes.

His next words confirmed her fears. "Let's get out of here."

They were silent as they left the restaurant. She expected him to turn towards The Hotel, but instead he drove in the direction of the bay, following a dark highway. It was late and there were few cars on the road. James drove until the road ended at the quay, and he could go no farther. They parked and the water was right in front of them, the only thing separating them from its vastness was a concrete barrier.

It was dark and chilly outside so they sat in the car with the heater running. They were in the nicer part of the docks that had been renovated and now boasted expensive condominiums and hotels for the very rich. Lights were strung along a walkway that ran parallel to the water, but the cooler weather kept strollers inside.

Tiny lights in the distance seemed to float untethered in the darkness. Fishing boats and cargo ships, so far out to sea that their beacons looked like will-o-the-wisps dancing across the horizon.

Sofia thought it a very romantic setting, but James hadn't looked at her since they had left the restaurant. He was staring straight ahead when he finally spoke. "I don't like you doing The Wager, Sofia."

She huffed out a sigh. "I know you don't James, but what else am I supposed to do?"

He looked at her and his eyes were hard and determined. "I want you to come live with me."

"What?" She wouldn't have been more surprised if a mermaid had jumped out of the sea and sat on the hood of the car. "What are you saying?"

"I'm saying, come live with me. It will get you out of The Hotel and The Wager."

"And in exchange you want…what?"

"Nothing."

She narrowed her eyes. "Nothing?"

He laughed without humor at the shocked expression on her face. "Is that so surprising to you? Hasn't anyone ever done anything for you just because?"

"Never," she answered.

He sobered at that and looked in her eyes. "I'm sorry."

"You don't need to be sorry. I'm a prostitute, James. I'm used to people wanting things from me and not giving anything back. But it doesn't matter, I can't leave The Hotel. I'd never abandon Sami."

"She can come too."

Sofia stared at him, too shocked to speak. There had to be some catch, nothing in life was this easy.

As if he'd read her mind, he said, "I promise you there will be no strings attached, no expectations. I live in a big house with plenty of room, and I often travel for business. With any luck you won't even have to see me."

She didn't answer for a long time, and he stared out at the bay, giving her the space she needed. He had made up his mind that it was the best way to get her out of The Hotel, but he knew she would not be easy to convince.

"It's a very generous offer, James," she finally said, her

voice a little unsteady, "but this is all happening really fast. I need to take some time to think about it and of course talk to Sami."

He looked at her and the softness in his eyes almost had her saying yes without a second thought, but she pressed her lips together, refusing to let her emotions and developing feelings for him make this decision.

"Take all the time you need," James said, leaning over and brushing his lips against hers. He'd done everything he could think of to persuade her; she had to be the one to leave. He couldn't drag her away, as much as he wanted to.

He sat back in the seat and she put her head on his shoulder and for a while they sat watching the bay. At one point the clouds parted and the moon and stars shone down on the water in bright splendor. She relaxed into the warmth of him and closed her eyes. He kissed the top of her head.

"I think it's time to get you home," he said quietly. She nodded sleepily.

It was midnight when they got back to The Hotel. James left his car with the valet and walked her to the bank of elevators, holding her hand. The desk staff and some of the working girls, looking exhausted in their five-inch heels, watched them curiously as they walked by. Sofia gave them a little self-conscious wave.

When the elevator closed she asked, "Are you staying in the same room? Floor twenty-five?"

He reached past her and hit the button for the top floor. "Not tonight."

He didn't want to go back to his room? This night was

getting more bizarre by the minute. The elevator opened and they stopped in front of her door.

James took her hand and kissed it. "I meant what I said, Sofia. What's important is getting you somewhere safe. I hope you'll think about it. I'm leaving the city tomorrow."

What he didn't tell her, because he was too much of a coward, was that he wouldn't be back to The Hotel. He'd told his sister India about wanting Sofia to come live with them. India had thought it was a great idea but cautioned him not to pressure Sofia because he tended to be overbearing when it came to something he wanted. India's exact words had been, "And for goodness sake don't fuck it up by being a dick."

James had done his best and if Sofia refused, there was no longer a reason to pursue her. If she chose The Hotel over him, that would be the end of it. She would have made her decision and even if it ripped him in two, he would have to respect that.

He reached into his jacket pocket and pulled out a business card. It had his name and contact information for his law firm. He flipped it over and there was a handwritten phone number on the back. She took it and nodded.

He gave her a gentle kiss on the lips and then turned to the elevator. She watched him until the doors had closed and then she went to her room and flopped on the bed.

Sami was burrowed under the covers, but her head peeked out when Sofia joined her. "How was your date?" she yawned.

"It wasn't a date, it was work, but he took me to a fancy restaurant." That got Sami's attention. She sat up and wouldn't even let Sofia change until she'd told her every detail of what she saw and ate. Sofia told her everything that she could remember, but she left out the part about James' invitation. There was no point in getting her excited over something that probably wouldn't happen.

After Sami's curiosity had finally run its course and she was tucked back down in bed, Sofia lay awake thinking about James' offer. He said no strings attached but she didn't believe that for a minute. There were always strings attached and the obvious one in this scenario was sex. What other reason would he have for wanting her to live with him, she scowled to herself. Then her face softened and she thought, would that be so bad? Sleeping with only one man, and a man she happened to like?

At the same time it would be trading one master for another. Rufus and The Wager for James. She knew what was expected of her at The Hotel. As much as she wanted to believe James was the honorable man he seemed to be, there was no guarantee he wouldn't kick her out when he got tired of her.

She was going to miss him, and would have liked to see him again, but she had a good life here and had fought too hard to get where she was just to throw it away on a fairy tale. She got out of bed and went silently to her dressing table and picked up the card James had given her. She ran her fingertips over his name and then ripped the card in half and threw it into the wastebasket.

CHAPTER 14

SOFIA PACED BACK AND forth in front of the door, her high heels clicking on the hardwood floor. She went over her checklist; nice dress, fancy shoes, hair done up in an innocent ponytail. She would speak clearly and calmly. She would not lose her temper and she would not beg.

Things had taken a sudden and drastic turn which changed Sofia's mind about contacting James. It had come down to Sami. Sofia would risk anything for her and if being James' mistress was the price she had to pay, then she would, without question.

Sami had been approached in The Hotel by a foreigner with a thick accent. His white hair was thinning but was made up for by the bushy beard, the same snowy color, that hung to his chest. He had asked her if she was one of the girls available for the night.

"No sir," Sami replied cheerfully. "But if you talk to the front desk they can give you more information on the girls who are."

The man looked Sami up and down, stroking his beard with gnarled fingers. He hummed, turning from her and approached the desk. He asked to speak to the owner.

All Rufus needed to hear was the word foreign, because in his experience it was synonymous with rich. He came trotting out, all smiles and handshakes. They disappeared into Rufus' office and stayed there for over an hour.

Sofia and Sami had both been in the lobby when they finally emerged, laughing and smoking cigars. The foreign man had left with a satisfied look, stroking his beard lovingly.

Rufus scampered over to Sami and Sofia, smiling broadly.

"That, my darlings, was Mr. Boris Petrov. He's Bulgarian, very influential, very rich. He's heard wonderful things about The Hotel, of course, and plans on making it his stopover whenever he is in the city. He had one or two stipulations." He steepled his fingers and tapped them together.

"Sami," he said, and her eyes snapped from the floor to him. Rufus looked at her, his face an unreadable mask. Sofia had never seen him so expressionless.

"Do what you need to do to prepare for next Saturday. Mr. Petrov has requested you specifically, and you will be available to him when he visits then and in the future."

Sami's mouth fell open and her green eyes slowly grew until they were wide as saucers.

"You can't do that, Rufus. She's only fourteen!" Sofia cried.

Rufus got in her face, pinching her cheeks with his thumb and fingers in a painful grip and growled, "Say that a little louder and see what happens."

Sofia felt tears prick her eyes and she pulled her face away from him. Sami was trembling and Sofia held her tightly against her as if Rufus might try to snatch her away right then.

He ranted on. "Grow up and join us in the real world, sweetheart. You're not an idiot so don't act like one." He straightened up and readjusted his collared shirt. "And if I hear a breath of this from anyone, you'll be back on the streets before lunch. Now get out of my sight."

Sami had been shaking so badly Sofia had to support her as they made their way to the elevator. She was in a state of shock by the time they got to the room, and she sat down heavily on the bed, staring at the wall.

Sofia knelt in front of her and took her hands. "Sami… Sami look at me." Sami turned to her with a dull expression. Her face was bone white, and her eyes popped out like glassy marbles. "I will not let this happen, Sami. You don't have to worry. We're going to get out of here. I have a plan, I promise."

She tucked a trembling Sami into bed and went to the wastebasket by her nightstand. She dug through the discarded cotton balls and tissues and found the torn business card. She held the pieces together and looked at the number, then went into the other room, closing the door quietly.

Her hands were unsteady, and it took her three tries to dial the right number. His end rang several times, and for one heart stopping moment she thought he wouldn't answer.

"James Hardy," he said briskly. The sound of his voice made her weak in the knees with relief. She sat down on the edge of the couch.

"James, it's Sofia."

His voice came back alarmed and anxious. "Sofia? What is it? What's wrong?"

She held back a sob. "James, Sami and I need to get out of here before Saturday."

"I'll come get you right now."

"No, we need a couple of days. I have to talk to Rufus. Can you pick us up on Thursday?"

"Of course," he thought for a moment. "I have a meeting that day I can't get out of but my friend Rob Majors could pick you up."

"Oh…" Sofia hesitated. The last thing Sami needed was another strange man driving them away from the only home she'd ever known.

"Don't worry," James said, sensing her discomfort. "I trust Rob with my life…and yours."

"Alright," she said quietly.

"Are you sure you're going to be ok until then? Did something happen?"

"A man came to the hotel and wanted Sami. I don't know what he promised Rufus but he actually agreed. He'll be back on Saturday and will expect Sami…James, how could Rufus do this? She's like a daughter to him!"

James was quiet for so long, Sofia thought they'd lost the connection. Then he said, quietly and dangerously, "Because he's a narcissistic bastard." He continued to describe Rufus in more colorful language, and it made Sofia laugh despite her tears.

"I'm afraid he won't let us go," she said, choking out the words.

"He doesn't have a choice," James growled into the phone. "You're employees. He can't hold you there against your will. Call if there's a problem; I can be there in twenty minutes and personally escort you out of there."

"We'll see you on Thursday then, and James?"

"Yes?"

"Thank you."

Now she was standing outside Rufus' office waiting for an audience. She'd been waiting for twenty minutes; Rufus' way of letting her know he was not in a good mood. It was not a positive sign.

Finally he yelled for her to come in and she opened the door and stepped inside. She took a deep breath and clasped her hands together to keep them from shaking.

Rufus sat behind a desk, positioned in front of a large window that looked out onto the rainy streets. Gold drapes were pulled to the side, held back with red tassels. A red brocade sofa and two matching chairs were positioned facing the desk.

A decanter and glasses were arranged on a side cart. A small mahogany bookshelf in the corner held a handful of slim volumes, propped up by several fat, naked gnome figurines, their beards doing nothing to hide their genitalia.

A blue bean bag was in one corner, a treadmill in another. The room was impeccably clean. No books or papers scattered around, in fact no clutter at all. Rufus' desk held a computer, a pad of paper, and a cup full of pens. Near his elbow was a mug of tea, the steam from the hot water rising lazily to the ceiling.

He was tapping on the computer keyboard with his index finger, one key at a time. He'd been surly with her ever since she'd "made a scene" as he put it, in the lobby of his hotel.

He banged on a few more keys and then shoved the keyboard to the side. He rose in one fluid movement and gave her his cheek to kiss. He wore a black sparkling tank top and a pair of tight bicycle shorts that left no question as to his assigned sex at birth.

"I've been extremely busy or I would have called for you sooner." He sat her on the sofa and perched himself next to her. He held his head up regally and looked down his nose at her. "You've been very uppity lately."

"What do you mean?"

Rufus waved his hand in the air. "Making scenes, throwing tantrums."

"I don't throw tantrums," she frowned.

"I beg to differ. Slapping that silly little man at the ball."

"He pulled my dress down!"

Rufus waved his hand in a dismissive gesture. "You seemed to be quite pleased to be rescued by James Hardy." He narrowed his eyes at her. "Does your attitude lately have something to do with him?"

Sofia felt her stomach drop. The question caught her completely by surprise even though it shouldn't have. Rufus was intelligent and observant, especially when it came to The Hotel. "Why do you think..?"

"Well, isn't it obvious?" he said, cutting her off. "You've been sleeping with him like a randy teenager, and frankly I don't think he's a good influence. He has far too many scruples." Rufus wrinkled his nose distastefully. "Are you starting to have feelings for him?"

Sofia's heart skipped a beat. She felt her skin turn red and fought to calm herself, but she knew it was written all over her face.

"No!" Rufus' eyes grew huge and he stood up slowly, staring at her. "My little blaze of Glory! Has that man extinguished your magnificent flame?" He had both hands clapped over his mouth. He looked so ridiculous and dramatic that Sofia had to stifle a laugh.

"I can't believe you, a seasoned veteran, the pride and joy of The Hotel, would succumb to the charms of some man, no matter how good looking he is. You know better than to get personally involved. Did I teach you nothing?" He paced the floor, his movements becoming more erratic with each pass. "Well, what are you going to do about it?"

Sofia opened her mouth, but he interrupted her.

"Never mind, you've done enough. Of course he's going to fall for you, you stupid creature. They all do. That's the whole point! That's why they keep coming back to The Wager. For you!" He fisted his hands above his head as if grabbing invisible tufts of hair. "You can't have a lover and work here, you know this! Who is going to pay when they know someone else is getting you for free?"

"Rufus, I…"

"You can't ever see him again. We're going to snuff out this imbecilic infatuation and you'll forget all about him. He'll be banned from The Hotel, of course…"

"Rufus!" Sofia said sharply. He looked down at her, his

eyes rolling wildly. She looked straight at him and just let herself breathe out the words, "James has asked me and Sami to come live with him."

Rufus stopped, frozen in place, a mockery of a smile plastered on his lips. His eyes bulged and his head was shiny with perspiration. Sofia leaned back in surprise.

"Rufus!" She was truly concerned he was having a stroke or some kind of seizure. There was a faint ticking under one of his eyes and his upturned lips quivered as if it was all he could do to keep them in that position. She stood up ready to catch him if he collapsed. He was more likely to fall on top of her, she thought, bracing herself.

He came out of it as if he was waking from a dream. He laughed and his face softened and a brilliant smile full of teeth settled on his face. "Well, that's…awesome!" he cried, clapping his hands. "My little Sofia, all grown up and moving on in the world." He made a sweeping motion with his hand. "Heh heh, yes, well, well. I guess you won't be needing to work?" He looked at her with such innocence that Sofia almost felt sorry for him. She shook her head. "Oh well, no harm in asking, I guess. Congrats my dear, he's quite a catch."

He put his arms around her and exhaled heavily, patting her back. "We will miss you terribly. Get your things together whenever you're ready." He led her to the door with his hand on her back. "I'm sure he'll be sending a car around? Good, that's settled then. Do visit us sometime, after all, you are family."

She said she would and found herself standing outside the door of his office. He gave her another brilliant smile and shut the door in her face.

Sofia stood, confused, the slamming door echoing through the empty hallway. What had just happened? He almost seemed happy for her, she thought. Was that possible? It couldn't be that easy…or maybe it was. The Hotel was full of girls; they really didn't have anywhere to put her if they demoted her from the suite. Maybe he was tired of her. Maybe she'd become more trouble than she was worth. She was twenty-three and in her line of business that was getting toward retirement age. Rufus would find a new, younger protégé and would forget all about her. She looked at the closed door then turned and hurried down the hallway before he could change his mind.

She didn't hear the blood-curdling scream or the sound of tiny explosions as gnome figurines smashed against the door one after another.

CHAPTER 15

JAMES' FRIEND ROB WAS coming in two days to pick them up and Sofia and Sami were going crazy with excitement, and impatience.

Sami was a bundle of nerves, bustling around their suite, throwing things in a bag, talking incessantly until Sofia made her sit down before she hyperventilated. Sofia tried to be a calming influence, but her nerves were just as rattled. This would be the first time either of them had left the city and the prospect left her breathless and terrified.

When the day finally arrived, Sofia was blurry eyed with exhaustion. Sami hadn't slept at all and had kept Sofia up with her tossing and turning.

They had to say goodbye to the girls which took up most of the morning. Maryanne clung to Sofia and sobbed, and Sofia eventually had to gently pry her friend off and promise she would come to visit.

They had a quick lunch and said goodbye to a stalwart but teary eyed Chef. They were back in their room by one.

The thought of a nap was laughable, but Sofia laid down on her bed anyway and watched the clock tick by the minutes.

She was jostled awake an hour and a half later by Sami.

"It's almost three!" Sami squealed as quietly as Sami was able to squeal. She had been sitting in a chair, reading, but one eye had been on the clock the entire time. At three they gathered their few possessions and hurried to the lobby.

Rufus was there waiting for them. He was wearing shorts that rode up his thighs, cowboy boots and an oversized sweater. Mascara stained his cheeks with coal-colored smudges as his tears fell. He had a large red and blue checkered handkerchief that he was using to blow his nose violently. He was drawing odd looks from guests who, passing by, gave him a wide berth.

"I know I said I wouldn't make a scene, but this has to be the saddest..." He paused to choke in a sob and put a hand over his heart, "the saddest day of my life." He took Sofia in his arms and cried into her shoulder. Sofia looked at Sami and raised her eyebrows.

"It's ok, Rufus," she said, rubbing his back. "I promise I'll come back for a visit."

"I'm going to hold you to that!" he exclaimed. He turned to Sami. "And you, sweet little Sami." He held her for a long time and then took her by the shoulders. "It's a big bad world out there, cherie. If you ever need sanctuary, you come running back to Daddy Rufus."

Sami nodded and returned his hug, then went to stand beside Sofia, her closeness soothing her vibrating nerves. They watched out of the window; hands clasped, their small bags waiting at their feet. Sami was trembling.

"It's going to be ok," Sofia whispered encouragingly. "You know James. He wants to give you a wonderful life."

"I know," said Sami with a shaky smile. "It's just I've never slept in a different bed before."

Sofia smiled and squeezed her hand. "I think you'll find it easy to get used to."

They passed a weeping Rufus and walked through the swinging doors. The rain was falling steadily and people rushed by with umbrellas.

When Sofia was standing next to Sami on the rain-slicked sidewalk, she gave a shaky laugh. She truly hadn't believed Rufus would let them go. She realized she had spent the last three days waiting for him to do something or say something, to burst this dream-like bubble she was in; but here she was, outside The Hotel and about to get into a stranger's car. She laughed again at the absurdity of it.

A young man was leaning against a car that was parked out front, his arms crossed. He looked about James' age, maybe a little younger, but where James was lanky and lean, this man was built like a wrestler with broad shoulders and thick legs. His flannel shirt was rolled up at the sleeves revealing tan forearms corded with muscle.

A backwards baseball cap covered his brown hair and as Sofia approached him nervously, she noticed he had the softest, kindest eyes she'd ever seen. His eyelashes were long and dark and the combination could have been described as beautiful if his other features hadn't been so rugged and masculine.

She found herself smiling; his open, friendly expression

putting her at ease. He held out a hand, large and calloused.

"I'm Rob Majors. I take it you're Sofia?"

"Yes," she said shyly. She was so used to being brazen and playing the ditsy sex kitten, that it was always an adjustment when meeting new men who didn't behave like she was a possession. "And this is Sami."

Sami just stared at him with huge green eyes, everything happening too quickly for her to process.

"It's a pleasure, Sami," Rob said smiling, and took their small bags, putting them in the trunk.

"Is it alright if I sit in the back with Sami?" Sofia asked.

"Absolutely," Rob said, opening the door for them. "There's a cooler in there with water and sandwiches. Freddy never lets anyone drive farther than fifteen miles without packing food."

"Who's Freddy?" Sami asked, curiosity overcoming her shyness. She put on her seatbelt and rolled the window down.

"She's James and India's housekeeper and she does most of the cooking too. She comes in during the weekdays to help out." Rob pulled away from the curb and into the slow moving traffic.

Sofia watched The Hotel out of the back window as it got smaller and then disappeared from view. She blinked several times, not wanting to embarrass herself by breaking down in front of James' friend.

She was excited and terrified. "I can't believe this is happening," she said quietly.

Sensing the waves of emotions that were seizing her, Sami put her hand in Sofia's and squeezed.

"A new adventure," Sami said confidently.

Sofia kissed her head. "A new adventure."

Rob stayed silent, giving them time to adjust to what must be a mind-altering experience. To leave the only home they'd known, to start a new life in a basically foreign land with people they didn't know. It took a lot of courage, Rob thought.

When James had told him about Sofia, he thought his friend had lost his mind. James had always been stoic and purpose-driven to a fault; most likely a byproduct of having to grow up too fast and take on huge responsibilities at an unreasonably young age. Rob had rarely seen him lose control, but these past weeks James had been like a caged animal, restless and irritable; undecisive for maybe the first time in his life.

Rob couldn't believe that James had fallen so hard for a girl he'd just met, not to mention what she did for a living. It was a little shocking to find out his best friend was in love with a prostitute, but Rob held no prejudice. He rarely went to the city, but he was well aware of the conditions and lack of opportunities for so many living there.

He came from a working class family, who had owned the local car mechanic shop for four generations. The only reason he was fortunate enough to live in The Lake District was because his great-grandfather, an entrepreneur from an early age, had bought the lot when real estate was cheap.

Now that Rob had met her, he could see why James was drawn to Sofia. She was obviously physically stunning, but as he watched her in the rear view mirror, he noticed a softness to her, a vulnerability that would have brought out every protective instinct James had. His friend was in big trouble, Rob thought with a chuckle.

James had told him that he had no intention of making a move on Sofia. She was going to live with him to get her away from The Hotel, no other reason. Rob shook his head. He wondered how long that would last.

The city streets were clogged with congestion. They moved at a snail's pace, past honking horns and shouting vendors. The smell of sewers and hot dogs and exhaust fumes combined into one odiferous cloud which assaulted them through the open windows.

They drove the short distance to the city limit and the road turned from cracked pavement to gravel. Sofia realized that this was as far as she had ever gone outside the city. She had a moment of panic when the car turned onto a black topped highway that went on as far as she could see. Driving off with a complete stranger went against every survival instinct ingrained in her. But when she thought of James at the end of the journey, her heart sped up for a different reason. She hadn't allowed herself to dwell on how excited she was to see him.

Rob pointed out bits of scenery to them and answered Sami's non-stop questions about The Lake District. Every once in a while he would make a silly joke and Sami would giggle, putting her and Sofia both at ease.

They went north for another thirty minutes. The fog dissipated and Sami breathed in the fresh air, laced with a sharp and tangy scent.

"What's that smell, Rob?" she asked, sticking her head out the window and letting the warm breeze ruffle her hair.

Rob frowned and sniffed out of the window. "What, the pine trees?"

"Pine trees," Sami said, as if committing the words to memory, and inhaled deeply.

The trees thickened and the road looped left and right, curling around on itself. Sami's slight body swayed side to side, churning her stomach. Rob noticed in the rearview mirror that her pale face had turned pasty.

"Just a few more minutes of this," Rob said, concerned for his cargo, but also for the car which he'd borrowed from James. His truck wouldn't have been comfortable for the long ride.

The road finally straightened, and they came out of the thick grove of pines and into bright sunshine reflected off blue waters. Sami sucked in a breath. She had never seen anything so beautiful in her life. Stretching for miles, and sinking into the purple mountains beyond, the lake shimmered in the sun as if the surface was speckled with tiny diamonds. It was like Dorothy opening her front door and revealing all the colors of Oz for the first time.

As they drove, the water seemed to shift colors from sapphire to turquoise. Sami could imagine the lake was made of glass if it wasn't for the boats dotted throughout, churning out their white wakes.

A steep downgrade brought them to lake level, and the expanse of water grew in size as they drove nearer. It seemed to go on forever. They passed a grocery store on their left, and to their right, the lake, looking close enough to touch. They sat at a traffic light and Sami could feel the coolness coming off the cobalt waters. Nothing like the grey-green sludge she was used to at the docks. She'd never seen anything like it. Everything around her was brighter, and more colorful than she ever could have imagined.

Across the water was a mountain range; dark purple with a wall of furry trees climbing up the hillside. She couldn't believe how many different types of greens there were. She'd always thought green was green, but she had been so wrong.

They turned on to a two-way road flanked by more trees and beautiful homes, but Sami could still see the flash of blue as they drove parallel to the lake. Rob pulled off the road onto a gravel driveway that sloped up in a curve. Flowering shrubs lined each side, hiding it from the main road. Sami's heart fluttered as the car came to a stop in front of a large, two-story house.

"Did you catch any bugs in your teeth?" Sofia asked. Sami turned to her, a huge smile on her face, her hair sticking up in fluffy waves. "What?"

"Nothing," Sofia laughed as they got out of the car.

She and Sami stood in front of the house; hands clasped. It wasn't flashy, but it was beautiful, and the combination of wood and brick left no doubt in Sofia's mind that it was very expensive. Hydrangea bushes flanked the white stone steps leading up to the porch and double doors.

Rob pulled their bags from the trunk as the front door flew open and a tiny, thin woman stood beaming at them. Her white hair was done up in a bun that had lost whatever shape it had started with and now looked like a melted ice cream cone. She was wearing a calf-length skirt and sneakers and an apron tied around her waist.

"Oh, come in, come in!" she cried, grabbing them by the hands. She had a thick German accent and a strong grip for someone so little. "I'm so pleased you're here. How was the journey up from the city? It must be such a relief to get out of that smog. I'm Frederica, the housekeeper, but please call me Freddy, everyone does. Rob," she said, turning to him as he came into the house with the bags, "put those upstairs and then there's apple cobbler in the kitchen."

"I knew there was a reason I love you, Fred."

"Oh bah." She made a guttural sound of exasperation but there was a twinkle in her eye. "He's a good boy," Freddy said after Rob had disappeared up the stairs.

They were standing in a large entryway with glossy hard-wood floors. To the left through an arched doorway was a bright room decorated in sea greens and blues. The stairs Rob had gone up curved to the left leading to what Sofia assumed were bedrooms.

Freddy gestured, holding her arms out wide. "Well, here we are. This is your new home, and I hope you'll be happy here. If there's anything you need just let me know. James will be down shortly. He's been in meetings all day."

A Siamese cat came slinking into the room and rubbed itself along Sami's legs. "Oh look!" she cried. "Isn't he cute!" She knelt down and the cat allowed her to scratch behind its ears.

"That's Maurice," said James coming down the stairs. "He

runs the house. I'm surprised he's come up to you so soon. It usually takes him a good week to warm up to strangers. And even then I use the term 'warm up' loosely."

Sofia's heart gave a little skip when she saw him. He was wearing black slacks and a blue dress shirt that did amazing things to his eyes. As he came towards them, his movements casual and relaxed, she realized how much she had missed him.

"Glad to see you ladies made it. Sorry I couldn't pick you up myself." He put his hand on Sami's head and looked at Sofia. "No complications?"

"None." She shook her head. "I can't believe he just let us go like that."

"Hmm," James said. "Well, Sami, I'm going to let Freddy here show you your room. You can have a bath and a nap if you'd like."

"I'm not sleeping with you?" she asked Sofia, alarmed.

"You get to have a bed all to yourself, and a room all to yourself." Sofia reassured her.

"That's going to make it harder for me to wait on you," Sami said, frowning.

"Sami," Sofia said gently, "you don't have to wait on me. That was your job at The Hotel, but we don't live there anymore."

"But who's going to lay out your clothes and run your bath?"

Sofia smiled. "Believe it or not, I am capable of bathing and dressing myself."

Sami scoffed, doubting this, but she followed Freddy up the stairs, her curiosity getting the better of her.

James smiled at Sofia. "She's going to be fine."

"I think she is," Sofia said.

He held out his hand. "I'll give you a quick tour." She took his hand and immediately felt her face go hot. His hand was so familiar, and it felt good to touch him again.

He led her down the hallway which was covered with a beautiful blue and white rug. The kitchen was large and well lit, with a marble counter running down the middle, chairs lining one side. Loaves of bread wrapped in towels released a mouth-watering, buttery smell.

Every modern gadget she could think of was lined with precision along a counter, probably in some kind of ranking order, like a stainless steel army. The walls of the kitchen were painted sunshine yellow with white trim. It was a loud color, but it suited the room. She wondered who had been responsible for the décor. In an alcove was a rectangular wooden table with four chairs around it.

"We have a dining room, but there's just the two of us and I don't remember the last time we ate together. I guess now we can graduate to the grown-up room."

"I like this," said Sofia, running her hand down the smooth wood. "It's cozy."

There was a back door that Sofia assumed led to the lake. A large window overlooked an expanse of grass occupied by a white gazebo with couches and chairs set inside it.

James led her back toward the front of the house to a large room off the entryway. This was what the books would have called a drawing room. What the hell was she doing here, thought Sofia self-consciously. The room was furnished with two cream-colored couches, and several deep, plush chairs. A set of French doors and several large windows made up one side of the room. Against another wall was a fireplace; logs stacked neatly in the swept grate waiting to be lit when the weather cooled. A long bar in the corner was covered with bottles that shone in the low light coming from several lamps on side tables.

"For the most part we stay pretty quiet around here. I hope it won't be lonely for you."

"Are you kidding? Some loneliness sounds great," she said.

He led her to the French doors and they stepped out onto a gravel path that disappeared behind a bank of rose bushes, their buds just starting to open. Sofia could hear birds singing and she closed her eyes and immersed herself in the sound. It was so beautiful and innocent. It was as if the birds were celebrating being alive.

James watched Sofia; her eyes closed, face angled toward the sun. The light shimmered off her glowing skin. She had a faint smile on her face and her lips were parted. He didn't think he would ever tire of looking at her. Every day after he left the city, he had hoped to hear from her, and for each day that he didn't, he grew more withdrawn and irritable. The feeling that he had lost her, that he should have done more to convince her; and the knowledge that she was still doing The Wager, ate at him like a cancer until he was ready to come out of his skin.

India, in her infinite wisdom, told him to get his head out of his ass and quit with the pity party.

When he had heard Sofia's voice telling him she wanted

to take him up on his offer, he sighed in giddy relief, only to be replaced with an unfamiliar rage when she told him about what Rufus was planning for Sami. It had taken every ounce of self-control not to get in his car and pull them out of there himself.

As he gazed at Sofia's serene face, her lips glossy in the waning sunlight, he realized how difficult it was going to be to keep his promise to her. He wanted her in every way, but he'd told her there would be no expectations from him.

He thought of the first time he had seen her that day in the market, laughing with Sami and talking with vendors, her smile lighting up the darkest corners. He had fallen in love with her on the spot and was determined to find out who she was.

James had heard of The Hotel, just like everyone else in the city, but he was not the kind of man to ever consider using a prostitute. When he found out about the heinous Wager and that she was the prize, he'd felt a knife had twisted in his gut. Not revulsion, not pity, but something else.

Remembering her golden smile and the way she had put her arm around Sami and pulled her close; how open she was with everyone she met at the market, he knew she must have a will of iron. Women don't go into prostitution because they want to, they do it to survive. Whatever Sofia had been through that brought her to that point, James wanted to know so he could keep it from ever happening to her again.

He'd had no intention of sleeping with her that first night he had won The Wager, he thought wistfully. Going to The Hotel had been pure impulse, the desire to see her, talk to her, know her had become an obsession. He was obviously physically attracted to her, she was the most beautiful woman he'd ever seen, but her intelligence, humor, and compassion for those like her had pushed him in a direction he hadn't seen coming.

Her presence had been intoxicating that first night and the electricity between them, even as he touched her feet, was palpable. He wanted to rip that beautiful dress off her and possess her body until she cried out his name.

It had taken every bit of will power he possessed to wait until she had wanted him. After that his mind had been on her alone. When he wasn't with her he felt like a piece of him was missing, a phantom ache.

Now she was here he felt better, but still not complete. He wanted to take her in his arms; to tell her he loved her and that nothing would ever separate them again, but he hadn't brought her here to be his mistress. He had sworn to her that she was safe with him, and he would honor that if it killed him.

Sofia opened her eyes and saw him watching her. A faint blush came to her cheeks and she said simply, "birds."

He chuckled softly and she felt an overwhelming urge to kiss him. She looked away quickly.

James cleared his throat and pointed.

"There's a path that leads down to the lake. The water's cold but it's safe to swim. Boats don't come into the cove unless they have a reason to."

They stood for a moment; Sofia taking in the beautiful simplicity of the landscape. Other than the roses, which James told her was Freddy's other passion, the plants and flowers all seemed to grow wild in no particular pattern, scattering colors, shapes and textures on either side of the path and along the border of the lawn.

Holding her hand, he led her back inside to the foot of the stairs. They turned as the door flew open blowing in a girl dressed in a purple skirt, black leggings and a shirt that had the name of what Sofia assumed was a band. There were tiny hoops pierced in her nose and lip and Sofia could see part of a tattoo peeking out of her shirt sleeve. She wore her dark hair in a braid which showed off her studded ears.

Sofia's first impression was how much she resembled her brother. The striking combination of black hair and rich blue eyes.

The young girl bounded over to them. "You must be Sofia! I'm India. I'm so glad you're here." She gave Sofia an enthusiastic hug. "I hope you like boring because that's what you're going to get. James has been moping around like a lost puppy. Now he has a friend, maybe he'll stop butting into all my business." She gave them a wink and scurried up the stairs. It felt to Sofia like energy personified had just entered the house.

James smiled softly. "Yes, well, that was India. With her best manners, believe it or not."

"I think she's lovely," said Sofia.

He gestured up the stairs.

When he opened the door to her bedroom, Sofia's heart began to pound. She turned to him. He moved with a sleepy casualness, but his eyes were burning with energy. He followed her into the room. It was a big room, but he seemed to fill it. His body was between her and the door.

"There's a bath through there." He pointed to an adjoining room near the bed. "Take your time, get some rest. We'll have dinner in a couple of hours. If you need anything, just holler. Freddy or I will be around."

He went to the door and paused, his hand on the knob. "I'm glad you're here, Sofia," he said over his shoulder.

"I am too, James."

He gave a slight nod and left the room, closing the door behind him. She stood, confused. She thought he'd want to sleep with her right away. They had been apart for some time. Maybe he wanted to wait until tonight?

Rob had left her bag on the bed and she opened the clasp and looked down at every possession she owned in the world. She took out the few modest dresses, and other casual wear she had brought with her. She hoped James wasn't expecting glamorous because all those fancy outfits had belonged to The Hotel.

She walked to the window and loosened the catch. It swung out and the cool air filled her lungs. From the second story she could clearly see the path that wound through the rose bushes. It circled a grassy area where the gazebo stood, then traveled back down to the lake.

The incredible blue sparkled in the late afternoon sun. A wooden pier traversed the water thirty feet out from the shore, pylons positioned every yard or so. The water rushed at the thick posts, splashing up and then retreating, pulled by an invisible force. A mile or so in each direction, the land jutted out making a natural cove. Far out on the lake Sofia could see the white sails of boats drifting lazily across the water.

She left the window open to let in the delicious lake breeze and the smell of wet earth. She undressed and ran a bath. She soaked for a long time in the tub. Her body ached with exhaustion, but her mind bounced from one confused thought to another.

She couldn't believe that it was over; The Wager, The Hotel, all of it. Tears stung the back of her eyes, but she took a deep breath and didn't let them fall. It was such a relief and at the same time she felt on edge, uncertain of James' intentions. What did he want? Why go to all this trouble to get her out of The Hotel?

Rufus had asked her if she had feelings for James. Her body certainly reacted when he was near her, and she felt extreme gratitude. She enjoyed his company, but was there something else? She'd never been in love. She'd never even really liked a man before, she thought ruefully. She wouldn't know love if came up and slapped her. She trusted James, he made her feel safe, but she couldn't read him. Part of her success in The Wager was knowing how to read men and what their wants and desires were. He continued to be a mystery to her.

Her fingers were wrinkled by the time she climbed out of the deep tub. She slipped a thick, warm robe over her naked body, fell onto the soft, welcoming bed and closed her eyes. In minutes she was asleep.

CHAPTER 16

SOFIA WOKE, FEELING BETTER than she had in days. She brushed her hair, put on jeans and a sweater, and went to find Sami.

She was in the kitchen with Freddy. Sofia could hear her voice from the stairs. She hoped Sami wasn't pestering Freddy on their first day. Sofia went into the brightly lit room to find Sami standing at the long counter that extended halfway across the kitchen. Maurice sat on a chair next to her.

A large board was covered in a thin layer of flour and Freddy was working a thick ball of dough through her hands. She kneaded with vigor, flipping and pounding. She broke off a small piece of dough and handed it to Sami who flattened it with the palm of her hand. Flour poofed into the air and cascaded onto her hair and Maurice's nose. The cat sneezed and jumped off the chair to find somewhere safer to sit. Freddy opened the oven and peered inside.

"Anyway," Sami was saying, "then she told me that the guy's dick was so small…"

"Sami!" Sofia broke in. "Some stories are not appropriate to repeat." She looked nervously at the housekeeper.

Sami looked innocently at Freddy, whose backside was sticking out of the oven. "What's that, dear," she said straightening up and bringing with her a sheet of puffed-up biscuits. "Oh hello, Sofia. Did you have a nice nap?"

"I'm helping make the biscuits for dinner," Sami announced proudly.

"I can see that. Freddy, don't let her get in your way and please excuse her language."

"I love listening to the little thing chatter. It's like my garden fairy has come to life." She whispered to Sofia, "I'm mostly deaf anyway." She wrapped the biscuits in a moist towel.

"How long have you worked here, Freddy?" Sofia asked.

The housekeeper stopped what she was doing and put a finger to her chin, leaving a smudge of flour. "Hm, I believe it's going on ten years now. My India had just turned seven. Precocious little thing she was, still is," she said fondly.

Freddy told Sofia she had moved to The Lake District with her husband of forty years after he had retired from the military in Germany. He had died a year later from cancer. They never had children. They had moved from place to place and been so wrapped up in each other that it had never seemed a priority. They'd always say, "next year" and leave it at that.

When he was gone the loss and loneliness nearly destroyed her. She had her husband's pension to live on, and she didn't need to work if she didn't want to; but she was conscious of the fact that if she didn't get out and be with other people, she would soon follow her dear George to the grave.

Every morning, as was her habit, she drank tea and read the newspaper. She had come across an ad that read simply, 'housekeeper and cook wanted'. Freddy had been the oldest of seven and with two working parents, she had been running a household for the better part of fifty years. It was familiar to her, and she was good at it.

When she had met her potential new employers, she thought it was some kind of joke, sending the children in to do the interview. James and India asked her questions about her experience and background, two pairs of stunning blue eyes assessing her. They were so serious and professional that she found herself responding likewise. It wasn't until they hired her that she learned they were, in fact, her new employers.

It hadn't taken long for Freddy to realize that she had needed James and India as much as they had needed her.

"You mean it was just the two of them for five years?" Sofia asked, shocked. "How on earth did they manage?"

"James has a good head on his shoulders," said Freddy, going back to her kneading. "When he wants something, he doesn't stop until he gets it." She punched the dough again as if emphasizing the point.

Sofia smiled. "I've noticed that about him."

Freddy looked up at her with a twinkle. "That boy has been wandering around this big house like he's lost something and can't remember where he put it. His heart has been in the city for many weeks."

Sofia raised her eyebrows, startled, but Freddy began

humming and scurried to the oven with another tray of biscuits.

Sofia left the kitchen and wandered down the hall thoughtfully. She knew James had been jealous, but she thought that was just because she was sleeping with other men. It never occurred to her that it went deeper than that.

The drawing room was warm; the sun was setting and sending its rays streaming through the windows. James was at the bar. She approached him and he asked what she'd like to drink.

"White wine, please." She studied him as he poured her drink. He had bathed too, the ends of his hair were still damp. He wore slacks and a long-sleeved collarless shirt.

So far he'd been welcoming and polite but hadn't given her any indication that he had feelings for her. He was a rich man who didn't want to share his toys, that's all this was. She could understand that; it made sense to her. Anything more was complicated, and dangerous.

He handed her a glass, and he clinked it with his own.

"Cheers," he said. "To new beginnings."

"To new beginnings," she toasted, smiling. "Is India going to join us for dinner?"

"To celebrate your arrival, yes. It will be a rare treat to see my sister at a meal."

"I was talking to Freddy just now. I can't believe you went all that time with no adult in your life. How were you able to raise India when you were so young?"

He looked down at his glass and swirled the liquid. "I can't really take any credit. She pretty much raised herself."

"James, three year olds don't stay alive if left on their own. You obviously did something right or she wouldn't even be here."

He looked at her with amusement in his eyes. He stared at her for so long she started to feel self-conscious. She ran a hand through her hair and resisted the ridiculous urge to giggle. Sami rescued her by dashing into the room, a cloud of flour in her wake, announcing that dinner was ready.

Freddy, done for the day, said her goodbyes and with a beaming smile left for home. The four of them opted for dinner in the kitchen. The windows faced the setting sun, bathing the room in orange and gold. The effect against the yellow walls was stunning, like being inside a sunflower. While they were setting the table Sofia said to India, "Don't tell me your brother decorated this house."

India spluttered. "Heck no, are you kidding? If he had been in charge every room would be a charming shade of slate gray. That's how much imagination he has. He let me have free rein as soon as I knew my colors."

Sofia smiled, imagining James letting a preschool India choose paint at the hardware store. "Well, it's all beautiful."

"Thank you!" India beamed. "James says this room gives him a headache."

"Only when I'm hung over," James said, entering the kitchen and approaching the table. Sami was already seated with Maurice perched regally on her lap, his head level with the table.

"Uh, no," James said.

Sami puffed out her bottom lip and set the cat on the

floor. Maurice looked up at her sullenly and then curled around her feet.

James shook his head in amazement and took a seat across from Sofia.

The food was even better than Chef's and for a while all Sofia could think about was how good everything tasted. She hadn't eaten much for days, her nerves too rattled to risk putting anything in her stomach.

Everyone made a big fuss over the biscuits which were delicious, if a little lopsided.

Sofia tried not to look at James, but her eyes were drawn to his face and when she glanced at him, he was watching her, his finger making lazy circles around the rim of his wine glass.

She turned quickly to India. "Do you go to school, India?"

"Here we go," mumbled James.

India put down her knife and fork and addressed Sofia across the table. "I've just finished high school, and I refuse to go to some overly priced university run by a bunch of old men with no imagination. The curriculums are outdated with useless information."

She looked at James as if daring him to contradict her. He chewed silently with a faint smile on his lips as India continued. "There's not a practical thing they can teach me. It makes far more sense for me to work in the real world and figure out what I'm good at and what I want to do. And then I might think about college." She speared a piece of broccoli with more force than necessary and put it in her mouth.

Sofia looked at James and then back at India. "I think

that makes perfect sense. I take it your brother doesn't agree?"

"James thinks I should follow in his footsteps. Earn a degree and run some stupid business. He doesn't even care that I might want to do something creative with my life," she said, sneering at her brother.

"I do care," James said, casually picking up his wine glass and taking a sip. "and I've never said anything about following in my footsteps. When have you ever done that, dear girl?" He set his glass down, ignoring India's affronted look. "My point is that university can give you tools the way working at Bob's Beastly Burgers can't."

Sami laughed.

"You," said India standing up and throwing her napkin on the table, "can be such a dick." She picked up her plate, winked at Sami and after depositing her dish in the sink, went whistling out of the room.

"Those are going to be her last dying words to me," said James.

"She'll find her way," said Sofia. "She's very young."

"I'm just afraid if she doesn't find her way soon she'll end up in a gang." He leaned forward. "Sami, has Maurice been showing you around?"

"Yup! He showed me his favorite hiding spots in the house, and we walked on the rocks by the lake. The water's freezing! I want to learn to swim, do you think I can do that? The flowers smell better than the ones at The Hotel, maybe it's because they're still in the ground." She paused to take a bite of her chicken and James smiled at her.

"I'm glad you're making yourself at home," he said.

The sun had set by the time they finished dinner, but the sky still glowed dusky blue. Sofia and Sami insisted on doing the dishes, so James made coffee and then wandered into the drawing room. They found him reading the newspaper in one of the plush chairs. Sofia sat in the matching one next to him, and Sami curled up at her feet. He had lit the fire and the room glowed cheerfully.

"Rufus always read the news on his phone," Sami said, grabbing hold of Maurice as he sauntered by and dragging him onto her lap. He made a cursory attempt to get away but then slumped against her legs and was soon purring loudly.

"I do that sometimes," James said. "But I still like holding a newspaper from time to time, though it does make me feel ancient."

Sami laughed, then looked up as India came into the room. She was wearing a very short, very tight dress with a leather jacket thrown over the top.

"I'm going out with Janis," she announced.

James looked at her over his paper and said, "Where's the rest of your dress?"

India looked at Sofia. "You see what I have to put up with?" she said and turned on her heel and was gone, slamming the door.

Sami stifled a giggle.

"Incorrigible," James muttered, going back to his paper.

Sofia watched the fire, a deep sense of peace and safety, for her and Sami, settling over her. She felt the burden that had been resting on her shoulders lift with an almost physical release. She combed Sami's hair with her fingers and smiled when the little blond head began to droop.

"Sami," Sofia said gently, "I think it's time for bed."

Sami yawned and said, "I don't want the day to end."

Sofia smiled and said, "Tomorrow will be a good day too."

"'K," Sami said sleepily. She stood up, to Maurice's dissatisfaction, and blew air kisses to Sofia and James. She stumbled toward her room, Maurice trotting along behind her.

James watched them go. "Extraordinary. Since that cat showed up on my doorstep as a mewling runt, he's never taken to anybody."

Sofia smiled, turning to him, "He's very selective, like Sami. Sami doesn't trust men, you know. She's spent her entire life being told what rats they are, thinking women are only good for one thing."

He folded his paper and tossed it on the floor. "And I fall into the rat category?"

"Well," she said smiling, "that might be true, but she cares about you and she feels safe with you. That's saying a lot."

"That makes me very happy to hear," he said, looking into the fire. A log rolled over sending sparks crackling and spitting. She watched his profile, the flames shadowing his cheekbones. They sat like that for a while, James staring into the fire and Sofia memorizing the curves and angles of his face from under her lashes.

"You mentioned you like to read," he said, suddenly turning toward her and meeting her eyes. She jumped guiltily and nodded. "I have some books in my study if you want to have a look at them."

She roused herself and followed him across the hall past

the stairs. There was an alcove that she hadn't noticed before and he opened a heavy wood door leading into a small room. It contained the standard desk and chairs, a sofa; she guessed for potential naps or lady friends. What if he brought women back to the house, she suddenly thought. They had no arrangement otherwise. She frowned.

"Sofia?" James was saying.

She started and looked at him. He pointed and her eyes widened when she saw the rows and rows of books lining the shelves across two walls.

"My gosh, James! This must have cost a fortune."

He looked around him. "Not really. I've collected them over the years. Some belonged to my parents, some I've had since I was a kid."

She looked through the titles on the bookshelf. He came to stand next to her and showed her a few of his favorites. She was very aware of his closeness, their shoulders brushing, and she was disconcerted at her body's reaction. She tingled from the heat radiating off of him, and the smell of him, masculine and spicy, sent her blood pumping.

She reached out quickly and chose a book at random. She straightened and looked up at him. His face was composed but his eyes were laughing at her again. Her lips parted instinctively. "I think I'll take this one," she said unsteadily.

"Good," he said, nodding. "I'm sure you're ready to rest and have some time to yourself."

"Aren't you going to bed?" Sofia asked.

"Eventually."

"James?" She didn't know what she wanted to say. Actually, she did know. She wanted to say, James, I want you to touch my body.

"Hm?" He was looking down at her. She took a few steps toward him, reaching a hand out to touch his chest. She thought she heard his breath catch. Heat warmed low in her belly and her desire for him flared. His tenderness, the sacrifices he must be making to have them here. She wanted to give him what she knew he wanted.

"You must get lonely in this house all by yourself." She looked around the study.

"I don't mind it really."

She stroked up and down the smooth fabric of his shirt, inching closer to him. "You must have lady guests all the time."

"Not as many as you might think," he laughed, but it sounded strained.

She ground her hips into his. He put his hands on either side of her neck, looking at her mouth. She was ready, waiting for his kiss, but he put his hands down and stepped away from her.

His breathing was steady as he straightened his shirt. He looked at her with a lazy expression, and it was impossible for her to tell what he was thinking.

"Good night, Sofia. I hope you sleep well." He turned and walked out, leaving her standing in the middle of the room, the book clutched in her hand.

She had no other choice but to go to her room. She tried to read but confusion kept her from concentrating. James had promised her no strings attached and he was obviously trying to honor that, but she was trying to show him that she was willing and grateful, ready to be what he wanted her to be.

Maybe he didn't really want her like that, she thought, staring up at the ceiling. Her bed was like a soft cloud, the most luxurious bed she'd ever slept on. She should have been asleep when her head hit the pillow. Still, her thoughts wouldn't rest. Maybe now he had her under his roof, the allure had worn off.

She'd finally gone to sleep about midnight when the figure slipped into her bed. She rolled over to meet it, anticipating an eager warmth. A pair of ice-cold feet landed on her thigh.

"Mary in a bathtub, your feet are cold!" yelled Sofia, jumping to the farthest side of the bed. Sami had her mouth covered, trying to contain her giggles.

"I'm sorry," she said, still snorting. "I was so freaked out in that room by myself. How do people sleep alone? I don't get it. I was scared to death."

Sofia got out of bed and rummaged around for a pair of socks. She threw them at Sami who put them on happily and scooted under the covers.

"I don't care if you stay in here, but you've got to settle down," said Sofia getting in beside her.

They were quiet for a while and then Sami rolled over to face Sofia. "I think this house is haunted," she said deliciously.

"Go to sleep!"

CHAPTER 17

THE NEXT DAY SAMI and Sofia went to the local stores with Freddy. They were amazed at how much food she bought; the packages barely fit in the trunk of the car.

James had also told Sofia to take his credit card so she and Sami could go shopping for more clothes. Sofia's response had been an adamant no; she wasn't taking more from James than he was already giving them. He had finally convinced her to do it for Sami's sake and for Freddy's, who did the laundry.

"You need more than two pairs of pants or they'll be rags in a month," he insisted.

So they had visited the endless shops along the boardwalk located in the touristy part of town. The weather wasn't warm enough yet to attract too many visitors, so they had the shops mostly to themselves.

Everything seemed exorbitantly expensive and Sofia tried not to go overboard, but she had to admit, having so many clothes to choose from was exciting. It had been a long time since she'd dressed in a way other than to please a man. Her wardrobe had been specially designed to make a man spend money the minute they set eyes on her. It was a whole new experience trying on clothes with so much fabric and realizing she felt pretty, despite how much skin was covered.

Sami, on the other hand, had no qualms about spending James' money. She loved clothes and had been mostly responsible for ordering the gowns and lingerie at The Hotel. She'd never had much money to spend on herself.

As soon as they got home, Sami disappeared upstairs to show India her purchases. There were a few hours before dinner, so Sofia changed into one of her new outfits. Dressed in a pair of black slacks with black boots, and a green sleeveless collared shirt, she went to the drawing room where she found James.

"I take it the shopping trip was a success?" he said, turning off the news he'd been watching.

"Sami was in her element," Sofia said, sitting in the chair next to him. "You're sweet to indulge her. You'll spoil her if you're not careful."

"She deserves a little spoiling; don't you think?"

Sofia smiled at him and nodded. Her stomach fluttered as she watched the man who had become so much more than attractive in her eyes. It was something that ran deeper, and she didn't know what to do with it. Worse was that she didn't know what he wanted her to do.

"You look very beautiful," he said, interrupting her thoughts. He took a sip of his drink and stared at her over his glass. It was a deep, penetrating stare that felt so personal, so sensual, she didn't know if she should swoon or slap his face.

She stood on unsteady legs, needing something to do with her hands. She chose a bottle at random from the bar and poured the contents into a glass.

"Do you like scotch?" he asked curiously, as she came back and sat next to him.

"I've never tasted scotch."

They clinked glasses and she put it to her mouth and took a sip.

James watched as the dark gold liquid touched her lips. They parted and she drank, her soft neck tipped back.

"Mm," she said. "Not bad. So, is this what life is going to be? Shopping by day, drinking scotch by night?"

"It can be whatever you want it to be. If you want to travel or take up knitting, I'll fully support you."

"James," Sofia said, reaching out her hand and touching his arm. She could feel his muscles tense but he didn't pull away. "I don't know how I'm ever going to repay you."

His hand tightened around his glass, and he set it down carefully before he broke it. "You don't owe me anything, Sofia," he said but didn't look at her.

"But I do. I've never met anyone as kind as you've been to us and I know I could never pay you back with money but...would you..."

She stopped.

He'd gone as still as stone and his jaw was clenched so hard that a nerve was jumping under his skin. He stood up and her hand dropped from his arm.

She looked at him. "I'm sorry. Did I say something wrong?"

He huffed out a laugh but still didn't meet her eyes. "No. You'll have to excuse me, I'm sometimes not very good company. You've had a long day. I'll see you in the morning."

With that he was gone.

That night Sofia dreamed of James. He slipped silently into her bed. His body was cold, and he nuzzled closer to her. He smelled like cedar and spice. He found her breast with his mouth. It was warm and teasing. As his tongue sent burning tendrils shooting for her core, she moaned and wrapped her arms around his neck. He slid inside of her until their flesh was one and she was building to a climax and cried out...

She woke suddenly and a whimper slipped out of her mouth when she realized she was alone. She knew it had been a dream, but she could still smell him, and there was a lingering ache in her stomach. She pounded on the mattress with her fists in frustration.

She sighed and flopped over to look at the clock. Two am. She doubted she was going back to sleep now. The house was so quiet and still. She wondered if she'd disturb anybody if she read in the drawing room.

She put on a thin robe over her nightshirt and stepped into the hall. There was a curve in the hallway to her left that led to James' room. She went to the door and put her ear to it. She touched the door handle and thought about entering but decided her mind was in too much turmoil. She shouldn't do anything rash until she'd had a chance to get a decent night's sleep.

She retreated from the door and went back down the passage. She crept past Sami's room. She had worn herself out and hadn't protested about sleeping in her own room, surrounded by her new treasures.

Across the hall was India's room. She had gone out again tonight. Sofia wondered where she went. She was out most nights, and James never asked. James adored her and indulged her because he had raised her when he was still a child himself. India was headstrong and independent; it can't have been easy for him.

Sofia crept barefoot down the stairs. She saw light streaming into the hallway from the drawing room. As she neared, she could see the moon shining through the open French doors that led out to the garden; the soft glow making a perfect path down the center of the room.

A shadow crossed the path of light making Sofia jump. Maurice prowled across the carpet, heading for the open doors. He stood blinking at her as if waiting for her to follow.

The air was still and cool. As she stood, undecided, a breeze came up and whipped her hair, sending chills running down her body. She peered out of the doors to see if there was a reason they were open. The trees and bushes danced in the breeze casting long shadows on the ground. She took a few tentative steps forward. The gravel was cold and damp under her feet.

Maurice, tired of waiting, trotted down the path. She followed him, crunching past the rose bushes and past the lawn. The gazebo was decorated with little blue and white lights that twinkled like stars in the early morning darkness. She trod carefully as the path dipped down slightly, stepping over roots that had infiltrated the walkway.

Ferns, wild daisies and reedy grass lined each side of the path and the gravel beneath her feet grew colder and soggy as she neared the lake.

Maurice disappeared into the undergrowth and Sofia looked up to see a figure standing on the shore. His back was to her as he gazed out into the water. She felt the pulse in her throat throb. He was so still, as if frozen in that moment. The water lapped up the shore as if time moved around him.

The moon was almost full and cast enough light so she could see the tension in the way he stood. His hands were in his pockets, and he stared into the water as if to find answers there.

The wind picked up and she shivered. She realized she was barefoot and only wearing a thin robe over her nightshirt. She was about to turn and go back when he swung around and saw her. He had such a look of anguished frustration on his face it made her want to run to his arms.

"I'm sorry," she stammered, "I didn't know you were out here." She felt her face grow hot as she started back toward the house.

"Sofia, wait," James said and came up the path to where she stood. "Is everything all right?"

"I couldn't sleep." She could smell the night air mixing with the subtle scent of him. That and the lack of sleep was making her light-headed. "I saw the doors open so I thought I'd walk in the garden. The lake is beautiful in the moonlight."

He looked at the lake, as if noticing the moon's reflection for the first time. "Yes." Then he turned to her, his eyes serious. "You'll have to excuse me earlier. I wasn't myself."

"Having Sami and me here, it's a lot. I'm afraid we're going to be a burden on you," Sofia said. He had moved closer to her, and she resisted the urge to touch him.

"You're far from a burden." There was that burning intensity again sparking in his eyes.

She was trembling, her whole body vibrating with adrenaline.

"Are you cold?" He took her hands and looked at them, his thumbs rubbing absently across her palms.

."No," she said unsteadily.

"You're shivering." His hands were warm despite the cool air. She never wanted him to let go.

He touched her wrist with his fingers and stroked her lower arm, sending bumps rippling up her skin. He guided her arms around his waist. She didn't resist, and she moved closer to him until her breasts were almost touching his chest. He stared into her eyes for a long time, like a lost man who has finally come home. He caressed her cheek, running his fingertips over her chin and jaw.

She took shallow breaths. She couldn't get enough air into her lungs. Her heart was pounding so hard against her ribcage she was sure it could be heard over the orchestra of crickets undeterred by their presence. His hand came to the back of her neck, cupping it firmly, and she shuddered when his mouth brushed her ear. His warm breath sent chills skating down her spine. His arm was around her waist, and he pulled her into him until their hips met.

She leaned her head back as he ran his lips down her neck, leaving her skin enflamed. Then his mouth came down on hers. She moaned and opened her mouth to his tongue. She felt her body quicken in response while he devoured her mouth, kissing her like he would take everything from her. His hands roamed over her hips and back, and then he pushed her away. He stepped back and almost stumbled in his haste to distance himself.

"I'm sorry," he said, in a hoarse voice Sofia hardly recognized. "I shouldn't have done that."

She tried to say something, but he turned away from her before she could speak. He walked up the path, his feet crunching on the gravel, his footsteps getting quieter, and then nothing, as he reached the house. She waited until she was sure he was gone before she let out a frustrated sob.

James retreated to his bedroom, furious with himself. He had to do better. If he pulled shit like that she wouldn't trust him and she'd bolt. He couldn't give her any reason to think she owed him anything, especially sex. She had to believe she was worthy of kindness without being expected to pay for it with her body. She had to believe this was a safe space.

He tossed off his clothes and went to the bathroom, turning on the water as cold as he could stand.

A week passed and Sofia had barely seen James. He had been the perfect host, making sure they had everything they needed;

new clothes, trips to the city. He was charming and polite and infuriatingly casual. For the most part she tried to stay out of his way and he didn't seem to mind.

The fiery moment they'd spent on the beach together had convinced Sofia that what she was feeling was far beyond gratitude or obligation. She had fallen in love with James. But he had pushed her away that night and had been distant ever since. She'd never been able to read him, so she had no choice but to accept that he was offering her a home, but nothing more.

To help distract herself from the unrequited feelings burning inside of her, she helped Freddy with the chores and cooking. The housekeeper protested at first, but she seemed to pick up on Sofia's restlessness, and soon they were working side by side, cleaning the house and weeding the garden. Sofia especially liked being outside with the plants. It relaxed her working in the dirt, spending time with wild, growing things.

Sami was a transformed girl since she had left The Hotel. She had lost the pastiness from city living; her face glowed pink, and her eyes shone bright with happiness and excitement. Every day was a new adventure of exploring and creating new routines.

She and Maurice would look for colored stones along the edge of the lake; she had built up a collection that she kept on her windowsill in her bedroom. She'd always had an infectious joy but living at the lake had unbottled something truly beautiful, a peace that made Sofia realize just how stressful life at The Hotel had been.

It would have been a storybook ending had it not been for the tension that thickened the air whenever James and Sofia were together. He seemed to avoid her at all costs, and when they were thrown together at meal times or ran into each other in the house, he would politely ask how everything was and she would politely answer that they were wonderful. But they weren't wonderful. She had an aching desire to be with him and his constant rejection of her made her depressed and confused.

James was due to be away on business and Sofia had been in a foul mood all day. She didn't know what was wrong with her. This wasn't the first time James had been away. Why did she feel so unsettled? She barely saw him to miss him, but she felt his absence, nevertheless.

The night before he left, Sofia went to his room before going to bed. She had been reading by the drawing room fire, and her robe clung to her skin in warm folds. James was packing, wearing only pajama bottoms and his hair was still damp from the shower. One small lamp burned in the corner and the light played over the angles and curves of his bare chest. It had started to rain and the drops tapped persistently on the window.

"What time's your train?" Sofia asked, picking up one of his shirts and folding it to give her unsteady hands something to do. She didn't want him to see how much his half-naked body affected her.

"Nine." He threw a pair of socks in the suitcase.

She nodded, folding another shirt. When she looked up, he was staring at her, frowning.

"What?" she asked. He didn't answer. He looked back down at his suitcase.

She waited to see if he would say anything. The rain was now drumming against the glass and James turned impatiently, pulling the drapes closed. Sofia tossed the shirt down in frustration. This was ridiculous, she thought. She couldn't make him talk to her.

She turned toward the door. "Alright. Well, have a good trip."

She stopped in the doorway, her hand on the doorknob. He turned back to his suitcase and stared at it like he'd forgotten why it was there. He looked lost and suddenly she'd do anything to touch him again, to ease the lines carved between his brows.

"James?" she said quietly.

"Hm?" He zipped up the suitcase and put it on the floor.

"You can have sex with me if you want to."

She waited, her heart pounding. He didn't look at her, but she knew he had heard her from the tightness in his jaw, and his hands fisted at his sides. The silence gaped between them like an impassable chasm, and she started to feel foolish. Heat stained her cheeks. What if he really didn't want her? Maybe he'd had no ulterior motive for getting her and Sami out of The Hotel. Maybe the tension she had been feeling, the stolen glances, the meeting in the garden, were just her own desires creating fantasies in her mind. She knew what she felt for him had been growing. She owed him everything, but it was more than that; she loved him.

She took a deep breath and prepared to leave the room

with what dignity she had left. He startled her when he spoke.

"Is that why you think I got you out of The Hotel? To have sex with you?"

"Well, isn't it? I mean, that's alright." She took a step toward him. "I don't mind…having sex. I mean…I want to." She sounded pathetic in her own ears. She wasn't going to beg.

His face was blank, revealing nothing and displaying no emotion, but there was a spark in his eyes that betrayed him. He was very aware of her, and the passion in those stunning blue eyes gave her courage. She came back into the room and moved towards him.

He watched her like a starving man. When she laid her palms flat on his chest she felt him flinch, but he didn't back away. His skin was cool and his heart beat rapidly under her hands. They stood that way for a long moment, staring into each other's eyes. Sofia moved her fingers, so that her nails scraped lightly on his chest. His hands shot up, gripping hers as he looked down at her with such intensity that her heart leapt.

"I don't want to have sex with you," he said.

Sofia felt the ground tilt under her, and she tried to pull away, shame burning her cheeks, but James didn't release her hands, if anything he clutched them tighter. His eyes looked haunted and as much as she wanted to rip away from him, to protect her shattering heart, she couldn't make herself move.

"Sofia," he whispered, "I've been yours since the day I saw you. I don't want sex, I don't want gratitude." He swallowed hard and brought a hand to her face. As his fingers touched her cheek, Sofia thought she felt them trembling.

"I want to make love to you." His eyes searched her face, as if expecting rejection. "I want you to choose me and only me. I want…" he shook his head as if unable to find the words. "I want you to love me."

Sofia smiled through the tears that coursed a hot path down to her chin. "I do love you, James," she said quietly. "Make love to me."

The astonished look on his face was so comical she almost laughed but any sound she was going to make was swallowed when his mouth covered hers. His hands fisted the material of her robe, drawing her closer. The loose tie came undone and the robe fell open. He groaned when he felt her naked against him. He wrapped his arms around her so his bare chest was pressed against the sensitive flesh of her breasts.

He kissed her for a long time, as if reacquainting himself with her lips, her tongue, the soft skin under her jaw and down her neck. He rubbed his hands over her shoulders and down her sides, pushing the robe off her. It fell at her feet, and he looked down at her.

He shook his head. "You are so beautiful," he said hoarsely. He put his mouth to her neck, put his arms under her legs and back and carried her to the bed, slamming the door closed with his foot. He dropped her unceremoniously onto the fluffy comforter. "Damn you're heavy."

She laughed and kicked out at him. He grabbed her feet, kissing the soles and then tracing his lips along her ankle and up her calf. He stroked the back of her knees with his fingertips, drawing a moaning sigh from her. He slid his tongue up her stomach to her breasts, chest and neck, taking his time, lingering over her flesh, worshiping her body.

He was trembling slightly when he stood and took off his pajama bottoms. His need for her was so overpowering he was surprised he hadn't exploded from it. He wanted to take his time, to savor every second, every moment, to make her feel the same aching torture that he did. He wanted her consumed with fire, liquid in his hands.

She watched him from her prone position on the bed. There was a light sheen of sweat over his tanned chest and his eyes burned with passion, making her hot to her core. She reached for him and he hovered over her, looking into her eyes. His body was flush with hers and a coiling ache quivered inside her. She put her hands in his hair, running her fingers through the silky strands, leading his lips back to hers.

"I don't think I can wait any longer," he gasped into her mouth.

He choked back a groan when she put her hand around him and guided him to her. Sex with Sofia had always been incredible, but it was different this time. His heart was on the line, but he was ready to give her everything; lay himself bare at her feet.

He moved slowly, absorbing the sensation of her around him. He kissed her languidly, relishing her taste. When she panted his name and moved her hips, urging him to go faster, he lost any fragment of self-control and plunged deep until she cried out.

As they moved in a steady rhythm, their eyes locked, breaking all of Sofia's rules and pretenses, and shattering what was left of the frozen barricade she had lived behind her whole life; the one James had been systematically tearing down since they met. Now it melted into a warm puddle deep inside as her body quivered, begging for a release.

She pistoned her hips and he matched her pace, breathing heavily, sweat dripping down his temples. At last her insides clenched and spasms crashed over her. James shuddered, moaning into her neck when she tightened around him and pulsed out her pleasure, undoing him.

They were both slick with sweat, their bodies fused together when James finally realized he was putting all his weight on her and slowly rolled off her onto the bed.

Their fingers were touching. He opened his palm and she put her warm hand in his. He blinked rapidly to clear the mist of tears that was forming over his eyes. He squeezed her hand, holding onto it as if he was afraid she would float away from him like a wisp of a dream.

Love wasn't something he'd contemplated. He had never felt the need for anything more than passing companionship with anyone. To him love meant loss, so he became a defender, fiercely protective of everyone else but never letting anyone too close to his heart.

Even India, who he loved so much it made his chest ache. He held her at a distance, treating their relationship like a crystal glass, that if shifted the wrong way would fall and shatter in a thousand pieces.

He had been attracted to Sofia, and he had to admit to himself that his first reaction was that he wanted to save her. Get her settled in an apartment, somewhere far away from The Hotel. But it had become so much more than that and it was no longer jealousy that drove him, but adoration.

As he turned to Sofia and she turned to him, he realized he had been right; love was fear of loss and a desire to protect but it was also a willingness to lay oneself bare to that person, to risk everything to have them by your side.

"I tried to stay away," he said, looking deep into her eyes, trying to see what she was feeling. She said she loved him, but he needed to know for sure.

"You don't owe me anything, Sofia, especially not sex. I will never force you to do anything you don't want to do. If you want your own room, if you only want to see me once a week, I will be at your beck and call."

Sofia laughed. "Are you going to be my concubine?"

James lifted himself onto his elbow so he could look in her eyes. "I'll be anything you want me to be. I just never want you to think you've bought your freedom."

"And what if I don't want to be free, James Hardy," she said with a coy smile. Her eyes shone bright with brimming emotions. "What if I want to be tied to you for the rest of my life?"

"Hm," he said, tapping her chin. "Then I guess I'd better not be your concubine…how about your husband?"

She swallowed hard as another tear escaped down her cheek. "I think I'd like that," she said.

CHAPTER 18

JAMES AND SOFIA WERE going to be married in two weeks, and James finally got his date at the market. The four of them took the train. Sami sat glued to the window, watching the scenery race by as they left the beauty of the lake and the trees and entered the gray pallor of the city, thick with smog and humidity. They walked from the train station, passing through one of the alleys that led to the market.

Sami and India ran on ahead, looking for their own treasures. James and Sofia walked with their hands entwined, looking at the different wares for sale. They each bought an iced coffee and Sofia filled her bag with freshly picked apples, tomatoes and cucumbers. Each vendor had painstakingly nurtured their small plot of cracked earth and in return harvested enough food to feed their families and a little left over to sell. Despite their meager beginnings, fruit and vegetables from the market were the freshest around.

James stopped at a stall selling bouquets of flowers, mostly cultivated from window boxes and tiny backyard plots. He picked out a bunch of carnations and handed them to Sofia. She smiled and put her nose to them.

India and Sami joined up with them, and they followed an enticing aroma to a vendor sweating over a wok, the contents of which he was tossing into the air and back into the pan. They were handed plates piled high with steaming noodles and tender spiced chicken and sat in nearby chairs to eat.

The train left at ten, coinciding with the market closing, so at nine thirty they made their way back through the alley toward the station. James and Sofia walked together holding hands and India and Sami followed behind them, their laughter echoing off the concrete walls.

As the lights from the stalls faded, the way in front of them darkened. There were only a few more steps and they'd be out of the alley and then the lights of the train station would be visible. James was slightly in front when a figure stepped out of the shadows and pressed a gun against his forehead.

The figure was huge; tall and bulky, but black clothes and a black ski mask helped him blend into the darkness.

"Sofia…girls," James said calmly, "get behind me."

Sofia grabbed India and Sami and they huddled together against the wall of the alley, too shocked to say anything. Sofia glanced back toward the market, but they were too far away for anyone to see and bring help.

After everything we've been through, Sofia thought, biting her lip to keep from crying, she was going to lose James to a mugging.

James had his arms spread out at his sides. "Take whatever you want. There's no need for anyone to get hurt. Put the gun down and I'll get my wallet."

"I'm not putting down shit," said the man in an unnaturally deep, gravelly voice. "Gimme your money. Reach into your pocket slowly and keep your other hand in the air. If you try anything your brains are going to be splattered all over these lovely ladies."

Sami squeaked out a whimper and India held her close and kissed her hair. The desire to run at this coward, screaming like a Valkyrie, and gouge his eyes out was so strong that India had to dig her nails into her palm. The guy would shoot James before she had a chance to get near him. Instead, she clutched Sami to her, ready to protect her with her life.

James did as he was told, unwilling to risk his family's safety for the sake of the contents in his wallet.

"Toss it on the ground," the masked figure said.

James dropped the wallet at the other man's feet and thought about kicking him in the face when he bent down to retrieve it, but the gun was still aimed at his head.

James tried to see the color of the man's eyes as he straightened to his full height, but it was too dark.

"This is just the beginning," said the gravelly voice behind the mask.

James stared at him in confusion. "The beginning? The beginning of what?"

The man pulled his hand back and hit James on the side of the head with the butt of the gun. James went down and Sofia screamed, falling to her knees at his side. When she looked up, the man was gone.

Sami and India were clutching each other in silent shock.

James staggered to his feet. "I'm ok," he said, holding a hand to his temple.

"You're bleeding," Sofia said, reaching up to his hairline but not touching the gash in the skin above his ear. "We should take you to the hospital."

"No," said James, moving his head back and forth slowly. The dizziness was fading and though the side of his head was on fire, he didn't feel like there was any permanent damage. "I'll be ok."

He put his arm around her and looked at Sami and India. "Everyone alright?"

"What did he mean, James?" India asked.

James frowned. He had his suspicions, but he didn't want to voice them until he had more proof.

"I don't know. Just some crazy guy, probably hopped up on drugs. Let's get out of here."

As they made their way to the train station Sofia held onto James' hand and spoke softly so Sami and India wouldn't hear. She didn't want to worry them until they knew more.

"Do you really think that was just a random attack? It's been years since I've heard of that kind of thing happening around the market."

James squeezed her hand; he wasn't going to lie to her. "No, I don't think it was random."

"Who would...?"

He looked at her.

"Rufus? Why? What does he have to gain?"

"Fear, intimidation, bullying; those are his weapons of choice. He's obviously holding a grudge."

"What are we going to do?"

"There's nothing we can do until we have some evidence that he's tied to what happened tonight," James said.

"Do you know where to find any?" Sofia asked.

"No, but I know who might."

———————————

Grandmother Linnie's apartment looked uncommonly clean. There was still laundry on most surfaces but instead of jumbled heaps they were folded neatly in piles. The kitchen sparkled and the smell of cigarette smoke was barely distinguishable through the cloying scent of lemon air freshener.

Linnie sat at the card table, arthritic fingers curled like talons around a coffee mug.

"It looks really nice in here, Maria," James said to the young woman who poured him a cup of coffee.

"Oh, thank you," she said with a pleased smile. "Nora's finally sleeping through the night so I actually have some energy to get off my butt and get things done."

"Are you planning on going back to work?"

Maria put the coffee pot down and looked at James shyly. "With the settlement you got us, I was thinking of taking some classes at the community college to get my Associates Degree. I'm really interested in computers. Do you think that would be ok?"

James smiled at her. "I think that's a fantastic idea. Hit

me up when you're done with your AA. I could always use a tech geek since I'm useless with computers."

Maria beamed at him and went to get Nora who had started making burbling noises from her crib in one of the bedrooms.

"You look happy," Grandmother Linnie said, narrowing her eyes at him suspiciously.

"You make it sound like a bad thing," James laughed.

"Not bad, just strange. You seem different," she said accusingly.

"Leave him alone, Gran," said Maria coming back into the room holding a swathed bundle in her arms. "You want to hold her while I make her bottle, Mr. Hardy?"

James didn't hesitate but put his arms out and, supporting the baby's head with his bicep, held her close.

He loved babies. He didn't know why, he was hardly ever around them. Maybe it was the fond memories he had of his mom showing him how to take care of India when she was born. He'd been ten and his mom had kindly yet firmly instilled in him the basic needs of an infant. It was almost as if she knew she wouldn't be around to raise India, James frowned.

India had been potty trained well before their parents died, but James had never forgotten how to change a diaper or hold a baby.

Nora had a thatch of dark hair and olive-toned skin, unlike Maria's pale complexion. She had never told him who the father was and he'd never asked.

While Maria mixed formula and water into a bottle,

Linnie rummaged through the purse at her feet. Maria came over and handed James the bottle. She looked at Linnie with a frown. "Gran, you promised!"

Linnie scowled and put her purse back on the floor. "Promised I wouldn't smoke around the baby," she grumbled.

James winked at Maria and popped the bottle between Nora's pursed lips. The baby clenched her hands into tiny fists as she sucked and looked at James with large brown eyes.

"I am happy, Linnie," James said. "Sofia and I are getting married."

Linnie let out a whoop and Nora, whose eyes had started to drift into a sleepy haze, jerked. Her face crumpled and turned scarlet as a huge wail escaped her small mouth. James raised an eyebrow and Maria swooped in to take her baby from him.

"Gran!" she scolded, carrying Nora back to the bedroom.

Linnie chuckled. "She'll be alright." She reached her hand out and James took it. The back of her hand was knobby with veins and brown spots freckled her skin. Her fingers shook slightly like a frightened bird trapped in his palm.

"I am so happy for both of you," she said unsteadily, her eyes glistening. "It's like Cinderella, a real life fairy tale."

"Thanks, Linnie, but there's still an ogre in this story," James said, squeezing her hand then sitting back in his chair. "I think Rufus is trying to get revenge for Sofia and Sami leaving The Hotel."

Grandmother Linnie showed no sign of surprise but nodded sagely. "What's he done?"

"Last night a man wearing a ski mask robbed us at gunpoint, one alley out from the market."

Linnie's eyebrows rose. "That took guts. Didn't they lynch the last guy who tried to cause trouble near the market?"

"Something like that. That's why I don't think it was random. He also said, 'This is just the beginning.' I want to find him because he's going to lead me right back to Rufus, I'm sure of it."

"I knew it was too good to be true," Linnie said, reaching for her purse. She put her hand in and then hesitated and slowly put her purse down at her feet.

"What do you mean?"

"I knew in my gut that Rufus wouldn't let Sofia and that poor child go so easily."

James leaned forward, his elbows pressing down on the rickety table. "Have you heard anything about Rufus hiring new muscle? Or maybe one of his lackeys bragging about doing a job?"

Linnie drummed her fingers on the table and pursed her lips, a myriad of wrinkles appearing around her mouth. "I haven't, but I don't run in those circles. You might try The Coral Tide."

James nodded. "That was going to be my next stop."

Maria came back into the room holding a baby monitor that hummed with soft static. "She's finally asleep."

James stood. "I appreciate your time. I'm glad to see you're both doing well."

"Good to see you too," Linnie said, staying seated. "Bring Sofia and Sami next time."

James smiled. "I'll do that. Maria, good luck with school.

I know you're going to do great. Call me if you need any-thing."

Maria blushed prettily and nodded her head.

James left and walked the half mile to the city limits where he'd be able to catch a taxi.

Grandmother Linnie always knew what was going on, regardless of the circle, thought James, and he trusted that she would tell him if she knew anything. The fact that she hadn't heard anything meant the people who did know were keeping a tight lid on the information. Finding evidence that Rufus hired the mugger wasn't going to be easy.

The Coral Tide was a bar located on the docks which ran along the city's east side. It catered mostly to fisherman and laborers who went there, or any number of other bars or strip clubs scattered in with the warehouses, to blow off steam after a long day.

James had been there many times before, so the clientele was used to him. It was a good place to get the latest news via secondhand conversations when he was working a case. Nothing he heard was admissible in court, of course, but hushed gossip resulted in leads which often led to evidence.

The first time he had entered The Coral Tide, all con-versation had stopped and every eye had turned his way. He was in casual clothes; boots, jeans, t-shirt and leather jacket, so he didn't stand out physically but somehow everyone in the bar knew he didn't belong. Many respected him for the work he did for the people of the streets, but that didn't make him one of them.

He didn't let it bother him and he didn't let it keep him

from going back. The first few times he'd ordered a tequila shot and a beer, and sat at the bar, keeping to himself and just listening. It wasn't long before the regulars got curious enough to approach him.

They were a friendly bunch; hard workers and hard drinkers, but James found it difficult to get answers from them. Even the most subtly phrased questions had their faces going blank as if he was speaking a foreign language. So he stopped asking questions and let them talk, becoming one with the bar stool until they'd forgotten he was there.

Tonight he needed specific information and it was going to be tough to get it without causing everyone in the bar to shut down. A few curious eyes turned his way when he entered but he ignored them and found an empty stool at the bar.

Gerald, the bartender, was a heavy set black man with a goatee and glasses perched below bushy eyebrows. He looked like a college professor, dressed in his sweater vest over a long sleeve button-down shirt. It didn't take long for James to learn the truth about Gerald; that he'd once been in a gang, had killed dozens of people and kept a loaded Glock behind the bar.

He was one of the nicest people James had ever met; intelligent, funny, and willing to talk about most things, but some topics he closed down with a severity that told James pushing wasn't a good idea.

Rufus was one of those taboo subjects. His reach was long and unforgiving and Gerald wasn't willing to lose his job or his tongue.

Gerald set a shot glass and a beer in front of James. James

thanked him, threw the tequila back, feeling it burn down his throat and lodge warmly in his belly.

"What's new?" Gerald said in his pleasant tenor.

"Got mugged last night at the market," James said, just loudly enough for the closest customers to hear. A few turned their heads to look at him but quickly glanced away.

"At the market?" Gerald said in a disbelieving tone. "Nah, man, you were dreaming."

"I didn't dream the gun in my face, or this." He lifted up the hair that hung slightly over his ear to reveal the nasty looking gash that he'd left purposely unbandaged.

"Damn, man," Gerald said, but wiped the counter without saying anything else.

"Know anyone stupid enough to rob someone in sight of the market?" James asked, talking more to his beer than the people around him.

The man sitting to his right turned to him. He was a big man, with a thick black beard and a skull cap pulled down to his dark eyebrows. His heavy coat was slick with moisture and smelled like fish and gasoline.

He laughed, revealing black gums and rotted teeth. "I know plenty of stupid people, but no one's going to risk being strung up by their balls by a screaming mob."

"Yet someone did," James said, glancing at Gerald.

Gerald's hand had stilled, his fingers clutched around the rag he was using to wipe the counter. He looked at James, his black pupils eclipsing any white. He gave the slightest movement of his head to the left and then to the right, warning James to tread no further.

That was all James needed to know. Rufus was behind the attack. If he could lead the police to the guy who did the actual mugging, they might get him to turn on Rufus for a deal.

James had nothing to go on, and no one was talking, so finding the masked man was going to be next to impossible. He had to try, he thought, tossing money on the bar and stepping out into the misty evening air.

Rufus was acting out because for once he didn't get his way, but James would be watching. Sooner or later Rufus was going to get overconfident, and he wouldn't be able to slither his way free.

CHAPTER 19

SAMI STEPPED OFF THE train and took a deep breath. The smell of diesel and cooking meat of nearby vendors, along with the noise of honking taxis, and obscenities being shouted out by the cabbies, assaulted her senses and she smiled. She loved being in the city. It had always been her playground and now that she lived in The Lake District, she enjoyed coming back and experiencing the unique chaos, knowing she had a safe haven to return to.

She and India had come to buy from the local food sellers who needed the business far more than big grocers. It was a short ride by train and gave them the opportunity to browse the market. They each bought a hot dog and soda and wandered the stalls, looking at the handmade crafts of every textile imaginable. Beautifully woven tapestries, wire shaped into intricate designs for earrings, stained glass that glittered with silver, red and blue, and rows of soaps and candles, their fragrance almost disguising the ever present smell of fish.

India wandered away while Sami watched a lady as she crocheted a blanket, or maybe a scarf. Her hands moved swiftly in a flash of gold and green and Sami could barely keep her eyes on the movement.

The man appeared at her side as if out of thin air. One minute she was alone in front of the stall, and the next he was there, hovering over her menacingly. She jumped and whirled on him, staring into a pair of dark, almost black eyes. The rest of his features were obscured by a hoodie and a bandana that covered his nose and mouth.

"Rhys?" she cried, "What are you doing here? You scared me to death!"

His eyes sparkled and there was laughter in his voice. He pulled down the bandana. "Pegged me that fast, huh?"

She smiled but didn't tell him she had memorized his eyes, every detail of their shape and color.

"It's good to see you. How's life in the country treating you?" he asked.

"I love it! But I love the city too. Especially now that I don't have to be here. You know what I mean?"

"I can only imagine. Must be quite a change. Is The Lake District as beautiful as everyone says it is?" he asked, fingering the soft wool of the blankets on display.

"More, so much more. You can't imagine the colors and the air, so fresh and clean."

Rhys smiled, her joyful enthusiasm always bringing a lightness to his soul. He'd missed seeing her around the streets, more than he cared to admit, but was glad she had found a safe place to call home. He hated to ruin her day but seeing her here was like fate nudging him to tell her what he knew.

He took one last, long look at her beaming face before glancing around, saying seriously, "So you live with James Hardy now?"

"Yes. He's amazing. I think you'd like him."

"He's been asking questions about the night you got mugged by the market. I'm really sorry that happened." He frowned. "I wish I'd been there."

Sami's heart had started pounding the moment she'd recognized him, but the more he talked the harder it beat until she felt it pulsing in her throat.

"I know who it was, Sami," Rhys said.

Sami's eyes widened. "What are you talking about?"

"The man in the alley, his name's Bruce. He's new. Rufus hired him since the last guy doing his dirty work got killed in a bar fight. Apparently robbing James and giving him that message was his first duty on the job."

"How do you know all this?"

Rhys grinned at her, and it was like a butterfly was released in her stomach. "There's not a lot that goes on in this city that I don't know about."

His hands moved down absently and took hers. They were warm despite the chill of the afternoon air. Startled, Sami looked into his eyes and instead of the warm, melted chocolate softness, they were rigid like dark stone.

"I've heard talk, Sami, and it's not good. Rufus is majorly pissed about you and Sofia leaving. He's making everyone's life a living hell."

Sami looked at him in confusion. "He seemed happy

for us, he cried…"

Rhys laughed with bitter and angry contempt. "He had no choice but to let you go. He could rant and rave all he wanted but he had no legal hold on you. He was just biding his time until he could get you to come back."

Sami scoffed but her voice came out unsteady. "Well, that's never going to happen."

Rhys squeezed her hands. She had started to shiver and she clutched onto him like a buoy in a storm. "He can't make us go back, can he?"

"No, but he's declared all-out war on James Hardy. The Wager's lost traction and everyone's laughing at Rufus for letting Sofia walk out right under his nose. You've hit him the two places it hurts the most, his pride and his bank account." He looked down at their clasped hands. "I'm worried about you."

"You are?" Sami said, looking up at him.

"Of course I am!" he said harshly and Sami jumped a little in surprise. Rhys put a hand on her arm and the softness returned to his eyes. "I'm sorry. I don't want to scare you. I just want you to be on your guard. Rufus is desperate and unpredictable."

"What do you think he'll do?"

"I don't know," he said, letting go of her arm and tucking his hands in his pockets. "Just tell your family to be careful and stay out of the city if you can help it."

"But…"

"Sami!" India called.

"Over here," Sami said, turning her head.

When she looked back, Rhys was gone.

"No more trips into the city. No more going out alone," James said, pacing in front of the window. India and Sofia were curled up on the couch, Sami on the floor at their feet. The French doors were open, letting in the evening breeze.

Sami had told James about her encounter with Rhys and what he had told her about Rufus. She also told him about Bruce.

"Sounds like a typical thug, ready to do anything for enough money," Sofia said. It was one thing to sell your body, she thought, another to sell your soul.

James nodded. "That's why you're staying away from your usual places, like the market. Just stay here in The Lake District until we get this figured out."

"Couldn't you talk to one of your friends at the police department here?"

"They have no authority in the city, and with the amount of corruption, they probably would come up against a brick wall anyway. No, Rufus would have to do something here before LDPD got involved."

Sami said in a small, trembling voice, "Rhys said he was really angry about us leaving." She looked up at James, the tears in her green eyes sparkling in the light. "What do you think he'll do?"

James crouched down in front of her. "I'm not going to let him do anything, so don't worry, ok. He can't touch us here and that's why he's trying all these desperate tactics. He knows his hands are tied."

She nodded shakily. She was terrified of Rufus, but she trusted James more. She believed he wouldn't let anything happen to them.

James sat down in a chair, his relaxed posture contradicting the rage boiling inside him. "I won't stand for my family being threatened. I'm going to talk to some more of my contacts in the city. Rufus won't be able to move an inch without me knowing about it."

CHAPTER 20

JAMES HAD BEEN GONE for a week. He was two days late. Sofia sat on the couch staring out of the window at her reflection, her image streaked with rain as drops settled on the pane. Her legs were tucked up under her and she hugged her knees. A cup of tea, cold and forgotten, perched on the table by her elbow. The clouds threatened thunder as the cool of the rain mixed with the hot summer night.

That's what was making her restless, she thought, the electricity in the air. There was no need to be worried; she missed him, that was all. She never got used to him being away and not being next to her in bed, but this had been an especially long trip and she was anxious to see him. The fact that he was late was the only thing keeping her from explaining away her trepidation.

She stood up and paced in front of the couch. She had thought of all the disasters that could have befallen him and dismissed them, knowing someone would have gotten in touch with her. His secretary knew her number so if something had happened to him in the city, she would have called her. He would have called himself if something had gone wrong with the trains or he'd had to stay later for some other reason.

She looked out of the window, her hands behind her back. Maybe he was having an affair with his beautiful secretary. The thought flitted through her mind and then out again just as quickly. It was unfair and undeserved. James had done nothing short of worship her since they got married.

One month and five days since they'd sworn to forsake all others til death do us part.

That had been a strange day. Her emotions had been all over the place, from, this is crazy you hardly know the man, to sweating at the thought of waking up tomorrow to find it had all been a dream.

They had been married at home on the pier as the sun lowered over the horizon.

It had been magical, and she was finally able to put away all the what-ifs and allow herself to enjoy her fairy tale.

James had the pastor of the local church officiate and a tearful Freddy had sat in a folding chair, smiling from ear to ear. Sami and India had made the most beautiful bridesmaids, and Rob had been James' best man. Sofia chuckled, thinking about the way India had teased him.

"Oh my gosh, Rob, what is that around your neck? Watch out! I think it's trying to strangle you!"

Rob had just rolled his eyes and adjusted his tie. India liked to call Rob a good 'ol boy but even she had admitted he looked dashing in his charcoal suit.

India and Sami had decorated the gazebo with garlands of ivy and baskets full of carnations. A table had been set up, piled high with food. James had suggested they hire a caterer, and Freddy had gone after him with a frying pan. She had cooked for two days and produced a feast. Canapes, roast pork that melted on the tongue and, of course, bratwurst and sauerkraut, and her famous German potato salad. Pastries filled with fruit and nuts were served with champagne, and they each took turns giving silly and heartfelt speeches and toasting everything they could think of.

The last place Sofia had wanted to go for her honeymoon was the city or a hotel, so the next day James had given India and Sami his credit card and told them not to come back until dinner. Then she and James had made love like it was the only thing keeping them alive.

Everything had been perfect since then so why was this burning in her stomach telling her something was wrong?

She flopped back down on the couch and stared out at the darkening sky. She saw the first flash of lightning, closed her eyes and counted. She got to five when thunder rumbled across the sky.

She loved living out in the country, but the storms had been surprising at first. The city had a constant mist whether it was warm or cold, but The Lake District had real weather; hot, cold, rain, wind, snow, and when the heavens opened and watered the earth and the trees whipped, threatening to come crashing down on the house, Sofia got antsy. Add a lightning storm and she was ready to take roost on the ceiling.

She picked up her phone for the millionth time and set

it down again. She flipped through pages of India's fashion magazine and then tossed it on the other end of the couch. Bed was out of the question, so she folded her arms over her chest and closed her eyes.

James had been in the city on business for five long days. Back-to-back meetings with clients and late nights at his office had kept him from returning home and he was looking forward to being there and seeing his girls. His heart felt light thinking about them. The commute took twenty minutes by train which would seem an eternity. He found the right platform and sat down to wait.

Over the last few months he had learned to navigate the joyous, if sometimes treacherous, waters of living with three women. Sami had taken about two weeks to sleep consistently in her own bed. She would come crawling in next to Sofia, ultimately pushing James to the floor. The bed in the guest room was very comfortable, and he was ready to give her all the time she needed. She had spent three years with Sofia, doing everything with her. He didn't want her to feel thrust aside.

Sami eventually learned to appreciate her own space and the creativity it allowed her. James was thrilled because not only did he get his bed back, but it meant that Sami felt safe, and that was what he wanted for her.

He had started teaching her how to swim, which was another leap of faith for Sami.

She liked everyone with an equally outgoing joy, but she didn't trust men. James didn't blame her, but when she'd asked him to help her, he fully appreciated what that meant. She believed in him enough to let him hold her above the water, her fate completely in his hands. It was a humbling feeling.

Sami spent her days wandering the gardens, rescuing birds and rabbits out of Maurice's clutches. She had created a make-shift hospital on the back deck, complete with chicken wire to keep Maurice and other predators out. She had suggested they start a farm. James shuddered at the thought.

She followed India around like she was the oracle, which was equally as frightening. But India also seemed to have benefited from Sami and Sofia's arrival. She hadn't been going out as much, she'd managed to say more than three words at a time to him on several occasions, she was even letting him teach her how to play chess. She and Sami played cards, read together in the drawing room and giggled when they watched tv. India seemed to be thriving under the new domesticity. Having a family suited her.

The day he'd married Sofia had been the happiest of his life. Even India had been glowing, and James felt his heart swell with how easily Sofia and Sami had fit into their little duo.

The first morning he and Sofia woke up together as husband and wife he had watched the pink and yellow glow that filled the sky just before the sun peaked over the horizon, filling the room with a muted light. James had never experienced such joy; making love to Sofia, knowing she was his, knowing they would never be apart again; touching her olive skin, her hands in his hair, crying out his name…

He woke with his head screaming as if a chainsaw was buzzing where his brain should be. He fluttered his eyelashes trying to open his eyes, and with an effort lifted his lids. Squinting in the low light sent an explosion through his head. His stomach lurched and he quickly closed his eyes again, taking deep breaths.

When he tried to put his hands on his pounding head, his arms only moved inches. He tugged at whatever was holding them down but only managed to jar his wrists. He forced his eyes open, ignoring the sharp pain that shot through his skull, and slowly moved his gaze down. His hands were cuffed, a chain binding him to the arms of a metal chair. He moved his feet experimentally but felt the unrelenting metal against his ankles.

He forced himself to look around even though the movement made his stomach heave. The only light was a bare bulb hanging above him that illuminated a small circle surrounding his chair. The rest of the room faded into shadow.

There were no windows, and he had no idea what time it was. His train had been at two. He had been getting on a train. His head throbbed painfully as he tried to remember. He'd been at the train station. Where was he going and how did he end up chained to a chair in what looked to be a concrete block? He could envision the platform at the station as it filled with people. He'd felt a sharp pain in the side of his neck like he'd been stung by a bee.

Sofia's face flashed in his mind, and it was like being doused with cold water. He'd been going home to Sofia. He felt a new wave of nausea as his stomach tumbled. He fought it back and focused. Someone had the balls to drug and kidnap him in the middle of the day in a public place. There was only one person who was crazy enough to pull that off.

He yanked on the handcuffs, shaking his arms, but it made no impact on the thick chains. He wriggled his hand, trying to slide it through the small opening. He felt the sides bite down and skin scrape off his wrist. He grimaced and pulled harder, twisting back and forth until his skin was rubbed raw and his hand was slippery with blood.

He rested for a few minutes, taking deep breaths and looking around the shadows. There must be a door somewhere, he thought. He spent the next few minutes peering into the darkness, searching for inconsistencies in the bare walls. He felt a small wave of triumph when he spotted the rectangular outline, the grey metal slightly darker than the concrete around it.

It had to be locked. He couldn't even tell if there was a handle, but it was the only way out. If Rufus was behind this, which James had no doubt he was, this was probably the basement of The Hotel. His only hope was that Rufus was too overconfident to have locked that door.

He leaned over as far as he could until the chair swept out from under him. His head and shoulder connected with the concrete floor, and he fought back black spots that threatened to pull him under. He waited until his vision cleared and then used his feet to push himself along the floor, pressing off his hip and shoulder like an inchworm. It was a maddeningly slow process, and his right side was numb before he was half-way to his goal.

James craned his neck up as the door crashed open. A mountainous man, tall and broad, his muscles straining against the fabric of his sweater and jeans, entered the room. James watched him approach, warily eyeing the man's very large fists. This must be the infamous Bruce.

The man moved toward James with a lumbering gait. He grabbed the arms of the chair and lifted it, and James, setting them upright in the middle of the floor, back where he had started.

"That was very impressive," James said, breathing heavily. "Can you tell me why I'm here?" The man paced silently in front of him. His hair was shaved close to his head, and his heavy eyebrows jutted out from his prominent forehead.

James winced, rotating his aching shoulder. "I don't think we've been introduced. You're Bruce. Am I right?"

The man curled his lip. "Keep your mouth shut."

"Listen, Bruce, I have money. I'm sure we can work something out."

The man called Bruce moved in until his face was inches from James. James could see stubble coming out of his individual pores. His face was pockmarked creating deep craters in his skin. He must have had severe acne as a teenager.

"I said shut up!" Bruce yelled in James' face, spittle gathering on his lips.

James hated bullies, they made his blood boil. He was also afraid of what this large man could do to him with no way to defend himself. The combination of anger and fear, together with the pounding in his head, made him belligerent and reckless.

"How much did Rufus pay you to rob me and give me that stupid message? Or are you just his puppet, dancing when he pulls the strings?"

His head snapped back when Bruce's fist connected with his face. For a minute James couldn't see anything but bright lights and black spots. Then pain exploded in his jaw as the fist made another pass. His mouth filled with blood as his teeth clamped down on his tongue.

A high-pitched siren went off in his brain and his head slumped forward, suddenly too heavy for his neck. He could only pry open one eye. He stared, fascinated at the specks of blood on the ground. Bright red, the only color in an expanse of grey.

He raised his head when he heard the door open again, and a blurry figure approached. As he got closer James could see that he wore an impeccable pinstriped suit and fedora pulled down, almost hiding his eyes "Aw, Bruce," said the disappointed voice, "you started without me."

James let out a croak of laughter and spat blood on the floor. "Playing gangster, Rufus? Where's the tommy gun and brass knuckles?"

"James Hardy, cocky as always, even when you're up shit creek; always the charmer."

Rufus bent down so he was eye level with James. He pinched James' chin and turned his head to the side. "I told Bruce to wait for me. Did you say something naughty and piss him off?"

"We were just passing the time," James said, running his

tongue over his teeth, thankful that none were loose.

"First, I must apologize for the snatch and grab," Rufus went on, viewing James critically as if he were a minor inconvenience. "I really didn't have time to send a formal invitation and then wait for a response and blah blah blah." He produced a long switchblade from his waistband and clicked it open. He looked at the knife appraisingly and ran a finger down its blade. "Damn!" he cried, sticking his finger in his mouth. "That's sharp! Did you know these things were that sharp?"

He pointed the knife directly between James' eyes. He slowly moved it down, inches from James' skin, until he came to his neck. "I bet it wouldn't take much to slit a man's throat with a knife this sharp," Rufus said in a soft voice, like a curious child.

James stiffened but didn't move. He stared at Rufus, knowing he wouldn't kill him. There was a reason he had brought him here. He'd be dead right now if that's what Rufus wanted.

"I've heard you've been asking about Bruce and the unpleasantness at the market," Rufus said, straightening and walking in a circle around James' chair. Bruce stood waiting, his hands at his sides and his feet planted, ready for anything. "What are you hoping to learn?"

"I'm hoping to find evidence that you were behind the mugging and seeing as Bruce is here, straining at his leash waiting for your command," James ignored the low growl that came from Bruce's throat, "I think my hunch was correct."

James knew there was no point in lying. Rufus never asked

a question he didn't already know the answer to. He knew asking around about Bruce would get Rufus' attention. Word would have spread before James had made it down the street.

Rufus' lips pulled back in a feral grin. "You arrogant man, you really have no idea how truly fucked you are."

"I'm starting to get an idea," James said, spitting a stream of blood onto the floor. Rufus gave him a disgusted scowl.

"Of course it was me!" Rufus said, coming to stand in front of James again. "Who else would send a masked man to deliver a cryptic message." Rufus shivered elaborately. "It gives me chills, it's so wonderful."

Rufus brought the knife back to James' throat and pressed the tip just hard enough to break the skin. A trickle of blood ran down into James' collar.

"But you weren't playing fair. You were supposed to cower in that lake house of yours until I could think up my next brilliant scheme. Instead you're out the next day, asking questions. What is wrong with you?"

James shrugged. His mouth tasted like iron and his face was throbbing. "Sorry to ruin your plans. Are you going to tell me why I'm here?"

"Oh, you didn't ruin them, you just expedited what was already to come. I was always going to get you into this room. You earned that privilege when you showed up and took what was mine."

Rufus lowered the knife until it was hovering over James' chest. He slid the blade under James' shirt and yanked until the top button flew off. "Let me give you a word of advice," he said, plucking the next button from the fabric. "You think you're better than everyone else and that's why you have no friends. Apparently you can't find your own women either. You have to steal from other people." He ran the knife down the shirt until the rest of the buttons clattered to the floor.

James sat helplessly cuffed to the chair, his fists clenching and unclenching, wanting to get his hands around Rufus' throat.

"Sofia was never yours," he said as calmly as he could. Rufus thrived on drama and James losing control was exactly what he wanted. "She left because she wanted to."

"Let's agree to disagree, shall we?" said Rufus. "But to answer your question. You're here because I want to remind Sofia where she belongs and I also want to slow you down. You're too inquisitive by half and I can't have you running all over the city asking questions about me."

James stared at the floor, contemplating the white buttons that stood out on the charcoal grey concrete. Rufus bent down in front of him so their eyes were level. He slowly pushed James' shirt off his shoulders leaving his chest bare, glistening with sweat.

"I can see why Sofia would be drawn to you," Rufus said, skimming the knife over James' skin, lightly, not making a mark. "You're a fine looking man." He casually drew the knife in the opposite direction, this time leaving a thin trail of blood behind.

James bit his lip and narrowed his eyes.

"It's no wonder you two were always going off together. I've been told she's a very good…companion," Rufus said, dragging the knife across James' skin, deeper this time, until blood oozed down his chest.

James strained against his cuffs, growling low in his throat.

"I thought about sending you back to her in pieces," Rufus said, a savage grin on his face, as if he knew James was nearing his breaking point. "You are, after all, the reason she left. Without you she'd come begging me to take her back and of course, graciously, I would."

He sliced through James' chest again, leaving several long cuts. He stood back, as if admiring a painting.

James was panting, sweat and blood running freely down his chest. His lungs bellowed in and out as he struggled to take ragged breaths. He tipped his head to Rufus and stared him down.

"But then you'd be dead," Rufus continued, "and I wouldn't be able to use you to torment her again and again for leaving."

He swung in a slashing arc and opened a gash across James' stomach. James doubled over in pain, cursing Rufus out in fury.

"There you are," said Rufus. "I knew you were in there somewhere. Now, you glorious specimen, I cannot hang out with you all night long as much as I would love to. I'm going to let you sit and stew on our conversation. Just chill for a while and I'll be back." He sauntered to the door, Bruce close on his heels. Without looking back, they left the room, the door slamming shut behind them.

James didn't hear a lock or a bolt slide home, but it didn't matter. There was no way he was moving now. His chest and stomach were on fire and his vision faded in and out. He wanted to be alert if anything happened, but despite his best efforts his eyes fluttered closed. His head slumped forward and he knew nothing.

It was over twenty-four hours before he saw Rufus again. By then the cold, damp room and the cuts on his body had left James trembling and weak. His head hung limply as he tried to get what sleep he could to preserve his strength.

He had no idea if it was night or day when the door banged open and Rufus swept in wearing a heavy, embroidered cloak, and a tiara that sparkled with tiny diamonds. In his hand was a mahogany cane topped with a golden lion's head. He rapped the cane on the concrete floor over and over like a metronome, each beat pounding through James' aching head.

"I've done a lot of thinking, and I have decided to spare your life and return you to Sofia with a special message," Rufus said with a small magnanimous nod of his head.

"This isn't going to change anything," said James, gritting his teeth so they wouldn't bang together. "They're not coming back."

Rufus admired the carved lion, turning it so it caught the light. "I'm not so concerned about Sami anymore. At first I was angry, but she won't be any real use to me for another four years. Maybe we'll negotiate something then."

"You fucking bastard," James growled.

"Now, now. That isn't going to get you any favors. I could always change my mind and make Sofia a tragic, grieving widow. I bet men would pay through the nose."

James shook his hands in fury, but the cuffs just gripped

his torn skin until blood trickled down his arms.

"Of course I would be a shoulder to cry on. That is, after all, what family is for."

"I'm her family." James rasped out. He had much more to say, and the curses and threats were on the tip of his tongue, but he was so tired. All he could do was keep his gritty, exhausted eyes on Rufus.

Rufus glared at him and circled the chair, his cloak swooshing against the floor. "Yes, I know how you would think that but it's not true, you know. She belongs with me. She has always belonged with me." He stopped and tapped the lion's head on his cheek.

He tilted his head at James and used the end of the cane to push back the sides of James' blood-soaked shirt.

"It's a nice touch, but I don't think it sends the proper message." He pondered a moment and looked into the eyes of the lion on the end of his cane. "I also don't think it's going to slow you down significantly enough."

Rufus held the cane up as if testing its weight. "It's much heavier than it looks." He pushed the lion's head into James' face. "Made of iron, coated in real gold. A work of art, is it not?"

He stepped away, swinging the cane, using the heavy lion's head to gain momentum.

"But I digress. Back to the message. I need more; more drama, more flair, a certain panache"

Rufus stared at James a while longer; the cane swinging, the iron sculpture on the end barely missing the concrete floor. For a moment James was mesmerized by the golden lion swishing back and forth; he moved his eyes up to Rufus to keep from passing out. He watched, in fascination, as Rufus' face went from contemplative to what could only be described as evil.

James barely had time to brace for whatever was coming, when Rufus swung the cane up in the air and brought the lion head crashing down on James' left arm so hard he heard the bone snap.

James screamed. Nausea swept over him and he leaned his head back, panting. The black spots that had been hovering around his periphery got larger and larger until it was just all black.

Rufus was slapping his cheek. "Come now James, no time for sleeping. You still need to get this message to Sofia. If you forget I will be very disappointed. Are you listening? Good. I'm going to have Bruce drop you off. You're going to deliver the message and that will help Sofia put things in perspective. She'll see she made a mistake and she'll come back home."

"She's not coming back," James said hoarsely, his breath hitching with every word.

"How much you wanna bet?" said Rufus, smiling.

CHAPTER 21

THE THUNDER WAS GETTING closer. Sofia saw the lightning bolt sizzle through the sky and counted one…two… CRASH. The rain had stopped and the sky was heavy with electricity. She kept her eyes closed, trying to rest between strikes.

Scritch

She looked up. That wasn't the storm, that was in the house, or in the walls. Seriously, if they had rats. What kind of millionaire had rats? She rolled up the magazine and carefully stepped onto the floor as if navigating a minefield. The thick rug was soft and warm under her bare feet, and she moved slowly around the drawing room, glancing quickly under chairs. She used the magazine to swipe under the sofa. She froze and listened. The sky lit up like a bomb and thunder boomed in a delayed reaction. She continued to stand still until the rumbling had moved past.

Scritch Scritch

She moved to the entryway, near the bottom of the

stairs, straining to hear. She clutched the magazine in both hands like a bat.

Thump Thump

If that was a rat she was a son of a bitch. It sounded like someone beating an object against a wall. She put her ear to the front door.

THUMP

She jumped and fell backwards, the magazine still clutched in her hand. She screamed up the stairs, "India! Sami!"

She whirled around as another bang came from the front door. This one was harder, more insistent. She looked around frantically for a weapon, but there was nothing. She looked at the magazine and threw it on the floor. She braced her feet and held up her fists and tried to remember every defense move she'd ever learned. She took a steading breath and yanked the door open. She screamed as a body fell to the floor at her feet.

She heard India and Sami cry out behind her. They were frozen on the landing, staring with wide eyes.

"Is it dead?" India asked.

Sofia had jumped to the first step and gripped the banister until her knuckles turned white.

"I think it's a he," she said.

The man had been slumped against the door and now lay half-in and half-out of the house, his body on its side across the threshold. His hair was dripping wet and covered his face. The air felt cooler and heavy clouds poured down rain again as if making up for lost time. Heavy drops splattered the tiled foyer through the open door. The man's clothes, what looked like a dress shirt and slacks, were drenched and plastered to his shivering body. He gave a convulsive cough and Sami squealed. India clutched her hand.

"Don't be afraid. He can't hurt you. What do we do, Sofia?"

"We need to see if he's ok," she said, shaking herself into action.

She knelt in the puddle that was forming under him and tried to wipe the wet hair from the man's face, which was muddy and scratched. "Mr," she said, nudging him gently, "can you hear me, Mr?...Oh my God!" She pushed the man over onto his back.

"James!" screamed India and raced down the stairs.

His eyes were closed, one crusted over with blood. His cheek was a mass of bruises, and cuts on his forehead and neck were still oozing blood. He was shuddering violently, his teeth clenched together so hard it was making the cut on his lip bleed.

Sofia put a hand to his chest and it came away, wet and sticky. The buttons on his shirt were missing, and the sides fell open, exposing his skin. It wasn't just rain soaking his body; long cuts, some superficial, some deep, crisscrossed his chest and stomach. Most of them were still bleeding.

Sami stood staring down at him, her eyes wide with shock.

"Sami, call 911 then get some water and a towel. I need to see how deep these cuts are."

Sami looked at Sofia and then back to James, her lips

trembling.

"He's going to be ok," Sofia said, reassuring Sami, and herself. "I don't think there's anything life-threatening. We just need to clean him up and make sure the bleeding has stopped." Sami nodded shakily and ran to get the phone.

India was kneeling on the other side of him, tears coursing down her cheeks. Sofia wanted to cry too; James looked so pale and helpless but breaking down wouldn't help anyone. She needed to be strong for India and especially for Sami. She took a deep breath and willed her voice not to shake.

"We need to get him into the house."

Sofia took one of his limp arms and started to pull. India stood and grabbed the other. James made a choking cry and sat up, gasping.

"What?" cried India. "What happened?"

"My arm's broken," he said. His voice came out raspy and faint.

"Here," said Sofia, "can you get to the couch? The ambulance should be here soon."

She and India helped him, avoiding his arm which hung uselessly at his side, and he sat down heavily, wincing. His face was bone white, and his eyes were glassy and overly bright. Sami scurried in with a bowl of water and a stack of towels.

Sofia's hands were shaking as she helped James take off his shirt. As she dabbed at the water and blood that soaked his chest, she could see the cuts on his skin more clearly. Bile rose to her throat when she saw the long slashes, that could have only been made deliberately.

"Who did this, James?" she whispered, choking on a sob.

He turned his head to where India and Sami were wiping up the water and blood off the floor.

"Who do you think?" he said, laying his head on the back of the couch. He cradled his broken arm close to his chest.

"Rufus? I didn't think he was capable of such…brutality." Her eyes stung with tears, but she brushed them away impatiently. "What happened?"

"Short story; he had one of his goons grab me at the train station. They've had me locked up for two days."

"Two days!" She gripped his hand and shuddered at the bloody ruined flesh on his wrists. "That son of a bitch," she ground out between clenched teeth. "How did you get away?"

"I didn't," James said groggily. "He let me go. I think I'm supposed to be a warning. What happens if you steal his girls."

Sofia felt such fury that she didn't stop the tears this time but let them rage down her cheeks, welcoming the hot sting.

"I'm not his girl! I don't belong to him!"

"He thinks I took his family away."

Sofia stood up and paced in front of the couch. She didn't have words for the absolute loathing she had for that man. Some of the girls at The Hotel had looked on Rufus as a father figure. He praised and disciplined the way a loving father would; but that had never been Sofia. She had tolerated his feigned affection, but he had always been just another man, using her for his own gain.

"Sofia, sit down, you're making me nauseous," James said.

Sofia looked at him. His face was pinched and strained, his eyes full of weary pain. She sat down next to him.

"I'm sorry. I guess getting angry isn't going to solve anything."

"Yet a very natural response. Don't worry, we'll figure this out. When I'm better…" he paused, seeming to forget what he was going to say. He blew out a long breath and muttered, "When's that damn ambulance going to get here? I think I need to pass out."

His head slumped forward, and Sofia gently guided his limp body until his head was on her lap. She ran her finger-tips lightly over his bruised jaw and smoldered in the burn of tears that slid down her cheeks.

James was sitting up in bed when Sofia entered the hospital room. He was wrapped mummy-like across his chest and stomach where stitches covered his body. Sami had said he looked like a rag doll that had been ripped apart and sewn back together. James had thanked her for her vivid description. His left arm was in a plaster cast. Dark blue and purple bruises stood out on his pale face.

"The doctor says you're dehydrated but not concussed. The cast has to stay on for six weeks." She sat down on the edge of the bed.

The wait in the sterile hospital room had cooled Sofia's anger until it was a low simmer. When she was finally able to see him, she felt drained and exhausted. The sight of her husband hooked up to every conceivable machine, bandaged and broken, brought fresh tears to her eyes.

"I filed a police report, not that it will do any good.

I'm sure if there were witnesses no one would dare to come forward. He's going to get away with this, isn't he?"

James looked at her with droopy lids. "Kiss me."

"No, you don't get to get out of this just because you're hopped up on morphine." She smiled, but it quickly turned to a frown.

He patted her hand groggily. "It's going to be fine. Rufus has had his little temper tantrum. Now that he's got it out of his system he'll move on to other pressing matters, like who's going to bankroll his new amusement park."

"We can't count on that. Maybe we should move to another part of The Lake District."

"He'd still know where I work."

"You could retire and we could raise chickens. Sami would adore that.'

James laughed. "I am not raising chickens, and I am not running from Rufus. Sooner or later he's going to do something that gets the attention of the police, and he won't be able to find a loophole to wriggle through."

Sofia wondered; Rufus didn't give up easily. When he wanted something, he usually went for it like a wild dog let off a leash. He had lulled them into a false sense of security, thinking that he supported their decision to leave. She didn't know what his long game was, because that's exactly what it was to him, a game. He didn't care about Sofia; he was just obsessed with winning. By taking her and Sami from The Hotel, James had made a move Rufus hadn't seen coming. Now he was lashing out like a child.

Maybe James was right. Rufus had lost and there was

nothing he could do about it. He was just trying to terrorize them. She held her sleeping husband's hand and listened to the beeping of the machines. Rage and fear still burned in her chest, and the sickening feeling that Rufus wasn't going to fold so easily.

———————

Sofia sat at the kitchen table alone, slurping coffee; it was the only thing keeping her upright. She had stayed at the hospital until almost dawn. It had been a restless night. James, despite the ability to pump morphine into his IV, was trying not to rely on it and was in considerable pain. He had finally fallen asleep, and she had come home to get what rest she could.

She couldn't get the image of James on the floor, bloody and unconscious, out of her mind. She had always suspected Rufus was a little insane, but she truly believed he'd gone over the edge this time. To go to these extremes to get her back were the actions of a delusional mind. The problem was, Rufus was also smart and savvy. He knew exactly what he was doing. Crazy she could deal with, but his intelligence, paired with a savage ruthlessness, made him even more dangerous.

She had finally fallen into a fitful sleep and had woken up to an empty mattress where James should have been.

She took another large gulp of coffee, refusing to let the tears that burned behind her eyes fall. She needed to dig for the strength that had kept her alive all these years. Rufus was a bully. He was a child who threw tantrums if he didn't get his way. He liked shiny toys and games he knew he could win.

Bullies went for the weak, the helpless, those who couldn't defend themselves.

Sofia smiled a little. Rufus should know by now that she was none of those things. If he wanted to play, she'd play, but he'd find she was a tougher opponent than he anticipated.

She pushed away from the table, letting anger boil off any anxiety, and went to get ready to catch the train.

Sofia had plenty of time to think about what she was going to say, but as she stood in front of the huge glass doors leading into The Hotel, her entire core clenched with fear. The shiny brass handles, the silver-plated lion statues on either side of the entrance; it was all so familiar, except for one thing. The framed advertisement for The Wager had been taken down. In its place was a slight weather stain showing the outline of where it used to be, like a ghost from the past.

She didn't recognize the doorman; he must be new. He stood, one gloved hand outstretched, unsure whether she wanted to go in or not.

"Ma'am?" he said tentatively.

"Sorry," Sofia said, clearing her throat. "Thank you."

He held open the door and her breath stopped as her throat went uncomfortably tight. The cloying smell, so sickeningly familiar, of tobacco, flowers and men's cologne, struck her like a force field. She almost turned and bolted, just from the images those scents unwelcomingly conjured up.

She took a deep steading breath and entered the opulence of the lobby. The chandelier with its multitude of tiny crystals painted a rainbow on the ceiling. Sofia pulled her eyes away from it in time to dodge out of the way of a bellboy pushing a cart full of luggage.

The sound of bells and music poured from the casino, mixing with the cacophony of ringing phones, mumbled conversations and carts rumbling across the black and white tiled floor.

"Sofia!" screeched a voice and before she had time to brace herself, was engulfed by a flurry of limbs and hair as Maryanne threw herself into her arms. "I can't believe you're here!"

Sofia hugged her tightly. She could feel Maryanne's tall, thin frame trembling. As was typical, The Hotel's lobby was kept at arctic temperatures, and she was only wearing a thin kimono that hung open showing lacy panties underneath.

"What are you doing?" Sofia asked, surprised to see her. Maryanne usually only worked nights. She had a regular clientele that kept her busy and she was rarely around during the day.

She pouted her perky pink lips. "Rufus is making me be the mannequin."

The mannequin stood in the lobby, unmoving; usually dressed in very little, to encourage those checking in to book a girl for the night. It was a task typically given to new girls who hadn't yet earned the right to have more interesting things to do.

"Since when do you have to be the mannequin?" Sofia asked, surprise in her voice.

"Rufus has been so mean since you left," Maryanne grumbled. "The smallest thing sets him off."

She lowered her voice and leaned in so her strawberry-scented mouth was next to Sofia's ear. "Callie, this new girl who came in last week, a guest complained about her crying the whole time they were doing it, so Rufus had her beat up. Said he'd give her something to cry about."

Sofia was bewildered. Rufus cherished his girls and except for a frustrated slap here and there he rarely touched them. They were worth too much to mar in any way. No one wanted to bed a bruised and battered girl.

Had Rufus really gone crazy from her leaving? Or maybe it was just the final push to send him over the edge he was already teetering on.

"I need to talk to him. He's threatening my family, Maryanne."

Maryanne's eyes grew wide and her mouth formed an o. "Are you sure that's a good idea? He's been so unpredictable lately. I'm afraid he might hurt you."

"He's not going to hurt me," Sofia said with more confidence than she felt. "It would defeat the purpose of trying to get me back."

"Maryanne!" Rufus' voice thundered through the lobby and Sofia watched her friend's face go white.

"I gotta go," she said frantically and scurried back to her station near the front desk.

Rufus walked up to where Maryanne stood, her eyes staring off into the distance, her hands on her waist, one hip thrust out provocatively. The only part of her body that moved was her quivering lip as Rufus glared at her.

Rufus was a tall man, but in her high-heeled sandals, Maryanne towered over him. She seemed to shrivel as she cowered under his scrutiny.

"Move from this spot one more time," Rufus bellowed, "and I'll have your head shaved. Do you understand me?"

Maryanne gave a shaky nod, her eyes still gazing over his head, not daring to look at him. Then he whipped his head around and his piercing eyes focused in on Sofia. He raised two perfectly sculpted eyebrows and his withering expression transformed into one of glee. He shuffled over in ballet flats and purple leggings that showed off his well-formed calves. An immaculate, pin-striped blazer hung to his thighs.

"Sofia, my treasure! How wonderful it is to see you! Come to my office. I'll have tea brought in." He grabbed hold of her arm and bustled her down the hallway.

She waited until they were in his office before she turned on him.

"This isn't a social call, Rufus. I'm here to tell you to back off. I'm not intimidated by you so stop the scare tactics. What you did to James was inexcusable and if it wasn't for your army of lawyers and crooked police, you'd be locked up for assault right now."

Rufus listened to her, his lips pursed. He exhaled dramatically and collapsed into his desk chair. He waved at her to sit but she remained standing, her arms crossed in front of her. Rufus sighed again and rolled his eyes.

"Very well, I accept your admonition. I was a bad boy and was too rough with my new toy. But it got you to come here, didn't it?" he said with an impish grin.

Sofia just glared at him.

"Well, what was I supposed to do?" he said, throwing

his hands up in exasperation. "He stole you! He brainwashed you into leaving!"

Rufus jumped out of his chair and kicking off his shoes, strode toward Sofia barefoot, his toenails painted peacock blue.

"You would have never left if it wasn't for him. Ok, so I went a little overboard, but how am I supposed to react when he took you from the bosom of your family?"

Rufus' eyes welled up. He spread his hands wide. "Darling, this is your home."

"Oh, cut the crap, Rufus," Sofia snapped, refusing to back up as he came near, though her every impulse wanted to flinch away. "This was a job and I left. You need to get over it and move on. Find a new girl for The Wager because it will never be me again."

She turned to leave but his hand shot out like a striking snake and gripped her arm, tightening until his perfectly manicured nails were digging into her wrist. She could feel her pulse pounding under his hand. She looked at him in surprise. His eyes were watery, and his lips were pulled back over his straight, white teeth. He looked insane.

"You think it's that easy? You think you can just walk away after I turned you into a legend? A pearl among swine; an untouchable goddess? That's what they all think and that's why they play. You are far too valuable to me, and I will do what it takes to get you back, make no mistake about that."

Sofia snorted. "Yeah right, that is not going to happen." But she felt a twinge of unease. Rufus looked truly unhinged. She tried to pull her arm away but his grip tightened.

"Do you really want to test me, Glory?" he said in a low, menacing growl.

Sofia, despite her determination not to let him intimidate her, felt her heart speed up and thump in her chest uncomfortably. He'd already proven he was capable of ruthless violence after what he'd done to James. How far was he willing to go?

The manic look in his eye had her swallowing real fear.

"How about if I wipe out your little family you've created?" he sneered, rubbing his hands together like a villain from a melodrama. If he had a moustache he'd be twirling it.

Sofia felt the floor sway, but she took a deep breath, knowing he was bluffing. "You can't go around killing off people in The Lake District, Rufus. You don't have the police in your pocket there. As it is, I hear you're skating on thin ice in the city too. Too many slaps on the wrist eventually leads to prison."

Rufus scrunched his face at the word as if he'd sucked a lemon. "True," he admitted, nodding solemnly. "No more abductions or torture sessions; I get it." He paused dramatically with his finger in the air. "But who's to say there couldn't be some sort of tragic accident? James has taught Sami to swim, hasn't he? A drowning accident would be so heartbreaking, just after the little thing has found a forever home. And India," he tsked, wagging his finger back and forth. "She's a wild child, isn't she? James isn't doing very well in the daddy department, is he? Why, she could just go out one night to party with her friends and not come home, never to be seen again. Or maybe an accidental overdose; poor troubled girl."

Sofia felt acid coat her throat and she had to breathe

through her nose to keep from retching. He'd been watching them. Or someone had and was reporting back to him. He seemed to know their every move and suddenly the idea of him making good on his threats didn't seem so outrageous anymore.

She held her hands together to keep them from shaking. "Sami and India are innocent in all this," she said unsteadily. "Not even you could be that evil."

His lips curled into a malevolent smile, "You should know me well enough, princess, that when it comes to The Hotel, I won't let anyone stand in my way."

His expression suddenly softened as if he had exchanged one mask for another. "The Wager has been a disaster since you left." He approached her gently and took her chin in his hand. "They come to see you, my *belle femme*. They won't come if you're not here."

Sofia whipped her head away, yanking her chin out of his grasp. "I won't work The Wager again."

His eyes narrowed in disapproval. "I wouldn't test my patience, if I were you," he said, getting close enough that she could smell his breath. It wasn't unpleasant, the lingering scent of coffee and licorice, but it was so hauntingly familiar that she had to hold back from gagging.

"I'm tired of asking nicely." He strode back behind the desk and sat down, steepling his fingers together. "This is turning out to be quite the chess match. It's your move, my dear. If you take too long I will consider your turn forfeit and I will make my next move."

Sofia leaned forward, laying her hands flat on his desk.

"This is not a game, Rufus."

His eyes turned cold and steely, and his lips formed an unsettling grin.

"It is most certainly a game, and I intend to win."

CHAPTER 22

SOFIA STARED OUT OF the window as the train glided away from the city and raced towards The Lake District. She watched as the dry, dusty ground became rich, dark soil, and the sky turned from gray to azure.

Her limbs were numb, and her heart thudded dully in her chest. Would he really go through with it? Would Rufus really kill her family if she didn't go back? No, she thought, Rufus might have a cruel streak, but Sofia could read his tells better than anyone and she was sure he was bluffing. He couldn't legally bring her back to The Hotel so he was throwing out threats to scare her. She'd always had a healthy respect for Rufus, sometimes bordering on fear, but she had never let him see it and she wouldn't now.

She got home in plenty of time to go to the hospital. She washed her face and put makeup on, trying to mask the stress that was pulling her skin tight and hollowing out her eyes. She had decided not to say anything to James. He needed all his strength to heal. He didn't need to be worrying about Rufus.

The next two days were occupied with getting James out of the hospital and back home. The doctor advised him to sleep on his own for about a week so his arm didn't get bumped in the night and his cuts could heal. James snickered at first but then scowled when the doctor looked at him sternly.

"You're serious?" James had said.

"It won't kill us to sleep apart for a week," Sofia reassured him as he pouted on the way home. She'd tried to be cheerful, but she was sure James would pick up on her tension. Thankfully he was too groggy from pain medication to notice much.

That night she fell into bed exhausted, but her mind did not want to shut off. It was beyond frustrating that James was right down the hall but she couldn't cuddle next to him and tell him all her troubles. He had done so much to protect them, it was her turn to shelter him from the truth so he could rest and heal.

She gave up on sleep and got out of bed. She went downstairs in her pajamas, took a blanket from one of the couches in the drawing room and quietly opened the French doors leading out into the garden.

She walked down the gravel path to the edge of the lake. The moon was full and it carved a path of white light across the dark water. The soft lap of the waves gliding up the shore and pulling back again was a comforting respite from her ravaged thoughts. She walked to the end of the pier and sat down, draping the blanket around her shoulders.

Calling Rufus' bluff was dangerous. He rarely said things he didn't mean, but would he come all the way out here to hurt them? It was one thing to kidnap James in the city, another to come to The Lake District and cause trouble where the police weren't in his pocket and he'd get treated just like any other criminal.

Rufus didn't like being told no and her refusal to let him intimidate her might just fuel his deranged fire, but she had made up her mind, going back to The Hotel was not an option.

———————

India had prowled around the house all day. She'd felt unsettled since the incident with James. She had never seen that kind of violence before. That someone could do those things to another person, let alone her brother, shook her to her core.

She wandered out into the garden and found Sami in the gazebo, sitting on one of the soft couches.

"How ya doing, kiddo?" India said, coming to sit next to her.

"I'm still freaked out," Sami said. "Why James? He's the nicest person I've ever met."

"Seriously?" said India, nudging her.

Sami grinned but her eyes were troubled.

"What is it?" India said.

"Do you think this has something to do with me and Sofia leaving The Hotel?" Her green eyes were huge, anxious for the answer.

"I don't know," India answered honestly, knowing Sami would not appreciate platitudes. "But if it is, James and Sofia will figure it out. They're two of the strongest people I know, and together I think they're pretty unstoppable, don't you?"

Sami smiled and nodded.

India jumped up and held out her hands, pulling Sami to her feet. "C'mon, let's go for a drive. I need some retail therapy, and I'll buy you an ice cream. It'll do us both some good to get out of the house for a while."

India was saving for a car, so she usually borrowed Sofia's, but as she and Sami approached the garage, India's lips curled up in a wicked smile.

"Let's take James' Beamer," she said.

"Really?" Sami grinned.

"Why not? He's not going to be using it anytime soon." India found the set of spare keys James had hidden for emergencies and jingled them at Sami.

They got in the car with suppressed giggles and India backed out of the garage. As soon as they left the driveway Sami turned on the radio. She grinned at India when a song they both knew pumped bass through the speakers. Sami rolled down the window and sang loudly as the wind ruffled her hair. The warm air and tangy scent of pine overpowered her worry, and she let herself relax for the first time in days.

Trees and houses flashed by as India accelerated, also feeling the release of stress, losing herself in the music. She adjusted the rearview mirror and quickly glanced at her hair. She looked back at the road and ran a hand through her black, messy waves.

The sun was lowering, and India popped her visor down when the rays glared through the windscreen. The automatic car lights came on, and the dashboard glowed in neon blue lines.

"Wow, it's like a spaceship!" Sami exclaimed.

"Pretentious," India scoffed, but grinned and pushed down on the gas pedal.

After a few miles the road dipped slightly, and India prepared for the approaching decline that would lead them to the lake and the boardwalk. Sami loved the tourist shops and especially the candy store that sold ice cream.

India put her foot gently on the brake, but the car didn't slow. She pushed harder, but instead of slowing, the car picked up speed as it started its descent.

"What's the matter?" Sami asked, when she saw India's panicked look.

"The brakes aren't working!" India yelled, pumping the pedal. Her stomach twisted painfully when she saw there was a truck, with a line of cars behind it, moving slowly ahead of them where the road evened out.

"We're going to hit those cars!"

Sami was clutching onto her seat belt, her eyes and mouth wide. They were approaching the other vehicles at a dizzying pace.

India looked to each side of the road, trying to stay calm and think. Trees lined either side of them, but the thick branches looked more forgiving than the cars they were barreling down on. She waited, glancing right and left, until she saw a patch that was more shrubbery than trunks. She cranked the steering wheel to the right. The car swung off the road, bouncing over a mound of dirt and plowing into the dense bushes.

Branches slapped against the windshield and the sides of the car. Sami ducked her head to avoid being slashed in the face by razor-sharp twigs dragging past the open window. The car tunneled through the undergrowth, the resistance slowing their speed, until they were stopped by a large pine tree, the bumper crumpling on impact with a sickening crunch.

India's neck snapped forward, and she cursed when her head hit the steering wheel. Sami screamed and her seat belt locked, knocking the air from her lungs, but holding her in place.

Thumping music filled the car. India opened her eyes slowly and put her hand to her forehead where the skin had been scraped raw. Her hand came away wet and sticky and she felt a little sick when she saw her bloody fingers. She snapped off the radio and turned to Sami, who had tears running down her face.

They stared at each other for a full minute, processing the shock, and then started to laugh. They both unbuckled and Sami leapt into India's arms.

"Are you ok?" India asked, breathlessly.

Sami nodded, her small body shaking. After a long hug, Sami sat back in her seat.

"That was terrifying!" India said, wiping tears from her cheeks. "Oh shit! James' car!"

That sent them into another fit of hysterical giggles.

"You're bleeding," Sami said, catching her breath.

"It's ok." India dabbed at the cut getting more blood on her fingers. She sighed and tried to open her door. The dense foliage pushing against the car only allowed her to open it a few inches.

"Can you get out, Sami?"

Sami tried to push the branches away from the window, but the thick pine was like a wall of needles. She climbed into the back seat and tried the other doors, but they were stuck fast, years of overgrown shrubs on either side. India pulled out her cell phone and called Sofia.

It had been about fifteen minutes, and Sami had to pee. The situation was getting desperate when they heard the unmistakable sound of a chain saw. India looked through the rear window and saw Rob, wearing his characteristic baseball hat, the brim turned backwards, a flannel shirt, a pair of grease-stained jeans, and safety glasses. He was creating a path through the thick bushes.

India and Sami whooped and whistled, and he gave them a thumbs up. He worked his way steadily through the wall of trees and brush, slicing through years of vegetation, until he was beside them. When they were finally able to open the door, chunks of shrubbery and branches littered the ground. Rob's truck and several other cars had been positioned so their headlights shone on the path Rob had made. The sun had gone down, and it was shadowy beyond the glare of the lights. Out of the gloom, Sofia rushed to them and gripped them both in a tight hug.

"What happened?" she cried, running her hands up and down India's arms as if to reassure herself she was still in one piece.

"I don't know. The brakes wouldn't work," India said shakily.

A man with long grey sideburns and a bushy mustache was standing by one of the vehicles, observing quietly. Sofia introduced him as Mr. Wilcox, the owner of the house on the other side of the grove of trees. India apologized profusely for taking out most of his backyard, but he smiled good naturedly and said he was just glad no one was seriously hurt. Sami, hopping from one foot to the other, asked if she could please use his bathroom.

After taking a quick look under the crumpled hood, Rob brought his truck around and pulled out hooks and towing cables. India watched, still trembling with adrenaline. Rob glanced at her and frowned.

"You ok?" He put his hands on her shoulders and examined her critically. "Come here," he said and drew her in for a hug. "I'm proud of you. You really kept your head. It could have been way worse."

India put her arms around him. Her heart rate gradually slowed as she clung to his solid presence.

"James is going to kill me," she mumbled into his chest.

"Nah," he said, "it's just a scratch. He might not even notice."

India hiccupped a laugh and pulled away.

"Thanks, Rob."

"Anytime." He gestured to her forehead. "That's a nasty scrape. You might want to get that checked out."

"It's fine," she said, touching the grazed skin gingerly.

He turned to his truck and unwound the heavy chains, securing them to the back of the car.

"You might have a concussion."

"I don't have a concussion," India said with a scowl.

"And you've suddenly become a doctor in the last fifteen minutes?" he said, pulling a lever that had the chain shortening until the car dragged reluctantly closer.

"Ha ha," she sneered peevishly. "I see you've developed a sense of humor in the last fifteen minutes."

He laughed and walked to the cab of his truck. "I think you're going to be just fine."

When they got home, James sat in stony silence as India told him what had happened. He had gone pale as she relayed the story, and the dark bruises on his face looked almost black in the dim bedroom light.

After being reassured that neither of them were hurt, he told India he was proud of how she handled the situation. He smiled at her fondly when she got on her knees by his bed and begged forgiveness for smashing his car. He placed his hand on her head, telling her all was forgiven. She kissed him on the cheek before leaving the room, the trauma from the evening already melting away.

James stayed awake fuming. He wasn't going to say anything to the others until he was sure, but brakes didn't just stop working, not in his world. Rufus had gone too far; coming to his home, putting his family in danger. He clenched his uninjured hand. He needed to get out of this bed. He needed to get back out there and find the weakness in Rufus' armor.

The next morning, he was determined to get up and eat

breakfast in the kitchen, maybe get started on some phone calls. Sofia blocked the bedroom doorway, her hands on her hips.

"You are not leaving this room," she scolded. "You've got four more day's bed rest."

"Doctors don't know everything," he said, swinging his legs off the bed and getting to his feet. He took three steps and stopped, turning a sickly green color. Sweat broke out on his forehead and chest. Sofia raced over to him before he fell down.

"Damn," he said, looking at her.

Sofia nodded and helped him back to bed.

She went downstairs to make him some toast. India was sitting at the long counter, poking at a plate of scrambled eggs.

"How are you doing this morning?" Sofia asked, putting two pieces of bread in the toaster.

"I have no appetite, that's for sure," India said. "I'm still pretty freaked out."

"I can imagine," said Sofia, coming to stand at the counter across from her.

India heard the front door open then the friendly, "'Lo?" from Rob.

He came into the kitchen dressed in a pair of baggy cargo pants and a t-shirt that India couldn't help but notice fit his biceps and chest very nicely. He wasn't as tall as James but was more compactly built.

For as long as India could remember Rob had always been around. He and James had met shortly after her parents died and she had clung to him and her brother like a burr.

She smiled down at her eggs. Rob had the patience of a saint.

"At least you still have your sense of humor," Rob said, pouring himself a cup of coffee. "What are you grinning about?"

"Nothing. How's James' car?"

"It will live. You may want to stick with the bus from now on."

He laughed at India's affronted expression.

"How's James doing?" he asked Sofia.

"The stubborn man tried to get up this morning and practically keeled over."

Rob chuckled. "I wondered how long it would take him to get fed up with being stuck in bed."

Sofia put toast slathered in butter and a cup of coffee on a tray. "He'd better get used to it. He's not going to get better if he doesn't rest."

"Mind if I come up with you?" Rob asked as Sofia headed to the door with the tray.

He patted India on the head and laughed when she scowled at him, then followed Sofia up the stairs to the guest bedroom. When he saw James, his face turned grim.

"I didn't want to scare India," Rob said, leaning against the wall. Sofia set the tray on the nightstand.

"What is it?" James asked. Sofia sat down next to him and took his hand.

"You were right. The brake line was cut; there's no doubt about it. This wasn't an accident."

James cursed and Sofia felt the bottom drop out of her world.

"Rufus?" she said in a small voice.

"Who else?" said James.

"He actually targeted Sami and India?" She whispered the words past the agonizing pulse thumping in her throat.

"It was my car," James reminded her.

"He couldn't guarantee you'd be driving it," Rob said with a scowl. "Obviously he doesn't care who he hurts."

Sofia kept her face neutral, keeping her thoughts to herself. If James knew that Rufus had threatened her, he'd be on the next train to the city, doctor's orders be damned.

She needed time to think. She had sworn she wouldn't let Rufus bully her, that she would never go back to The Hotel, but at what cost? She would not let Rufus hurt her family again, not when there was something she could do about it.

"Sofia! Tell Sami that's not how the game works!" laughed India, throwing down her cards.

"You always say that when you lose," said Sami.

"I swear you cheat."

Sofia smiled. She'd been staring across the room at them. Two beautiful girls who would never have to live a life of poverty or sell their bodies to survive. She felt she had done right by Sami, finding her a home. If that was all that came of this then it was worth it. She knew she would be cared for. James loved her like another sister; he would see she had a good life.

She watched for a moment as Sami shuffled the cards.

Sofia would miss her so much. She blinked several times, stuffing down the useless tears. She had already made the decision; it was the only way to keep them all safe.

She put her book down and walked over to where the girls sat. She kissed the top of their heads. "Good night," she said quietly.

"You ok?" India asked, taking in the dark circles under Sofia's eyes.

"Yes," she smiled. "Just been quite a week."

They had decided not to tell India and Sami about the brakes being deliberately tampered with. James didn't want them frightened any more than they already were. He was confident that if he dug hard enough, he'd find something on Rufus that would finally put him away. Then it would all be over.

Sofia admired his courage and tenacity, but she knew he was just fanning the flames and that Rufus would only continue to retaliate. James couldn't save her, not this time. This time she would save him.

She went up the stairs and to the guest room doorway. James lay watching the news with his arm propped on a stack of pillows. "Oh, wonderful," he said, clicking the remote to turn the tv off. "You've come to keep the invalid company. How noble of you." His face had turned a mottled purple, but at least he could see out of both eyes now.

"You can't whine that you haven't had any visitors," she said. "Sami played cards with you yesterday."

"Sami cheats," he said, reaching for her. "And I miss your warm body next to mine."

She folded herself into his arms, her head laying on his chest. The rhythm of his heartbeat was so familiar to her and his scent was like coming home. She blinked several times and took a long deep breath.

He pulled her closer. "Everything's going to be alright, you know," he said.

"I know," she said and looked up at him.

His blue eyes pierced her with a mix of passion and tenderness that made her stomach tumble and her core tighten. He brought his lips down to hers with a firm and demanding kiss, promising so much more.

He clutched her to him with his good arm and moved his lips along her jaw, nibbling as he went. Sofia felt warmth spreading through her limbs and she leaned into him, needing to be closer.

When their tongues met and James deepened the kiss, she sighed with pleasure. Growling, he tried to flip her over on her back but yelped when his broken arm came in contact with the mattress.

Sofia choked back a sob and forced a laugh. "We can't do this!" She got up and moved to the other side of the bed to prop his arm back on the pillows.

"You started it," James pouted.

"I did not!"

"Yes, you did. You walked into the room. That's all it takes for me."

She smiled and stood over him. "Three more days and then you can move around to your heart's content."

"Then you promise we can sleep in the same bed?"

It was a sincere question, asked like a trusting child. Sofia had to swallow hard before answering, fighting back the tears that threatened. Still her voice came out hoarse and shaky. "I promise."

When she reached the door, she turned and said, "James, I love you."

He gave her a charming half smile and said, "I love you too."

She left him and hurried back to her room. She went in and closed the door quietly. She leaned against it shaking, taking breath after breath, each one catching painfully in her throat.

She felt sick and put her hands on her knees, hanging her head. Her uneven inhales became hysterical gulps, and her heart was beating as if it would pump right out of her body. The pressure on her chest was too much; it was going to crush her. Covering her mouth with her hands and pressing until her lips bruised against her teeth, she let out a strangled scream and released the tears that had been choking her all night.

She slid down to the floor and cried like she hadn't since she was a child. She wept into her hands, trying to quiet her sobs. She knew this had been too good to be true. She knew she didn't deserve a second chance. She was such a fool! She thought she could leave that old life behind; what an arrogant, naïve, stupid little girl. All these years and she had learned nothing. The worst possible emotion was hope; it ate away all sense until fantasy and reality blurred into a jumbled mess.

She'd given up hope the day her mother had died. To hope was to live in fear of disappointment. Hope that she'd find something to eat; hope that it didn't rain when she had no shelter; hope for a better life. Hope for love? It was insidious. It took hold and grew despite one's best efforts to squash it. Who was she to think differently? Who was she to think she could outrun the odds? She'd dared to hope and now it was over.

She knew with certainty that Rufus wouldn't stop until she was back at The Hotel. He could do anything he wanted in the city, and he'd just demonstrated his ability to stage an accident right where they lived. Nothing daunted him, nothing could crumble his kingdom.

The only time Sofia had ever seen Rufus show real fear was when rumor got around that he was prostituting underage girls. In a city full of debauchery, using children for any kind of sexual gratification was looked upon as inexcusable and extremely illegal.

He denied it emphatically, insisting he would never do anything so vulgar. The rumor didn't stop the pouring in of guests; those already bent on immoral behavior didn't judge others for their individual tastes. It did, however, attract the attention of the FBI, and the threat of them shutting down The Hotel if there was even a whiff of underage prostitution, had Rufus terrified.

The FBI tried raids at first, but either the rumors weren't true, or Rufus had been tipped off and had removed any damning evidence beforehand. The authorities moved on and turned their sights to lower-hanging fruit, like the dozens of underage girls hanging out on street corners every night. The Hotel soon fell off their radar with no one coming forward with new evidence and no one willing to talk.

James and Rob were on a fool's mission if they thought they could find a way to stop Rufus. Sofia knew he'd been willing to prostitute Sami, but it was her word against one of the most well-known men in the city, whose clientele included judges, police, and even FBI agents. They were just poking the hornet's nest and the sooner she put a stop to it, the safer everyone would be.

Sofia had no tears left and her bout of crying had left her shaky and tired. She found a piece of paper in her nightstand and scribbled a note, leaving it on her bed. She looked around her room. This was home. She couldn't take anything that reminded her. She needed to let it go. Move on. It had been a beautiful dream but reality had woken her up like she knew it would, so she walked empty-handed, soundlessly from her room and down the stairs.

She could hear India and Sami laughing in the drawing room. She stopped for a moment, listening to the music of their laughter. A tear escaped and rolled down her cheek. She wiped her eyes and then quickly opened the front door and slipped out into the night.

CHAPTER 23

"WHAT THE HELL DOES this mean?" yelled James, pacing back and forth in the drawing room. He held a piece of crumpled paper in his hand and flicked it with his fingers. "I changed my mind?" His face was drawn and pinched, his eyes bright with anger and confusion.

He had been pacing for fifteen minutes. It was three am and Sami, who'd had a nightmare, had slipped into Sofia's room and found the note. She had immediately woken James. It was still dark outside but the house was ablaze with light as James had gone room by room, turning on lights, looking for Sofia. He hadn't bothered to turn any of them off.

Sami was cowered in the corner, sobbing, and India was trying to calm James down. She'd sent for Rob who was leaning against one of the sofas, watching his best friend kill himself with exhaustion.

Rob stopped him in mid-pace and put his hands on James' shoulders. "Do you realize," Rob said, shaking him a little, "when we find her, you're going to pass out at her feet?

That's not going to be helpful."

That seemed to sink in, because James looked around as if waking from a dream. India was flushed, her hands on her hips and Sami was trying to melt into the wall. He nodded his head and sat down.

"She's with Rufus. I know she is," James said resting his head in his hands. "It's because of what he did to me. She thinks going back will make him stop coming after us."

"We could leave now and drive, but you'll be in no shape to do anything when we get there. The first train leaves at five," Rob said. "We'll be on it. Until then there is nothing we can do so let's all try to get a little rest."

India took Sami by the hand to take her upstairs. "It's going to be ok," she said firmly, looking into Sami's pale, tear-stained face. "There's a reasonable explanation and we're going to find out what it is."

Sami nodded and let India lead her up the stairs.

James poured himself a scotch and handed one to Rob. He went to the window, sipping his drink. The sky was still dark and he could see his own reflection in the glass. His arm was throbbing and his stomach was tied in a tight knot. The alcohol sat in his gut, churning. He hadn't felt such deep fear since his parents had died. That had been a sharp, painful grief that dulled with time. Sofia leaving felt like a part of him had been ripped away, leaving a gaping hole that was too big to ever heal.

"Why didn't she come to me?" he said in a rough voice.

"She's only had herself to rely on up until now," Rob said quietly. "She's used to dealing with things on her own."

India had rejoined them and was picking at a nail. "James?"

"Hm?" he said, not looking away from the window.

"What if she got freaked out with everything happening so fast? Coming here and then getting married…"

He turned on her fiercely. Rob stepped forward as if to put himself between them. "What are you saying?" James said coldly.

India wasn't intimidated and she stood her ground. She knew her brother better than he knew himself. Right now he was like a wounded animal, ready to lash out at anyone who threatened to harm him further, but she knew he'd never hurt her.

"Maybe it was all too scary for her and she went back to The Hotel because it was familiar. Maybe she just changed her mind about wanting to be with us." Her voice trailed off and James looked at her fully. His blue eyes had darkened almost to black but they softened and his voice was calm and matter of fact.

"I don't believe that for a second. Something else is going on. Don't worry, I'll bring her back."

———————

Sofia lay in bed listening to her roommate snore. She had been demoted and was now on the tenth floor sharing a room with a new girl named Bridgette. Rufus had been overjoyed to see her, insisting she get some rest and they would talk in the morning.

Sofia missed Sami bitterly. She knew she was going to be upset. She'd feel as if Sofia had abandoned her. The one person who was always going to be there for her sneaks away in the middle of the night without even saying goodbye. She would probably never forgive her.

Sofia bit down hard on her lip to keep from sobbing. James would know what to say to her. James always knew what to do. So why hadn't she just told him? Because he would have rushed in, one gun blazing, the other arm in a cast, planning on taking down the whole of Rufus' empire. He would find a way to get her out but at what expense? They would be terrified all the time, always looking over their shoulders until the day came when Rufus did manage to hurt or even kill one of them. That was no way to live. She had gotten Sami out and that's all that mattered. What happened to her was inconsequential compared to her family staying safe. She could handle The Wager.

She thought of James and looked at the clock. Six am. Had he found the note? Would he take it at face value and leave well enough alone? She prayed he would.

She listened to Bridgette's heavy breathing and watched the clock. Ten minutes later there was a knock on the door.

"Sofia," said one of the maids through the door, "there's a visitor for you."

Sofia's heart started pounding. It had to be him. She threw on a thick robe and took the elevator to the lobby, clutching her hands together to keep them from shaking. She had to be convincing. She had to stay strong for her family.

James was waiting for her in the lobby, his arm in a sling

and the colorful bruises on his face making a stark contrast to his pale skin. His eyes were sunken, and he looked weak and frail. He shouldn't have even been out of bed. A few feet behind him stood Rob.

"How could you let him come like this?" she said, frowning at him.

James said quietly, "This was my idea, not his. Is there somewhere we can talk?"

"No, this will do." She crossed her arms hoping she looked confident and uninterested. Inside she was trembling, especially when his brows knit in hurt confusion. She longed to hold him, to reassure him, but he had to believe this was her idea otherwise he would never stop.

"What does this note mean?" He held up the piece of paper. It was crumpled, the writing smeared and illegible.

"What does it say?" she asked, as if she didn't know.

"You changed your mind."

"Well?" she said, frowning up at him. Her look of contempt took him aback for a moment. She saw a flicker of doubt on his face as if for the first time considering that she might be sincere. She held back tears with everything in her.

"Well, what?" he said. A shutter came down over his eyes, hiding the vulnerability, the sadness. "Changed your mind about what? Us? Marriage? Your living arrangements?" He motioned around the room.

"About all of it," she said. "I decided I don't want to be anyone's kept bride. I've survived my whole life by myself, doing what I needed to do. I don't need a man in my life and I don't need you thinking I'm yours now. I don't belong to anyone."

"I never said you belonged to me, Sofia. You know that's not how I feel. And if you want to work, I'm not standing in your way." He looked around The Hotel lobby. "Just maybe not here." He took her hand. His was shockingly hot and dry in her cool, soft one. "I know you don't really want to be here. Rufus has convinced you somehow that you had to come back but whatever it is, you don't."

Her pulse quickened at the touch of his warm flesh, the sound of his soothing voice, the reassuring words. She stared into his eyes and it almost broke her.

"Don't you get it," she said angrily, shaking off his hand. "This is my home. It always has been. This is where I want to be."

He pointed at her. "That's Rufus talking. That is not how you feel, you're just afraid to admit it. You're afraid of anything you can't control."

"You're talking to me about control? What happened to you; never place a bet you can't win? Well, you bet on me and lost."

His eyes widened but she went on relentlessly, knowing she might as well have been throwing daggers at his chest. "You don't want me, James. All you see when you look at me is something pretty in a cage that needs to be rescued. That's what you do, James. You go around trying to save everyone because you couldn't save your parents."

He took a step back as if she'd slapped him and she sucked in a breath, hating herself. He looked at her for a long time. She blinked and willed herself not to cry. His face was calm but his eyes were lit with anger.

"I don't believe you, Sofia. Something else is going on. Is it because of this?" he said, gesturing to his arm.

"It's because I don't want the life you're offering me. You think you know me, but you don't."

"I know you, Sofia. I've known you since the day I saw you. I know you wouldn't do this if you had a choice. You would never leave Sami."

She closed her eyes and took a shaky breath. "Sami will be fine. I know you'll see to that."

He opened his mouth, but she interrupted him, saying, "Please, James, it just won't work. You have to let me go." Her voice hitched and she cleared her throat. "It's over."

He gritted his teeth. "I don't believe that."

"Is there a problem here?" Rufus sailed in on wedge heels, wearing cargo pants that cinched at his ankles, and a fluffy white sweater. Rob took a few paces forward.

"No, Rufus," said Sofia. "James was just leaving."

"I was not just leaving," growled James.

"Oh, but perhaps you should," said Rufus, snapping his fingers. Five armed guards materialized out of the shadows. Rob looked at James who shook his head.

"You don't have to stay here, Sofia," he said. "This is your choice."

"You're right, James, and you are going to have to come to grips with the fact that I didn't choose you." She turned and walked to the stairs.

He watched her ascend the stairs, her auburn hair flipping behind her. She didn't flinch and she didn't look back.

A tiny piece of him wondered if he was being an absolute fool. Why wouldn't she change her mind? Like being married to him was such a prize? He was helpless as a kitten right now. In fact he was fighting with all his dignity not to faint, but he had to keep believing that she was here under duress. He didn't think he could survive if the alternative was true.

"Ouch!" said Rufus, laughing. "That takes the stuffing out of a fella. Now, Mr. Hardy, the lady has made herself quite clear that she doesn't want to talk to you. I'm afraid I'm going to have to ask you never to return to The Hotel. Are you going to be leaving under your own steam or do my boys need to help you out?"

"I'm going," said James, half turning. "This isn't over, Rufus."

"Oh, but I think it is. Boys? Please see Mr. Hardy and his friend out. Do take care, Mr. Hardy, those bruises look nasty!"

———————

Days went by and it was getting harder for Sofia to come up with excuses why she couldn't work The Wager. First she was on her period and then she had a stomach bug, which was not far from the truth. The thought of sleeping with another man made her want to throw up, and Rufus noticed that she'd hardly been eating.

"You'll get too skinny," he said to her distastefully. "Nobody wants to screw a carcass, my dear."

She could tell he was getting impatient. She really needed to figure something out. She couldn't put him off forever.

She looked out her window at the darkening sky. It was getting late, but she felt antsy and knew she wouldn't be able to sleep. She threw on a light sweater over her t-shirt and jeans and hurried down to the first floor.

Rufus was in the lobby talking to a group of Japanese men in business suits. He would have towered over them anyway, but the roller skates on his feet gave him another six inches. His pants were yellow and flowy. His shirt was blue and bedazzled and showed off his sleek, waxed midriff.

She tried to rush by him but he rolled over and did a hockey stop in front of her, blocking the way to the door. "Where are you going in such a hurry, my darling?" She pushed by him and he skated backwards next to her as she stormed toward the door.

"To the market," she said, glaring at him.

"Well, don't be too long. It's getting dark and there are some unsavory people out there this time of night. I wouldn't want you to be molested." He put the emphasis on the first syllable and wiggled his eyebrows at her.

"I'll be fine," she said, stepping out of the door. She could hear him laughing as she left The Hotel and walked down the sidewalk.

It was dark when she reached the market, but the vendors were still open to accommodate those who worked late. She didn't really need anything, and she could hardly call it getting fresh air, but something about being around these people soothed her. They were a portrait of resilience and strength, the ability to overcome whatever life threw at them.

She had to remember that she'd relied on that resilience

and strength her whole life. Now was no different. She had to take the cards she was dealt and do something with them.

She smiled at the pun and couldn't help but think how Sami would have laughed at the reference to The Wager.

She'd come to the end of the line of stalls, and there was a dark patch that had to be crossed to get to the next aisle over. She had just stepped slightly out of the light when an arm grabbed her around the waist and swung her into the alley.

CHAPTER 24

A DRY, HOT HAND clamped down over her mouth as she was dragged into the darkness. She kicked out behind her and heard a satisfying "son of a bitch!" as her foot connected with a shin bone.

She was whipped against the alley wall and pinned by the heavy body pressing into her. She struggled against the hand that pushed down on her mouth, trying to bite it, trying to scream.

"Sofia, it's me!"

Her eyes widened and she shoved his hand away. "James! What are you doing here?"

He looked awful; the dark circles under his eyes, against the unusual paleness of his skin, looked like gash marks. He was sweating in the cool evening air and when his fingers came around her arm, his flesh was hot and feverish.

"We need to talk," he said, and she didn't miss the waver in his voice.

"There's nothing to talk about, James. I told you, I

changed my mind and you just need to accept it."

His chest was pressed against hers and she could smell the leather of his jacket. She could also see his eyes that sparked with unnatural brightness.

"That's bullshit," he growled. His pulse was beating at his neck, alarmingly fast.

"James, you're sick. I think you need to go to the hospital."

"Tell me you don't love me," he said, shifting his feet closer until the length of him was against her.

She blinked and inhaled quickly.

"Did you really think it was going to work between us?" she said, desperately trying to ignore his body, flush with hers and his mouth, inches away. "You're living in a fantasy."

"Am I?" he said. He swayed slightly and put an arm against the wall by her head as if bracing himself.

"James, I…"

The hunger in his eyes stopped her words as he bent and kissed her neck. The prickle of his rough unshaven face against her skin made her shiver; at the same time warming every inch of her. She knew the heat that scalded her flesh was not natural. He was burning with fever, but she couldn't get herself to make him stop.

She was breathless when his mouth took hers. She opened her lips to him as her pulse thundered in her chest. Her arms came up around his neck. She kissed him hungrily, her hands moving to his face.

"Tell me you don't love me," he whispered into her mouth.

For a moment more she clung to him with every part

of her and then sobbed, "I don't love you," and she pushed him away.

He stepped back. She could feel his eyes on her but she wouldn't meet them. She was afraid of what she would see there. Disgust, sadness, regret. She didn't think she could handle any of it. But when she looked up at him his face was blank and emotionless. It was worse.

He looked as if he was ready to drop but he said in a clear, precise voice, "I guess the matter is settled then. I won't be bothering you again." He turned on his heel and left the alley. Sofia watched him walk away. She heaved a shaky sigh, and tears ran down her cheeks. She squatted against the brick wall, wrapped her arms around her stomach and wept.

Sofia was dreaming. She was walking hand in hand with James on the beach. On his other side, a little girl skipped along beside him. She had auburn hair and eyes like blue-bells. The little girl said something and James laughed. Sofia's heart constricted and she felt a pang of sheer joy, mixed with crushing sadness.

She woke suddenly and touched her wet cheeks. The window had been left open and the room was cool. She reached over for James, but her hand only met the empty sheets. She let out a shaky sigh and a few more tears escaped. It had been five days since the night in the alley, and she'd been in a constant state of anxiety, wondering if he was alright.

It wasn't close to dawn yet; the sky was still black but

plenty of light shone in her window from the buildings where bright neon signs and billboard-sized advertisements lit the sky all night long.

The door handle moved and she held her breath. Is that what had woken her? Someone was trying to get into the room. Bridgette was working and Rufus was the only one with a master keycard. She heard a click and the subtle swoosh of the bedroom door opening.

Her back was to the door and she lay still, barely breathing. She formed her hand into a fist and when the shadow crossed over her she twisted and struck. The figure caught her hand and she struggled to pull away from him.

She tried to scream but lips clamped down on hers. It only took her a moment to know who it was. She fought him and thumped on his chest with both fists. He let out a mangled groan and fell to the floor.

"James!" she cried and threw back the covers, crouching at his side.

"Woman, you're so violent," James hissed, clutching his chest.

"I'm sorry," she said, not sounding sorry. "But if you will creep up on me in the middle of the night. How did you get in here, anyway?"

"I bribed a very tired night clerk to make me a keycard. Rufus really should vet his employees more thoroughly."

"Well get off the floor," she said, helping him up. He winced and she started unbuttoning his shirt.

"Um, not that I object but…"

"I want to see the cuts. I want to make sure they're not

infected." She pushed his shirt back over his shoulders and it fell to the ground.

Sofia scanned his body. The stitches had been taken out, leaving angry red marks across his chest and stomach where Rufus had cut him. A few were going to leave scars.

"Are you really ok?" she said softly. She put out a hand and touched one of the long red gashes on his side. She felt the muscles ripple under her fingers when he trembled. She traced the length and then moved to another, this one faint and almost flush with his skin. She laid her palm against it and looked up at him.

"Yes," he said, putting his hand over hers. "It didn't take me long to recover after Rob and India forced antibiotics down me."

"I'm glad," she whispered.

"Are you?" he asked, bringing his mouth closer to hers.

"Of course I am. You think I want you to be hurt?"

"I'm not sure what you want, Sofia," he whispered against her cheek. She closed her eyes when he said her name, his warm breath caressing her skin. "But I'll give you anything you ask for."

She shivered as his lips moved softly over the outside of her ear. "This isn't a good idea, James," she said, tilting her head to give him better access to her neck. "If Rufus catches you in here."

"Is it a crime to make love to my wife?" he said. He moved in closer and Sofia backed up until the back of her knees were against the bed.

"No, but I…"

He gripped her waist. "Tell me to stop, Sofia," he whispered, capturing her mouth with his.

An involuntary moan was pulled out of her and she put her arms around his neck.

"Don't stop, James," she murmured, and sighed when he put his hand in her hair and devoured her mouth.

Their tongues did a slow dance and she clung to him as if his kiss was the oxygen she needed to survive. Keeping his cast out of the way, he lowered her with one arm onto the bed.

She was only wearing a thin camisole and he could see every curve of her breasts, where her rib cage created an indentation down her stomach, and the flair of her hips. He stroked his hand down her torso and she arched her back like a cat being pet.

"You're so beautiful, Sofia," he said, moving his hands over the silky fabric covering her skin. He cupped her breast and his thumb rubbed a slow circle through the thin material. She gasped and her hips thrust toward him.

He stood up and Sofia groaned, frustrated at the loss of the pressure of his body against hers. One handed, he pulled down his loose pants and shucked them off his legs.

"You're also brave and strong; you don't need this place." He drew his boxers down and Sofia just stared at his toned, lean body. The welts on his chest and stomach did not deter from the beauty of his sculpted frame.

"You don't need Rufus," he said, kneeling on the bed. He hooked her panties with his fingers but had trouble pulling them down with only one hand, so he grabbed the material in his teeth and dragged it down her legs.

"And you certainly don't need me. I'm not here to rescue you, Sofia. You don't need rescuing," he said, positioning himself between her legs so his mouth was near her stomach. "I believe you can do or be whatever you want. But I made a vow to you, and I will worship you…" he kissed right below her belly button. "Your body…" he nipped at the tender flesh, bringing a sharp cry from her. "Your mind…" he moved lower and kissed her inner thigh. "Your soul."

She gasped when he kissed her between her legs and then whimpered as he moved on, climbing back up her body, kissing and touching as he went until they were face to face, eyes locked. "Until my dying breath," he whispered.

He kissed her and Sofia felt like she was flying. She knew this was a mistake; it was just fanning the flames for both of them, but she couldn't bring herself to make him stop. Her body took over and she arched into him, inviting all of him.

With a growl he wrapped his uninjured arm around her waist and drove into her. The sensation of him moving inside her brought stinging tears that she blinked away. It was too familiar, too much like home. It was a mistake; but still she didn't stop him. In fact she moved with him, the way she had countless other times, their bodies melding together as one in a sensual dance.

She put her arms around him and moved her hands up his back, feeling the muscles ripple with each thrust. A light sheen of sweat on his skin moistened her fingers as she stroked along his sides. Bringing her hands to his chest, she laid them gently against his skin. Another guttural sound rumbled in his throat and he crushed his mouth to hers, biting her lip, sucking her tongue into his mouth.

This time she let a moan of pleasure escape as that familiar coil of tension rolled through her core, demanding release. Her hips moved frantically and she clasped her hands around his neck. "James, I'm…" she panted.

"I know baby, let it go. I've got you."

The words and the feel of his body, fitting to hers so perfectly, sent a shiver down her spine and with it her body convulsed and a breathy sob tore from her throat as all the tension and all the fear exploded into a mist of glorious surrender.

When the room stopped spinning and the reality of her surroundings planted itself in her befuddled mind, Sofia felt a tear slip from the corner of her eye and trail its way down the side of her face.

James had rolled off her onto his side and he caught the tear with his finger before it disappeared into her hair.

"Why are you crying, Sofia?" he asked gently.

"I'm not crying," she sniffed and rubbed a hand over her eyes.

He traced a lazy finger over her bare arm. She shivered, pushed his hand away and sat up, wrapping the sheet around her and drawing up her knees. He propped himself on his elbow and leaned his head on his fist, watching her.

"What?" she said, refusing to meet his eyes.

"I'm dying to know what you're thinking," he said.

"I'm thinking…this was a mistake." She tucked her face down and put her forehead to her knees. "This doesn't change anything…It can't change anything."

"Why not?" he said it casually, but his insides were strung tight as a bow. He could feel her slipping away again and as much as he wanted to grab her, sling her over his shoulder and carry her home, this had to be her decision, her choice.

She raised her head and looked at him. He needed a haircut; his hair was messy and falling on his forehead. She clenched her fists to keep from brushing it aside. His eyes were soft and lazy, but she knew him too well. He couldn't hide the spark of anxiety burning under the surface of those sapphire irises.

She knew the words she was about to say might very well end her dream of a happy ending once and for all, but the poor girl didn't get the handsome rich prince in her reality. The poor girl had to stand on her own two feet, no matter what it took. She'd worked her way to the top, and she could do it again, but first she had to convince James to leave and forget about her.

She flung the covers aside and stood up, taking her robe from the hook by the side of her bed and throwing it on.

"I don't know why you came here tonight," she said, going to stand in front of the window, putting distance between her and the bed as if proximity made any difference when her heart was shattering.

James sat up and began putting his clothes on. "I would think I made that pretty obvious." As much as his body pulled toward hers like a magnet, he stayed where he was instead of moving closer to her.

She felt like butterflies had been released in her stomach as she watched him carefully move his arms, his scarred chest and abdomen flexing, as he put on his shirt. She wanted to take him in her arms and devour his body and love it like no woman had ever loved a man. Her breath caught and she resisted, squeezing her stinging eyes shut. Instead she steeled her will and stared at him across the bed.

"I'm not going back with you," she said, tossing her head back, determined to see this through. "This," she said gesturing to the bed, "what just happened, doesn't change anything. I don't love you. I don't want to be married to you. I don't want you, period. Next time you want to screw me, sign up for The Wager like everyone else." She spat the words at him like darts.

He crossed his arms and looked at her with faint respect. "Damn, Sofia, I never realized what an extraordinarily good liar you are. But I guess in your line of work that starts to come naturally. I mean, you lie to yourself all the time. You think you hold all the power, but that's a lie. You tell yourself you're not terrified all the time, another lie. You think you're in control, that's definitely a lie."

"Get out!"

"Everything's a lie," he said, walking toward her. "It has to be, otherwise you might actually feel something in that frozen heart of yours."

She slapped him hard across the face, leaving a red blotch on his cheek. "I said get out!"

He stared at her silently, his face full of grief and regret and then walked to the door.

"Don't you pity me!" she snapped, real anger bubbling out of the crack in her heart.

He reached for the handle and turned to her. "I don't pity you, Sofia. You're the strongest woman I've ever met. And I promise you this, I will find a way to bring Rufus down and bring you home."

The door shut behind him and she was left standing in the middle of the room, shivering in the cool night air. She climbed into bed and curled into a ball. She lay there, staring out of the window until the sun came up.

———————

A week later, and she had heard nothing from James. She hadn't really expected to but deep in her heart she had hoped. She'd just returned to her room after a shower. She didn't have a private bathroom anymore; she shared with the other girls in this section of the floor, so it had taken a while to get a turn.

She stood in front of the window and brushed her hair. The sun had finally made an appearance, so she stood in the square of light with a towel wrapped around her wet body. The heat felt like an embrace, and she closed her eyes and let the warmth soak into her skin. There was a knock at the door. She turned and said, "Come in."

"Are we decent?" sang Rufus, opening the door. "Oh, I do like the fresh out of the shower look. You could certainly sell that one." He giggled at her.

"What do you want, Rufus?" She turned back to the window.

"What do I want? I want you to earn your room and board, my precious. It's long overdue, young lady. It's time for you to get to work!" He clapped his hands enthusiastically. "In fact, there is a perfect guest for you coming in tonight. A real high roller."

"Tonight?" She turned to Rufus with wide eyes, putting a hand to her neck as if to still the pulse jumping there.

"Yes, and don't pull that innocent young thing act with me. You and I both know that ship sailed long ago."

"I just don't know if I'm ready," Sofia said, looking at him with watery eyes.

The slap was so sudden she didn't even have time to flinch. Her cheek exploded in pain, and she put her hand to her burning skin.

"Do you think I care if you're ready?" he snarled. "This is a business, not a spa. Now get your little tush moving. No more excuses!"

Sofia, still stunned, could only manage a quiet, "Okay."

"Excellent!" Rufus beamed. "That's my girl."

He blew her a kiss and left the room.

Sami came into the drawing room and threw herself into the chair next to where James sat, the tv remote held loosely in his hand. He was trying to find the energy to turn it on. Even though he wanted to spend every waking moment in the city, digging into Rufus, he knew he had to rest. His sickness had caused him valuable time, and he knew pushing himself too hard would just weaken him.

He'd spent countless hours on the phone, calling in every

favor he could think of. He prowled seedy bars, willing to talk to anyone who had information. With each passing day came another brick wall to bash his head against. Rufus and his financial transactions appeared so squeaky clean even James' contact with the feds had given up.

Rob and India had convinced him to stay away from The Hotel in case Rufus got him arrested for trespassing. He was about ready to go there and break the man's neck, to hell with prison.

"Everything ok?" he asked. It was a stupid question, of course she wasn't ok. Sami put on a brave face, believing James with her heart and soul that he would bring Sofia home. He just prayed he didn't fail her.

"I'm not sure. Too many thoughts in my head, I guess."

"Have you and Maurice finished exploring the house?"

"Yep," she said, brightening, "top to bottom."

"No buried skeletons?"

"Sadly, no," she said, pretending to sulk. "You're really going to need to do something about that."

James laughed, glad their conversation seemed to be distracting her from her gloomy thoughts. He scrubbed at the thick stubble on his chin, watching her and thinking.

"Sami…"

"Hm?" she said, kicking her foot back and forth against the chair.

"What about The Hotel? Did you find any skeletons there?"

Sami considered the question. "No skeletons, but there were secret passages."

James felt the fine hairs on the nape of his neck prickle and rise. He slowly leaned forward in his chair, almost as if he might startle her away.

"What do you mean?"

"They ran behind the rooms and went all over." She spoke casually, scratching at a mosquito bite on her elbow, oblivious to how still James had become.

"That's interesting," he said, tapping his index finger on the arm of the chair. "I wonder what those are for."

Sami perked up, pleased to know the answer. "I know exactly what they're for; they're for hiding the girls."

James swore his heart stopped for a full thirty seconds and when it started back up again it was beating at double its normal pace. He leaned forward, looking intensely into Sami's bewildered eyes.

"Tell me."

CHAPTER 25

THAT NIGHT SOFIA STARED at her reflection in the mirror. She was going to do The Wager and that meant giving her body to someone other than James. She'd known it would come to this eventually but now it was here she didn't know how she was going to go through with it.

She thought about walking out and never looking back, but where would she go? She couldn't go back to James, that would just put them all in danger. She had no money, no food and no shelter. She was every bit a prisoner as if manacles encircled her wrists and ankles. She knew she wasn't going anywhere.

She looked at her wedding ring. The band was thin and delicate around her slim finger. The diamond was beautifully cut in an oval that sparkled even in the dimmest light. The morning after they had said they loved each other, James had disappeared for a few hours and returned with a red velvet box. He had taken her to the edge of the lake and knelt in the sand.

James, who was always so confident and in control, had been shaking with nerves. He'd taken her hand and asked her to marry him.

For a moment she had been breathless and unable to speak; the excitement and implausibility of the whole situation striking her momentarily dumb.

She had seen a flash of concern in his eyes and blurted out, "Yes! Of course, yes!"

"Oh thank God," he'd said, stood up and kissed her.

Sofia smiled sadly as she slid the ring off her finger and set it on the table. She stared at it for a full minute, taking one last look at her old life, and then turned away.

She didn't have a fireplace in this room, so she sat cross-legged on the bed to brush her hair. She closed her eyes and counted the strokes. With each stroke her mind slipped further away.

"One." *She was rising through the floors and out of The Hotel.* "Two." *She was soaring to the clouds* "Three." *She was floating in the sunny air.* "Four." *Her mind was sitting on a cloud. She could barely see her body through the haze.*

She hovered in that space for as long as she could and then reluctantly came back to earth. She uncrossed her legs and stood in her bare feet, squishing her toes into the carpet, trying to relieve the tension humming through her.

She looked at the clock and sighed. It was time and she was out of excuses. She looked at her reflection one last time. She wore a teddy that covered her chest and stomach in thick lacework, the most conservative thing she could get away with, and topped it with a sheer robe.

Her makeup was caked on thick and dark to hide the signs of the hysterical sobbing she had been doing all day. Her eyes were rimmed black with eyeliner and mascara, the foundation on her skin creating a flawless canvas. She had bronzed her cheeks and contoured certain areas to bring out the interesting shadows and angles of her face. Her lips were wine red and her hair hung sleek and shiny down her back.

There were no signs of the desperate girl from an hour ago who had wept until her pillowcase was warm and soggy. She had no tears left, just a crushing fatigue that went deep into her bones.

She took the elevator to the wagering room, the smell of cigarette smoke and cheap cologne sickeningly familiar. She walked up the stairs to her balcony and peered over the edge. Don and Jack had been celebrating her return through the preliminary rounds and they entered the wagering room unsteadily, leaning on each other for support.

When Jack looked up and saw her his face beamed. "Glory! It's glorious to see you!"

Don giggled, waving enthusiastically. She wiggled her fingers at them and tried to smile seductively but it was lackluster at best.

They took their places at the table, talking and laughing boisterously. Five minutes passed and another man came into the room wearing a dark blue suit. It fit him as if it had been made for him, which it probably had. This must be the high roller, she thought. They usually dressed to impress.

For one fleeting moment she thought James might walk through those doors, but when two strangers came through instead, she knew it had been a stupid thought. Even if James wanted to join The Wager, Rufus wouldn't allow him back in The Hotel.

She sat numbly, staring down, not really seeing. The room was warm, and she was so tired. As the sweat trickled down her spine she thought back to a time before this nightmare had begun. When she and James were married, and she was living her happily ever-after, naively thinking it would last the rest of her life.

It had been the middle of July, and temperatures had reached record highs. India and Sami had been invited to an overnight pool party at India's friend Janis' house, so James had taken Sofia to a burger place on the boardwalk. They had eaten cheeseburgers and drank beer while country music played in the background.

They had gone home and made a fire on the beach. They'd made love in the sand, the heat sticky on their skin, pasting tiny rocks to their bodies. By the time they were sated, they had sand in every crevice imaginable. They'd dove into the ice-cold lake and washed each other's bodies…

Sofia felt that icy water shoot through her veins as the high roller roared in triumph, tossing down his three fives, beating out every other hand. The rest of the men grumbled in reluctant defeat, and they all glanced up at her as they left the room. Sofia should have smiled coquettishly to encourage them to come back and try again, but she sat dully, no longer caring.

Rufus was clapping the high roller on the back and offering him a cigar. That was Sofia's cue, and she got up from her seat, moving like an invisible string was tugging on her, forcing her limbs to move.

Without looking at the men below her, she began her descent down the stairs. It felt like a death march.

***

When Rufus left the wagering room, he went to the lobby to find James Hardy being blocked entrance by one of The Hotel's security guards. James waited patiently, leaning against one of the large carved pillars. The guard stood with his beefy arms crossed as if James might rush him at any moment.

"Says he needs to talk to you, sir," the guard rumbled, eyeing James suspiciously.

"Well, I'm not so sure I want to talk to him," Rufus said with a sniff, looking James up and down like he was some kind of vermin. "I thought Sofia told you to get lost."

James had one hand in his pocket, the other, with the cast, hung at his side. His stance was relaxed, almost lazy. "Oh she did, in no uncertain terms. I'm here to extend an olive branch in the form of a business proposition."

Rufus shrugged indifferently, but the glimmer in his eyes betrayed his interest. He'd partner with the devil if he thought it would make him money. Many said he already had.

"Fine. Thank you. That will be all," he said to the guard who was happy not to have to listen to his boss talk business.

James pushed off the pillar he had been leaning against and walked toward Rufus. "Thank you for trusting me," he said.

Rufus scoffed. "I don't trust you. I don't trust anyone. But you're not going to hurt me." He twisted his mouth in a feral grin, his red lipstick cracking, leaving fissures in the perfect veneer. "I hold a very precious commodity in my hands that you want. And don't think for one minute that I wouldn't destroy you both, if it came down to it. I don't care how beautiful she is, I would sacrifice Sofia on the altar of Beelzebub himself if it meant saving my hotel. So try anything and I will show no mercy."

Rufus had been inching forward, his finger stuck out in front of him until it pressed against James' chest. He had to lift his head slightly to look James in the eye and that made Rufus equally furious.

"So dramatic, Rufus," said James, trying to suppress a yawn. "I told you, I have a business proposition, that's all. Can we get on with it, it's way past my bedtime. I don't know how you vampires can function staying up all night."

Rufus tried to hold his scowl, his finger still extended, but his mouth broke into a grin and then a full belly laugh. "You are a charming man, Mr. Hardy, but like I told you before, I'm immune. Now what do you want?"

"You want to discuss this in the lobby?" James asked, lifting an eyebrow.

"I need to make sure it's worth my while before I let you take up any more of my time. I'm a very busy man and do not have time to play games."

James barked out a laugh. "Rufus, you live for games."

Rufus snorted out a giggle. "I do, don't I? But not today," his face grew stern as if he were correcting a disobedient child.

"I don't have the patience for it. So tell me or get the hell out of my hotel." He admired his nails, sharpened to points and painted neon green.

James plastered a self-satisfied smile on his face. It took everything he had not to grab Rufus by the collar and slam his head into his fancy tiled floor. Blood red would go great with the black and white motif. He choked back the desire to put his hands around the filthy man's throat.

"I concede defeat as far as Sofia," James said, his stance relaxed. "She's made her decision to be here and there's nothing I can do about it. But she's still my wife and I expect her to be treated right and have comfortable accommodations. I am willing to give a generous donation to The Hotel, but I want Sofia moved back into the suite."

"Done!" said Rufus, holding out his hand.

"I'm not finished," said James, holding up a finger. "I want back in The Wager so I can have a chance to be with her."

Rufus' mouth stretched in a savage smile. This was a scenario he hadn't thought of. James Hardy paying him to sleep with his own wife, it was just too delicious.

"You know, let's go sit in comfort while we talk. In fact," Rufus said, patting James' shoulder, "I have a thirty-five year old bottle of scotch collecting dust. I've been waiting for an excuse to open it."

Rufus led him down the hall to his office. He opened the door, turned on the lights, and gestured for James to enter.

James took in the immaculate room. Despite the gold curtains and fancy red furniture, the room was more conservative than he would have imagined. Apparently, Rufus took the business side of running The Hotel very seriously.

Rufus waved James towards a chair and went to the cart that contained several decanters filled with liquids ranging from pale gold to walnut brown. From the bottom shelf he chose a bottle and pulled out the cork. He inhaled the aroma and closed his eyes and sighed.

"Heaven," he said. "Absolute heaven."

He splashed the contents into two crystal tumblers and handed one to James. He sat down in the chair opposite him.

"So, what should we toast to? New ventures on the horizon?" Rufus said cheerfully.

James raised his glass, forcing a smile, and took a sip.

"Now," said Rufus leaning forward, his arms resting on his knees. He wore a pair of jeans that were rolled up to his hairless calves. His feet were clad in canvas boating shoes. "Tell me more about this generous donation."

"Sami's doing well, by the way," James said, leaning back in his chair.

Rufus' eyes flashed with impatience at the change in subject, but he smiled with delight. "Yes, of course! Little Sami. Such a dear thing. She was raised here you know, yet she still turned out completely unjaded. So pure, so unspoiled." Rufus looked at James and for a moment, the pleasant mask slipped. Irritation and loathing crossed his face. "She was going to make me a fortune when she was old enough."

James' hand clasped so tightly around his glass he was afraid he was going to break it. He had to resist the desire to grind his fist into Rufus' face.

"I'm surprised you were going to wait that long," James

said, as calmly as he could.

The cheerful smile was back in place and Rufus answered good naturedly. "Yes, well, you may not know this, but we have a strict over eighteen policy here at The Hotel."

James raised his eyebrows. "Really?" he said. "I could have sworn Sami told me some of your working girls are fourteen, fifteen years old."

"Well, that's just a filthy lie," Rufus said, setting his glass down hard on the table. "How could my little Sami say such vicious things about me after all I've done for her?"

"C'mon Rufus, you can tell me. I'm an investor now."

Rufus narrowed his eyes and then seemed to make up his mind and sat back, relaxed again. "Are you telling me that your interests run in that direction?"

James had to swallow the vicious retort that was burning like lava in his throat.

"I'm not saying that. I just want to know what I'm getting into before I put down what will be a significant amount of money."

"I can assure you," Rufus said, practically salivating, "we at The Hotel hold discretion at the utmost, highest level. Um...how significant are we talking?"

James scratched his chin, ignoring Rufus' question. "I've heard you've had some run-ins with the FBI. They've threatened to shut you down if they even suspect you're working underage girls here."

"FBI?" cried Rufus. "James, how could you be so cruel! To come into my office, in my hotel, and utter those letters in my presence." He fanned himself with his hand. "Everything is above board, I assure you," Rufus said, his face reddening.

James tilted his head. "Is it?"

"Of course. What do you mean?" said Rufus, taking a large gulp of scotch.

"Sami's a smart and observant girl," said James. "Since she's been with me, she's searched my entire house from top to bottom. She knows the place better than I do and I was born and raised there. She knows every mousehole and every cranny."

As James talked, Rufus' smile remained fixed to his face, but the skin on his bald head had turned rosy pink.

"The other night as I lay recovering from my near death experience," James continued, "she told me about the things she'd found over the years here at The Hotel. Apparently, when she was bored, she'd go exploring. One night she found a door built into one of the walls. It was all but invisible. Inside was an empty room. Of course that spurred her curiosity, and she made it her mission to see if there were any more hidden rooms. And, in fact, there were."

Rufus looked at his fingernails as if he were only half listening.

"But there weren't just hidden rooms; there were whole passages, built into the structure of the hotel, some leading outside into the back alley." James said.

Rufus smiled politely.

"The FBI have suspected you of working underage girls for years. They've even done surprise raids but have never found anything."

"Exactly," Rufus said with exasperation, "because there

is nothing to find. Now can we get back to…"

"Sami was outside her room during one of these raids," James went on, as if Rufus hadn't spoken. "She panicked and ran for one of the passages and found a group of girls hiding but didn't understand why they weren't in their rooms. One of the girls said you would kill them if anyone found out."

Rufus picked up his drink and took another deep swallow. He choked a little and coughed, pulling a blue and white striped handkerchief from his pocket. He dabbed at his mouth, leaving splatters of crimson lipstick on the fabric. Beads of perspiration were popping out on his forehead.

"Sami is a troublemaker," he exclaimed. "She always has been. She lies about everything." He pointed his finger at James. "You'd better watch your back, having her in your house. I can't believe I kept her around for as long as I did. You know she arrived on my doorstep out of nowhere? A regular devil's spawn, I'm sure of it."

"I don't know," said James shaking his head, barely keeping a rein on his temper. "I bet the FBI would also be interested to know why girls are hiding in secret rooms."

Rufus' smile had wilted, and his eyes were large and wild. Unable to contain his agitation he stood up and went to the cart. He poured himself another drink out of a flashy green decanter, filled to its neck with dark liquid.

He took a long swallow, contemplating James through narrowed eyes. He gestured at him with his drink still clutched in an unsteady hand. "You tricked me," he said almost with respect. "You're not looking to invest at all, are you?"

"I'm afraid not."

"Well then, what do you want, money?"

James laughed. "You're not getting off that easily."

Rufus set his glass on the cart. "Fine, I get the picture," he said, running his hand along the various colored bottles. "You want Sofia back? No problem. She was getting bothersome anyway. And so old! She was really past her prime." Rufus waved his hand in dismissal.

"I'm glad to hear it." James said, not making a move to get up.

"What, there's more?" Rufus asked in a bored voice, playing with the top of the green decanter. He stroked the carved ridges on the glass, tracing his finger down its long length.

"You leave my family alone, and you stop using underage girls at this damn hotel."

Rufus rolled his eyes. "I suppose I'm doing all this out of the kindness of my heart?"

"You and I both know you don't have one of those," James said, setting down his glass. "You'll do it because otherwise I will make your life a living hell. I will have the FBI dogging your every move. No one will want to be seen here. The Hotel will be done."

"Alright." Rufus fluttered his handkerchief in the air. Sweat was dripping off his head and into his eyes and he wiped his face impatiently. "Truce, truce. You're a better man than I, James. You're a man of conviction. I admire that and will strive to be more like you. Let's drink to that."

Rufus turned to refill his glass. He grasped the green decanter around its neck and smashed it into the side of the cart. The contents splashed to the floor, soaking the carpet and releasing the sharp, spicy smell of alcohol. He whirled on James, still clutching what was left of the decanter; the jagged, deadly edges slicing the air. James jumped up from his chair, knocking over the side table and his drink.

"You!" Rufus moved forward, backing James towards the wall. "You come in here, take my family, threaten to destroy my livelihood." Rufus inched closer, swinging the bottle, the green glass shimmering in the light. James retreated another pace, his arms held out in front of him.

"My home!" Rufus continued his rant as blood dripped from his hand where flying shards had ripped through the flesh. He didn't seem to notice. "I created this place from nothing! Everything in this hotel is my idea, my plan. You think you can take all that away from me? You think you can just show up and destroy what I've spent the best years of my life building?"

He was heaving out breaths, jabbing the air in front of James, the spiked edges of the broken decanter like a gaping mouth full of teeth. James didn't move, he just watched Rufus, waiting for the lunge he knew was coming.

"You don't get to win!" Rufus snarled. "I always win!"

He was feet away from James, but he stopped and giggled triumphantly. "I have won, though. Sofia is with the winner of The Wager right now."

James' eyes darted to the door and back. In that split second Rufus was on him, snarling and slashing. James backed against the wall and held his cast up to block the blows. Rufus' hand came down again and again, carving grooves in the plaster, shattering more of the glittering glass. James grimaced, trying to keep his arm elevated but the pain was too much, and he dropped it to his side. He tried to whirl sideways and knock Rufus off balance, but Rufus thrust out his arm in a wide swing.

James felt searing pain tear down his cheek as the glass opened his skin and blood poured down his face.

"Mother fu-!" he cried and clamped a shaking hand over the gash. Blood seeped between his fingers and down his wrist.

Rufus was staring at the shattered decanter in his hand as if he wasn't sure where it had come from. He slowly looked at James, whose eyes were open wide with shock. Blood smeared his chin and neck. Rufus made a guttural sound in his throat; the snarl of an animal ready to finish its prey. He lunged, slashing and jabbing.

James forced his frozen limbs to move and stumbled back, dodging the swinging bottle. Using Rufus' momentum, James grabbed his shoulders and ran him face first into the wall. Rufus slammed to the floor and was still.

James stood heaving in gulps of air, fighting back waves of dizziness. He leaned over Rufus and fisted his hands in his shirt, dragging the top half of his body off the floor.

"What room, you son of a bitch, what room?" James yelled, shaking Rufus' limp form. He weaved and blood dripped from the gash and splattered onto Rufus's slack face. James dropped him in disgust and Rufus fell back onto the floor with a thud. James straightened with effort, the ground moving precariously under him.

A towel was spread out on the drink cart, and he whipped it off, sending broken glass flying. He pressed it to his cheek and looked around, swaying unsteadily. He went to Rufus' desk and started opening drawers. In the third one he checked he found a gun. His fingers curled around the cold metal.

CHAPTER 26

WORKING AT THE HOTEL was hard on Bobby Stapleton, and the pun was not lost on him. At the end of each shift he had to race to the bathroom, praying no one saw the tent he was making out of his slacks. When his friends had asked him if the girls really walked around naked in the lobby, his reply was, they might as well be.

He'd gotten the job as desk clerk straight out of college. He was one of the few who had made it through his entire school career without losing his virginity. This was partly because of his stigmatism and overbite, but mostly because he developed a stutter when he talked to the opposite sex.

The girls at The Hotel loved to tease him, but it was all in good fun and he took it as such. They were a great group of gals, and they would have been like family if they didn't give him a boner every time they strutted past.

Bobby was a cheerful type with a round face, made larger from the expanse of forehead. His hair had unfortunately started receding at a young age and showed no signs of halting its retreat.

It had been a typical Saturday. Men had poured in to do The Wager, but his shift didn't start until the excitement was over. Most of the girls had coupled up for the night, but a few still lingered in the lobby. Bobby could hear the buzzing and clanging from the casino down the hall, but he had learned to drown it out as he worked. He flipped through reservation cards and typed the information into the computer.

He glanced up when he heard an odd squealing noise like an injured bird. More voices joined in, and then a wave of shouts accompanied several girls who emerged from the hall screaming and waving their arms hysterically. They ran past him and out the front door.

"Wha…?" He got out, alarm making his voice climb. He turned to peer down the hall and saw what they had been screaming about.

A man with blood dripping down his face and neck, saturating his once blue shirt, was walking purposefully toward the front desk. One arm was covered in a plaster cast up to his elbow and was holding a towel to his cheek. In the other hand was a gun.

Bobby tried desperately not to pee himself as the man approached. Up close he looked even worse. The towel was doing nothing to stop the constant dribble of blood from a gash running from his cheek to his jawline. His nose, forehead and other cheek were also smeared red as if he'd run his hand over his face.

He propped the arm holding the gun on the counter, as if it was too heavy to raise.

"Hi," he said, squinting at Bobby's name tag. "Robert."

"It's Bobby," he said automatically.

"Bobby, Ok. I'm James." He spoke calmly and politely as if he didn't look like he'd painted himself with pig's blood for some sort of ritual. "Listen, Bobby, I've had a hell of a day, and I need some information. It would mean a great deal to me if you could give it to me with no arguments."

"W-what is it?" Bobby said, beginning to stammer under the man's deep blue gaze.

"I need the room number of the man who won The Wager tonight."

"You'll have to talk to my boss about that…"

"Your boss is unavailable right now," James said, trying to control the urge to come over the desk and put his hands around the kid's throat. "Give me the number and the key."

"I can't!" Bobby exclaimed, his words coming out in a squeak. "I'll lose my job."

"Bobby, do you see this gun pointing at your chest?"

Bobby nodded, his eyes bulging from his head.

"Do I look like a man who is concerned about your employment status at the moment?"

Bobby shook his head.

"Good. Now give me the room key."

"I-I can't…Wait!" he said, holding up his hands as James raised the gun. "A key won't get you in. For VIP clients only my handprint can override the lock, and I need express permission…"

"Consider this permission," James said, waving the gun at him to move.

Bobby stepped around the desk. There was no fear of exposure now; whatever had been up had shriveled and hidden a while ago. They entered the elevator and Bobby pushed the button for the twentieth floor. Orchestral music floated through the air as they began their ascent.

James leaned heavily against the wall. His face didn't hurt as much as he thought it should; just a strange throbbing numbness. He had given up trying to stop the blood, and the soaked towel hung limply at his side. He felt a little like passing out, but he knew he didn't have time for such luxuries.

"So Bobby, what's a nice boy like you doing in a place like this?"

Bobby shrugged. "Needed the job. I want to go to pilot school."

"Do you, now?" said James, clapping him on the shoulder, making Bobby jump. "Sounds like a great plan, but if I were you, I'd update my resume."

The man who had won The Wager was named Brody. He was tall and thin and wore his wealth like a badge of honor. Large silver and turquoise rings flashed on his fingers. His jacket was real cowhide and his huge bronze belt buckle caught the light like a beacon. He strutted away from The Wager table in a pair of pointy-toed boots, shined to a gloss. He tipped his Stetson in Sofia's direction as she waited for him at the bottom of the balcony stairs.

"Well, hey little lady," he said with an exaggerated drawl,

looking her up and down and blowing out a long breath. "Aren't you just a sweet little heifer. I got my work cut out for me, don't I? How's about you and me head back to my room and have a little fun," he said, taking her arm.

Sofia didn't bother responding. Every inch of her wanted to rip her arm out of his possessive grasp, but this was her job now…her life. She'd better get used to it.

Brody spent the ride to the twentieth floor talking about his wealth in the cattle business that he had inherited from his father. Sofia guessed he was in his thirties. He smelled like leather, denim and body spray.

"I don't actually work the ranch," he said quickly, as if to reassure her that he wasn't some common hired laborer. "I oversee the business operations. The place wouldn't run without me."

Sofia gave him a tight smile and stiffened when he rested his hand against her lower back, guiding her out of the elevator and down the hallway.

She shivered as they approached his room. As usual, it was on the cool side and she only wore a teddy with a filmy, short robe over it, but her pebbled skin and accelerated heart rate weren't because of the temperature.

She didn't bother looking around his room when he led her inside. It would be like every other room at The Hotel, and she had flashes of the first time she had been alone with James. She began to tremble and had to banish the thoughts from her mind. She took a deep breath and removed her robe.

Brody grinned at her as he took off his jacket. "You're really something to look at, you know? I think I'm going to make this last a very long time."

He kicked off his boots and began unbuttoning his shirt. He stopped with a sly smile, and said, "Why don't you come over here and do this for me, darlin'?"

Sofia moved mechanically, numb and expressionless. Her lack of enthusiasm didn't deter him. He kept the cocky grin as her fingers ran down his shirt, releasing the buttons as she went.

"That's it," he said, fingering the lace that ran down either side of her breasts. When she was done, his shirt hung open revealing a pallid, hairless chest that lifted and fell with his rapid breathing. She lowered her hands, like a slave awaiting her next command.

Without warning, Brody gripped the top of her bodice with both hands and tore the teddy in half, ripping the thin material straight down the middle. The ruined garment fluttered to the floor, and as Brody's eyes scanned her naked body, Sofia called on years of training and stuffed down humiliation and rage. He licked his lips and she clenched her hands, resisting the urge to slap him. She fought to stay numb as feelings of helplessness threatened to overwhelm her.

He put his hands on her shoulders and shoved her to her knees. The carpet was soft under her skin and she tried to imagine she was kneeling in a meadow, but she was too panicked to concentrate. Brody was panting as he quickly snapped open the buttons of his jeans and fumbled for the zipper. Sofia closed her eyes. Her own breath came fast and sharp, and she thought about chocolate ice cream cones and spring hillsides as tears coursed down her cheeks. She thought of James, India and Sami and the happy ending they had fought so hard for.

Brody's erection sprung out of his briefs. Sofia's eyes flashed open, and she knew she couldn't do it; would never do it. Ever. Again.

His eyes widened in surprise when Sofia stood up and pushed him in the chest as hard as she could. He swore and stumbled back, tripping on his jeans that were half-way down his thighs. Sofia turned and ran. She reached the door, but he had engaged the safety lock, and it required a key card to open. She wrenched at the handle, frustrated tears blinding her.

She looked around for a weapon. The logs in the fireplace were closest, but before she could move she was yanked backwards by her hair. Her scalp seared with pain and she cried out, reaching behind her, trying to grab his wrist. He wrapped his other arm around her throat, and she gagged as her breath was cut off. She scraped her fingernails down his arm and was satisfied with the slickness of blood under her fingers. Brody grunted and squeezed tighter. Sofia saw black clouds, like the coming of a storm, but then the pressure released, and she was flung face first onto the bed

She had seconds to suck in a breath before he was on top of her, sitting on her legs, pushing her head down so her nose and mouth were pressed against the mattress.

"Well, this little game is unexpected," Brody puffed, his eyes bright with lust. "Do I have to pay extra for this?"

"Get off me!" Sofia yelled, contorting her body, trying to buck him off.

"Now you just shut your mouth or things are going to get real interestin', ya hear?"

He grabbed Sofia's flailing arms as she tried to flip over, but his thighs were crushing her sides, pinning her to the mattress. He kept one hand pressed to her head and used the other to shove his pants down. She could feel him, slick against her skin.

"No!" she screamed.

James was coming down the hall with Bobby on his heels when he heard Sofia's scream. He raced to the door and pounded on it.

"Get this open, Bobby! " he yelled.

Bobby's hand was shaking, but he managed to press his palm to the digital plate on the wall. When it lit up green, James pushed open the door, almost knocking Bobby to the ground.

Sofia was naked, face down on the bed and a man was straddling her. One of the man's hands was pushing her head into the mattress, the other trying to keep his erection as he struggled to subdue her.

James wrapped his arms around Brody's waist and yanked. They were about the same height, but James was stronger and running on pure adrenaline. He half-lifted, half-dragged Brody off Sofia and onto the floor.

"Hey!" Brody cried when his bare ass hit the carpet.

"Get out of here," James snarled, trying not to weave.

He prayed he wouldn't have to fight.

Brody was indignant, but he wasn't stupid. The man standing over him was covered in blood and had murder in his eyes. Things had not gone as Brody had planned, and if the board of his company, a bunch of ancient farmers, found out he'd visited The Hotel, they'd probably take away his limousine again.

He scrambled backwards, away from James and found his pants. He didn't bother with his underwear but bunched them in his hand as he stumbled out the door, past an open-mouthed Bobby.

James sagged with relief. "Call 911," he said, handing Bobby his cell phone. "Tell them your boss is unconscious in his office."

Bobby looked startled but took the phone and went into the hall. James sat next to Sofia and pulled a blanket over her shivering body. He said her name and put a hand on her head, stroking gently.

Sofia's body was trembling violently; her eyes shut tight, her nose pressed against the mattress. But she wasn't aware of any of it. She was on the shore at the lake, basking in the sweet fragrance of roses and jasmine. The sun was setting, lighting the sky like a pillar of fire. The water sparkled as if mother nature had scattered a million diamonds over its surface; so bright Sofia had to shield her eyes. The smell of wood smoke drifted in the air. She smiled as James came up behind her, draping a blanket over her chilled shoulders. It was soft, and she clutched it to her chest.

He floated there in her periphery, like the fading memories of a dream. When she felt a warm hand caress her hair and heard her name whispered in a low, familiar voice, she squeezed her eyes tighter, trying to hold on to the illusion.

"It's ok, love, he's gone. You can open your eyes. You're safe now."

He repeated the words over and over, in that same deep, soothing voice, and how she wanted to believe him.

"It's over now. It's time to open your eyes and come home," he said quietly.

Home. Where she and James had started a life together. With India and Sami. Her family.

She became aware of his body near hers. He was sitting on the edge of the bed, his hand softly stroking her hair. He was real. She could feel the warmth of him.

The thought of what she'd done, what he must think of her, blew away any wisps of fantasy, burning her stomach like acid. She started to shake again, this time from shame. She didn't want to look at him, didn't want to see the disappointment or hurt in his eyes. Tears leaked from under her closed lids.

"C'mon babe, open your eyes. Come back to me, Sofia."

"How can you still want me after what I've done?" she whispered.

"What have you done, my silly love?" he said lightly, brushing hair from her forehead.

She covered her face and took a deep breath, letting it out with a shudder.

"I left you. I went back to The Wager. He was going to kill you. I thought this was the only way. I…I'm so sorry,

James. I should have told you."

"There's nothing to be sorry about. This was all Rufus. Do you hear me, Sofia?" His voice was stern, and when she still didn't look at him, he softened his tone.

"I understand why you came back. You sacrificed yourself for me and India and Sami. You're the bravest woman I've ever met, Sofia, and I love you so much. Rufus is finished. The Hotel, The Wager, it's all over. We're safe and we're going home."

His words made their way through, and they warmed every inch of her. It was over and she and James were finally free. She reached out a hand and James covered it with his own. She let out a long sigh and slowly opened her eyes, gazing at their entwined hands. She frowned. His fingers and palm were sticky and stained red.

She glanced up and screamed. He was streaked in blood from his hairline to his chin. Thick red drops fell from a gash on his cheek, dripping onto the front of his shirt, soaking it black. Under all the dark red smears his pallor was frightening.

For three stunned seconds she just stared at him, then she cursed and rolled off the bed, running for the bathroom. She stuffed her arms into a robe and swiped a towel from the neat pile by the sink.

She hurried back to James, who was staring at the wall and swaying slightly.

"What happened?" she said, kneeling in front of him and pressing the towel to his cheek. He winced and gripped the edge of the bed.

"Rufus and I had a little altercation. It's hard to tell by

looking at me, but I actually won."

"You stupid man." The towel was absorbing the blood at an alarming rate and her lips trembled as she fought back panic. "You should have said something!"

"I didn't want to ruin the mood," he said.

"Hold this. I'm calling 911."

"Already done. In fact they should be here any minute. At least I hope so," he said.

Sofia sat back on her heels, blinking back tears. The towel in his hand had turned the color of dark rust and the contrast to his white face was startling.

"Do I look that bad?" he said, his words slightly slurred.

"Nothing a little soap and water won't fix," she laughed shakily.

It was only a few minutes before the police and paramedics showed up. They stormed The Hotel while security held off dozens of reporters, who huddled around outside, peering in windows, hoping to be the first to discover what the excitement was about.

Rufus had regained consciousness and was screaming to anyone who would listen that the attack on him was unprovoked and that James should be locked up in an asylum. The fact that Rufus had a small lump on his head, while James was having his face stitched together, had the police doubting his story.

Rufus and James were loaded into separate ambulances, leaving Bobby standing in front of The Hotel, facing a swarm of cameras and microphones. He grinned, pushing his chest out as he told the reporters his crucial role in the events of the night.

Sofia sat next to James, looking out the window of the ambulance. Police lights flashed red and blue in front of The Hotel's entrance. White lights pulsed like a strobe from dozens of cameras and cell phones.

The Hotel became fully visible as they moved further away, and Sofia took in the splendor of it. It looked magical, towering over the buildings around it, bathed in soft glowing lights from hundreds of windows and sconces. The moon danced over brick and glass and wrought iron balconies.

The Hotel had always seemed alive to her, a living, breathing entity. But knowing Rufus wasn't there anymore seemed to have taken the soul out of it. Now it was just another building cluttering the city skyline.

There would be an investigation, and Rufus would finally be put behind bars where he belonged. She looked down at her sleeping husband; his hand held firmly in hers. The Wager was over, and in the end, she had won.

CHAPTER 27

SOFIA HAD A TEARFUL reunion at the hospital with India and Sami. India had come out of James' room pale and shaky. It was bad, but it could have been so much worse.

By the time James was released he was disgruntled and sulky. There was a large bandage covering the right side of his face and it hurt every time he moved his mouth.

"I want a drink," he pouted.

"You'll get one," said Sofia, helping him into the car.

"And I want my own bed, with you in it."

She smiled and said, "We can sleep in the same bed, but that's it. The doctor said you can't exert yourself until the stitches come out."

He grumbled and looked out of the window.

When they reached the house and got out of the car, Sofia almost wept from the familiar feeling of home. The unique lake smells of wet rocks and breezes blown over fresh water, with a hint of smoke. The rich blue sky and the sound of sparrows.

"Where is everyone?" James asked as they entered the quiet house. "I expected banners and fanfare."

"The girls went to the store with Freddy, so they could make us a welcome home dinner."

James smiled. "India cooking? Another first."

He sat down on the couch with a rough exhale. Sofia curled up next to him and put her head against his shoulder.

"Can we be a boring married couple from now on?" he said.

She laughed. "I'd like that."

James' cell phone rang and he picked it up.

"Are you watching the news?" Rob said.

"Um, hello to you too, and yes, I'm doing fine," James said, while pointing the remote at the tv.

The screen showed Rufus walking out of the courthouse with four men in suits surrounding him. Reporters swarmed them, and one of the men tried to shield Rufus, but he waved him aside and smiled widely as flashes went off all around him. He'd obviously anticipated the crowd because he'd taken the time to apply blue and green eyeshadow, and his lips were tinted pink.

"It was all one big misunderstanding," he gushed into the microphones. "All charges have been dropped, and I have been exonerated of any wrong doing.

"Can you believe this shit?" Rob said angrily.

"I'm not surprised, really," James said, the rage in his voice barely contained.

Sofia leaned into him, and her hair brushed his cheek. He closed his eyes and breathed her in, letting her scent calm him as it always did. The red mist receded, and he focused on the questions being fired at Rufus.

"The FBI is saying underaged girls were found this afternoon during a raid," said one reporter, zooming the camera in on Rufus' shocked face. "Do you have any comments?"

"Absurd," he said, laying his palms on his chest as if stilling his heart. "Utterly absurd. I don't know why they would make up these stories about me. Nothing illegal has ever gone on at The Hotel." He wagged his finger as if scolding a child. "My lawyers can attest to that'"

As one, the men in the suits nodded, and Rufus smiled angelically.

"Anyway," he continued, straightening his yellow fluorescent tie; he thought it had paired nicely with his dark blue suit. "I've decided to sell The Hotel and retire."

The reporters exploded. They shouted questions at him, each trying to drown out their competition. Rufus didn't say anything, letting the moment build. He faced one camera with a coy smile and then turned to give another his profile. He angled his head at each lens, making sure every station represented got a good shot, before waving his hands to quiet them down.

"Yes, it's true. I've decided to retire on some beautiful island somewhere. It's been a delight to serve the members of this community."

James lowered the sound, not wanting to hear any more of Rufus' lies.

"At least there's that," Rob said on the other end of the phone.

"Mm hm," James said, watching cameras trailing Rufus as he and his lawyers climbed into a large black limousine and drove away.

"You don't think he's going to retire?" Rob said.

"I don't think Rufus would be able to stand not being the center of attention. I think retirement would bore him right back into another twisted venture."

"Well, don't let it drive you nuts. Get some rest." Rob clicked off and James put the phone on the table.

He chewed on his bottom lip and then winced as the movement tugged on his stitches. He doubted they'd seen the last of Rufus. He might go away to lick his wounds for a while, but he would be back. He was too narcissistic to stay hidden for long.

James clenched his fist, feeling that familiar rage. He'd be damned if he let Rufus open another hotel. When he resurfaced, because James knew that day would come, he'd be watching. Rufus wouldn't be able to buy a pack of gum without James knowing about it.

He felt Sofia looking up at him, and he forced himself to relax his jaw. He put his arm around her and drew her close.

"Whatever happens," Sofia said quietly, knowing in which direction his thoughts were going, "we have to put Rufus behind us, or we'll never be free from him. He would get a lot of pleasure knowing he was a shadow hanging over our lives. I refuse to give him the satisfaction."

"I know," James said. He turned so he was facing her. In his blue eyes she saw tenderness, but also electric heat that had her breath stopping halfway up her throat.

"I love you, Sofia."

She smiled and felt relief, almost like shackles releasing from her wrists. She was finally free from Rufus, The Hotel, and The Wager. She'd never felt so safe and so in love.

"It's getting late," she said, standing up and holding out her hands. He let her pull him to his feet and she led him by the hand to the stairs.

"Are you putting me to bed? Because I'm not sleepy," he complained.

"I think we can come up with some activities that will help you sleep," she said, towing him up the stairs.

"But I'm not supposed to exert myself; doctor's orders."

She opened the bedroom door and tugged him inside. "Doctors don't know everything, and anyway, I'll do all the work."

He laughed and she closed the door.

COMING SOON

The Game

ACKNOWLEDGEMENTS

I started writing The Wager in May of 2024. It was the first piece of fiction I'd sat down to write in over thirty years. It started out as a short story full of rollicking sex and plenty of ripped bodices; something to read to my husband and make him laugh, but as I gave my characters personalities and histories, I ended up falling in love with them and felt they deserved more to their stories.

God only knew how that summer would unfold and how writing would become my solace, my comfort, the peace I needed during difficult days for my family.

My parents were the first to read my scribblings. They were gracious with their critiques and indulged my creative process with enthusiasm and encouragement. I don't know if I would have pushed myself the way I did if it had not been for their sincere interest.

My Dad has had my back in every way possible, and he is the reason I know anything about poker. My Mom, editor extraordinaire; I wouldn't want to walk this road with anyone else.

Thank you, Jesus, for the seasons that you give us and see us through.

Thank you to my husband who doesn't like to read but always listens.

To my children, who are the greatest gift I have ever been given.

To Andrea and Lou for reading my drafts and all the fabulous input.

To Megan, for another brilliant cover. (She did my book Wildflower, too)

And to my cats, for keeping me company while I work, and for graciously allowing me to use their videos on Facebook and Instagram.